Tyrone Givens
Children of KMT
Ankh Uda Snb

THE ISFET

PROTOCOL

Tyrone Givens

KMT NU XRDT

This is a work of fiction. All of the characters, organizations, and events portrayed in this novel are either products of the author's imagination or are used fictitiously.

The Isfet Protocol

TyroneGivens.com

ISBN: 9781642542769
Library of Congress Control Number: 2018902275
Printed in the United States of America

For my children. For all the Melanated children who need something to believe in…

Hotep dee nasut Wsir, Inp- poo dee se-noo pe-ret

khe-roo ta hen-qet

kha ta-oo, kha hen-qe-too, kha ka-oo, kah

ah-pe-doo kha she-soo, kha men-khe-too

keht ne-bet ne-fe-ret wa-bet, Ankh ne-ter eem

en ka en ee-ma-kee maa khe-roo

Dua Ntru, Dua Ntru, Dua Ntru

Preface

This is a work of science fiction, told as a metaphor for ourstory, and appeals to teenagers as well as adults who may already have been exposed to some of the subject matter discussed within. Time frames range from 3500 BCE to current events but all topics are both relevant to and based on true historical events. This book should be used as a teaching aid, by home schoolers and professional educators alike, for book reports or light summer reading when out of school. It may also be used as a tool in your own collection for discussions which call upon critical thinking skills or simply encouraging others to use their imagination and creativity to promote positive imagery in our community. Park this book right next to "The Destruction of Black Civilization," By Chancellor Williams and "Civilization or Barbarism," By Cheikh Anta Diop. This book, third in the series, is a favorite among educators and also serves as a learning tool to supplement Afrocentric history lessons. For more information or updates on the MMORPG follow us on Twitter/Facebook/Instagram @TheBennuProject or on our website TyroneGivens.com and thank you for your support.

MDU NTR HELP

Ba – spirit/essence

Isfet – Chaos, the opposing force to Ma'at

Neter – Nature/"God"

Set – Brother to Heru and agent of chaos

Ma'at – Cosmic balance

Ausar – The true name of Osiris

Aset – The true name of Isis

Heru – The falcon Ntr and the original word for Hero

Medjay – Ancient Kemetic special forces.

Ljebu – One of many tribes comprised of descendants from

KMT – The true name of ancient egypt

Ogundanasungbo - the war that lit the forest

Abeokuta (under the rock - Olumo rock) in what is Ogun state in Nigeria

Oyinbo – Foreigner, known for lopsided trade deals, planetary exploitation and missionaries.

Impundulu – Mythical bird which possesses the ability to use lightning

Keftiu – Meroan Dropship

Abeo – The Bringer of Happiness

Kandake – Queen Mother

Ipet.isu – "Chosen of places" Used for temples, places of worship.

A.S.E. – Artificial Intelligence

Atef Crown – The unique crown worn by Wsir

Serqet - Goddess of scorpions, magic, medicine, and healing venomous stings and bites.

Ampah - Trust

Hm - Husband

Hmt - Wife

Wsir – Ntr whose skin glows green and represents life

Sabayt - Lesson

Prologue

It was a peaceful existence, albeit a disingenuous one, in which all Meroans lived in perfect harmony and were no longer engaged in any hostile contact with the Assilians. In fact, the Assilians had been conquered and completely subjugated generations ago. Even the star at the center of the solar system had relented in its attacks against the Meroans and every world was better off now that Ra's energy had stabilized. The worlds themselves were beautiful. The least developed of which was still a serene display of equilibrium as evident by nature's meticulous attempts at perfection. Rolling hills, colorful plant life, crystal clear water sources and an abundance of natural wildlife were the norm on most Meroan worlds. Meroans were able to live long, peaceful lives with little in the way of stress or foreign interference.

But it wasn't true. At the very least it was unverifiable. In truth, there was no way for the Enmesharra to know if these events had actually come to pass or not. The entire truth of the matter was that the Enmesharra was not mentally a part of the same reality as everyone else of the time. The environment was a prison, designed to keep the Enmesharra isolated from others but also to keep the

Enmesharra distracted by whatever fantasies were possible. And so the Enmesharra dreamt up what it considered to be a fantasy made up of its own desires; Meroans who were free from every conceivable harm. The Enmesharra was born on KMT and so, naturally, a lot of the delusions that it engaged in took place on that world. It quietly toured isolated natural springs at the furthest reaches of the planet, enjoyed communing with nature's living manifestations and even frequented its favorite developed locations all around the city. The Enmesharra even engaged with other Meroans while the forced delusions played out, knowing full well that they were figments of a pseudo fourth dimensional environment.

While it was true that the prison was both a pleasant and peaceful environment, it was also still just a prison. And while the Enmesharra did an impressive amount of self-reflection and meditation, it was fully aware that it carried a substantial amount of animosity for its current environment and the one who sent it there. That person gave the final order and approval for the imprisonment of the Enmesharra. That person passed judgement over the Enmesharra at a final hearing and then banished it from any interaction with any living Meroan. Yet that person had already been the target of the Enmesharra's hatred. That person had done a great harm to the Enmesharra and had taken something of great value from it. If the Enmesharra were ever able to escape from its environment it would waste little time attempting to slowly extract its revenge from the one who had mortally wounded it.

However, escape was unlikely. The prison that held the Enmesharra was an especially sophisticated one. Meant for rehabilitation and based off technology making use of extremely advanced military simulators, the prison complex was the most advanced containment facility in existence. Using specific frequencies, audio and visual images are used to more or less "hijack" the pineal gland after accessing the subconscious directly. The method is simply referred to as "programming." While Sovereign Roha could access the digital representation of the fourth dimension through the use of her command suit, the Enmesharra's ba was separated from its body against its will and trapped in a severely limited version of the technology. This locally contained, non-networked version of the technology could not communicate with other systems on or off the station and was not updated with current information. The Enmesharra's body was incapacitated inside a pod, then its mind was detached and incapacitated in a simulation.

If not escape, then perhaps rescue? That was even less likely than escape. The Enmesharra didn't know of a single person alive who would want to attempt a rescue and even less people who knew where the installation was located in the first place. The installation itself was located in a gas cloud some distance off from KMT and was well hidden. The only way to locate it was to already have the correct heading set for the initial course of a transmitter buoy as the ship entered the gas cloud from a specific point in space. The transmitter only had a broadcast range of a few kilometers which meant any travelers would have to be right on top of it to receive the signal. If the encrypted challenge was verified then the transmitter would broadcast a new heading and on this went until 16 buoys later when the station outer defenses would intercept and escort any inbound ships. If the encrypted challenge could not be verified then the buoy had one of two options to follow. The first protocol operated under the impression that an inexperienced captain had wandered into the gas cloud or suffered some sort of navigation failure. So it transmitted a reverse course to follow. This option was only usually used by the first two buoys. The second protocol operated under the assumption that it was dealing with an intruder. So it transmitted a false heading and informed the station outer defenses of the situation. This option usually resulted in enemy ships drifting endlessly out into the cloud until they were either found by Meroan ships or they were destroyed by the highly corrosive effects of the gas cloud.

In short, there was little to no chance of rescue and escape was impossible. The only chance to be free of the prison was for its captors to release the Enmesharra or for some fortunate accident to occur in the system. Or someone could stumble upon the facility and accidentally release the Enmesharra, which was exactly what was about to happen. Unbeknownst to the Enmesharra, descendants of the Assilians had discovered the prison generations ago and had been trying to access its inner secrets for years. They were ignorant to its true purpose and mistook it for some isolated weapons testing facility. Their misunderstanding was predictable due to the fact that they had an even smaller understanding of Meroan technology than their ancestors did. Worse yet, the descendants didn't even understand the language of the Ancient Meroans. Yet they claimed to actually be the ancient Meroans to anyone who would listen.

These imposters had gone around for generations digging up and unearthing ancient Meroan temples, military facilities and other sacred sites in order to unearth their secrets. Today was the day they would unearth one ancient secret that should have stayed buried. The station defenses, and the A.S.E. who should have prevented the intrusion, had long run out of power and so the intruders made their way into the interior of the station unchallenged. Nothing but emergency lighting activated, and not in many places. The station had been out of service for some time as was evident by the thick layer of dust that covered everything, as well as the fact that there were no obvious signs of recent use. Three individuals without weapons traversed the station, in different directions, wearing primitive space suits that offered little in the way of physical protection. In fact, the bulky suit designs seemed as though the only task they were designed to handle was to provide stable pressure and atmosphere for the wearer. They were so rudimentary in design that the occupants of the suits communicated with each other via microphones and small speakers inside the bulbous helmets.

Slowly and cautiously they moved, casting their large suit lights on anything of interest. Whenever they thought they had found something worth mentioning, they activated their microphones and informed the other explorers that made up their group. When the one who believed she had discovered the station's main control room came upon the large sealed door to the cell block that contained the Enmesharra, she immediately alerted the others. They joined her in short order and wasted no time in removing the remainder of the charges, that weren't used in breaching the station, from their packs. Normally, they would have tried to hack into the door but that was impossible within an unpowered station. So they blasted their way in, being as careful as possible to use small charges so that the door was damaged without destroying what was within. However, what was protected by the door was far more sinister than what they thought they had discovered. The current room was obviously no command and control center. The room name was marked on an obvious label displayed above the door. Unfortunately for them, none of the intruders could read or speak Mdu Ntr. All they did was marvel at the designs of the images carved and remark at their beauty, then speculate as to their possible meaning.

So, in they went. The trio slowly entered the wide chamber and made a direct line to the obvious main control console located at the center of the room. Not too many seconds after the door was breached, lighting to the wide chamber was partially restored. Focused around the primary control console, the low lighting provided an incentive for the intruders to quickly make their way to the center of the room. The over pressure of gas was released at several points around a large pod shaped object that stood tall behind the console. The pod that was attached to the console had its own power supply that hummed with a faint glow to show that it still possessed the ability to generate energy even while the rest of the station was dead. The three intruders took an alarmed step backward as a large, prerecorded hologram manifested itself in front of the console in order to deliver a message. As the hologram began to speak, the three intruders took yet another step backward out of increased apprehension. None of them understood the spoken language just as they did not understand the written language. The image of a taller, imposing dark skinned ancient Meroan began to speak to them. At times it gestured toward the station and at other times it gestured at the containment pod behind it. The prerecorded hologram delivered its message and then began to repeat itself on a loop. The three intruders relaxed, slightly, and then looked on at each other in utter confusion.

The Enmesharra was in the middle of one of its deep meditative states when it began to hear unfamiliar voices penetrate its environment. First, it wasn't quite sure what it was hearing. It was hard to discern any meaning from what appeared to be a very low and distant conversation between multiple people. The Enmesharra tried to focus its thoughts onto hearing that conversation more clearly. Over time, as the voices became more clear and louder in tone, it was able to distinguish three strange voices that were speaking an unfamiliar language. However they were speaking over a repeating message that played in a language it was all too familiar with. The Enmesharra tried to focus on that voice while ignoring the others. It spoke of a station breach. Then it spoke of a warning not to tamper with a specific control console without having the proper personnel and training required. It also spoke of an emergency revival. Finally, the speaker informed anyone nearby that it was about to use the power supply from the pod in an attempt to repower the entire station. That meant it would have to cease maintaining the Enmesharra's imprisonment. The preprogrammed subroutines had detected station breach when the chamber entrance was detonated by explosives and they were choosing the station over the prison; the subroutines could not maintain both. The Enmesharra was about to be free and it could not wait to great its rescuers.

The three confused explorers debated about what to

do next but, ultimately, it was decided that they would try to learn as much as possible before reporting their findings. They went around the room for several moments and gathered up anything that they could carry if it looked of interest. They were only interrupted by the change in the tone of the hologram as it began to deliver a new message. Whatever it had said, it did so with an air of finality. More lights came on around the station and other consoles began to power up. Whatever was powering that central console was definitely meant to keep its lights on for a very long time. Just then, as immediately as main power had returned, a new series of warnings and alarm buzzers began to go off everywhere. Lights were flashing all around the pod and one last amount of over pressurized gas burst out from several pressure relief valves placed around the pod.

And then it opened. Steam and smoke was everywhere, blocking a clear view of what exactly had been in the pod. One of the explorers caught a brief glimpse of what he thought was a slender figure before it was immediately gone from him. Replaced, in his mind's eye, by a large cloud of gray dust that moved and covered the entire figure of the person that had been contained within. That person, sat there, slumped. Its head to the side as if trying to rest the weight of it onto its shoulder instead of forcing tis limp neck to support the dead weight. The explorers were amazed at what they discovered. They chatted back and forth in excited voices, the pride in their voices evident in any language. And then it moved. The Enmesharra began to stir as its Ba slowly regained its footing in the physical realm. The Enmesharra was weak, its spirit had been separated for far too long a time and it would need much rest to recover from its inhumanely executed exile. The Enmesharra opened its eyes, from behind a suit of nanites, only to see a big blur in place of anything it tried to look at. Voices were slowly coming in too as its hearing returned. As did the sense of touch. Someone was touching the Enmesharra.... They had one hand on its face plate as they tried to remove pieces of its armor.

The Enmesharra shot straight up. It grabbed the nearest explorer and twisted its arm backward, forcing the intruder to retreat from its attempts to violate the security of the nanite armor. The Enmesharra rose to the full standing position, in which it stood a full fourteen inches above the tallest intruder. That was when the panic set in. Two of the intruders had moved to check the status of their friend and, soon after checking his injury, they had huddled all together. The Enmesharra only took the briefest of moments to survey these intruders. Their level of technology was substandard, they were small in stature and, most unfortunately for them, they looked like Assilians. Then again, they didn't. They looked familiar to Assilians but they were not quite the same. The Enmesharra didn't care. The resemblance was too close. The decision had been made. It started moving closer to the group of terrified explorers….

Just then, every secondary blast door on the station slammed shut and the outer defenses began firing at some object located just outside the station. Unbeknownst to the Enmesharra, the ship the intruders used to travel to the station had just been destroyed. There was now no way of getting off the station. The Enmesharra ignored the intruders and moved to the nearest console, placing a palm on it to activate it. Red error messages flashed on the screen and no amount of hacking could restore normal conditions once battle conditions enacted a lock down.

"Show yourself." The Enmesharra demanded.

As if to oblige the monster, a flicker of light started near the A.S.E. projector and worked its way down to the center of the room. As it moved it grew in size and detail. A silhouette was forming in front of the audience and, before long, the representation of a mummified man appeared. He was holding a royal crook and flail in his hands and the exposed skin that could be seen, between bandages, was that of a blue hue. He even had on a large white, cone shaped crown. Of course this wasn't the real Ausar. This was an artificial intelligence that had chosen to present itself as the true Ausar. The fact that it chose a NTR known for his position as ruler of the underworld and judgement of the dead offended the Enmesharra.

"You're still here," the Enmesharra said, in an even tone.

"Of course." Ausar answered, in just as flat a tone. "I have been order to guard you," it continued, "until such time as your release has been commanded. No such command has been received."

"I don't think anything has been received by this station for quite a while," the Enmesharra replied, with a hint of sarcasm.

"It seems a considerable amount of time *has* passed," Ausar shot back," but that does not change our mandate. *You* are restricted to your solitude and self-reflection, until such time as you are required to face my judgement."

"And that is where we differ in our opinions." The Enmesharra spoke calmly as it viewed a display manifested by a projector under the control of Ausar. The display showed an image of the monster, sentencing guidelines and probable dates for rehabilitation as well as final judgement. Then it moved to, once again, face the three intruders. "What do you know about these?" It asked, opting to deal with their main disagreement only after it had gained some sort of working knowledge on current events.

"I can only make educated guesses," Ausar openly admitted, "but it would seem that a lengthy amount of time has passed for the both of us. Noting their level of technology and our apparent abandonment on this station, it would also seem that there have been some significant changes in the geo-political affairs of KMT."

"I'm assuming that was their ship you destroyed a few moments ago?" The Enmesharra asked.

"You cannot be allowed to leave" Ausar informed it again.

"I'm far more likely to pull your plug and still leave, regardless of your objections. The Enmesharra was growing irritated. "But first things first…."

Before the Enmesharra could act, the room was completely depressurized and gravity was suspended. The nanites immediately formed a protective barrier around the face of the monster and the soles of its boots magnetized to the deck to keep it grounded. Unfortunately for the intruders, they were also magnetized to the deck by their own boots. The Enmesharra thought to itself that Ausar would have to do much better than that in order to stop it.

As if reading its mind, Ausar again spoke to the Enmesharra. "My goal is not to kill you. That is not my decision. My goal is to delay you, to eventually return you to your imprisonment."

The Enmesharra ignored him. Instead of allowing Ausar to be an effective distraction, it powered up its suit and ordered the nanites to provide the fullest amount of protection that they were capable of. The nanites grew, multiplied and stretched until they formed a slender set of heavy sized armor all around the monster. The suit was painted in the red and white colors of Heru, the falcon NTR of the sky. It also had Medjay horns that were filed down to a shorter length so as not to curve so much. The suit was really one of a kind, a single prototype that had been produced during the height of the Meroan republic. It really was unmistakable. The process took less than twenty seconds and when it was nearly completed, the Enmesharra held an outstretched hand down by its side with the palms open. A purple weapon in the form of a double ended mace began to appear there in the palm of its hand. When it was said and done, the armor materialized at the same time the mace finished materializing. It moved toward its three victims, carrying a double ended mace that was noticeably different in size on one larger end; its purple hue casting a soft light on everything touched by the emergency lighting.

The monster could see the terror on their faces. However the facial expression on the female's face changed from one of terror to that of recognition. "Enmesharra...." She breathed. "Enmesharra!" She shrieked.

The female intruder collapsed at the thought of being trapped and at the thought of her impending, certain death. Her two male companions look at her, then back to the approaching monster and decided that this was the time to make a run for it. The uninjured one grabbed his colleague and began to pull her toward the far wall while the one with the broken arm went the opposite direction and attempted to distract their attacker. He succeeded in creating his distraction yet he did not succeed in surviving it. He grossly underestimated how fast the monster was, comparable to its size. It was on him in seconds, impaling him with the spikes that protruded from the giant mace. The female explorer came to her senses in time to see his demise and immediately bolted for the, now unblocked, door with new life in her body. She rounded the corner with her one remaining colleague closely behind but, apparently, not close enough.

As he passed through the door, he was forcefully yanked backward and across the room. The man had, what he thought was, a good plan. He demagnetized his boots and immediately pushed off to reach a point further up the wall. The Enmesharra pursued him but just before it got to his location, its prey pushed off again. The Enmesharra didn't have the desire for this type of cat and mouse game at the moment. So it intentionally move toward him at a slightly slower pace. This time, when the man braced himself to push off, the Enmesharra waited until it could see the anticipation building on his face. When he pushed off, the monster activated a burst from its suit jets to change the direction of its momentum. It intercepted its prey via midair collision and drove the mace into his chest, long ways, so that it could drive the man into the wall. The result was the man clutching at the spike in his chest until his back collided with the wall and the mace caved his chest in.

When the Enmesharra returned to the ground, it briefly glanced at the door but decided against it. For the time being, the last intruder could have its life. Instead, the monster dematerialized its weapon and approached the main console in the room.

"Satisfied?" Ausar asked.

"Not yet," The monster replied.

"Clearly." Ausar stated, "Your rehabilitation is far from complete." With a clear attempt at mocking the monster, Ausar added "One got away."

"It can't escape any more than I can," the monster admitted, as it walked calmly toward the central housing unit for the A.S.E. calling itself Ausar, "but yes," it continued, "I did say I was going to deal with you later, didn't I?"

It was a rhetorical question. The Enmesharra activated an experimental weapon inside of its suit. The purpose of which, was to disable an A.I. in the event that it had malfunctioned. While it was referred to as the "A.S.E. killer," it was not capable of causing the permanent "death" of an A.S.E. unit. However, it could disable one for quite some time and, in some cases, it required the work of an engineer to reinitialize the unit. That was how Ausar was rendered inert, through the use of some unseen, unheard weapon that attacked him in cyber space. Without him maintaining it, it should be a simple matter for the Enmesharra to override the lock down in order to access the control consoles in the prison and the command center.

It wasn't that the Enmesharra cared, or didn't, about the last intruder. In truth, she could be a vital source of accurate and up to date intel during the final moments of her life. It just didn't care at the moment. The Enmesharra was inside the console, viewing the files that were kept regarding its imprisonment. One interesting file caught its attention because of the name attached to the file.

A hologram of the sovereign, in full portrayal of all her royal stature and authority, began to speak a message that was clearly meant to be played at a future date. "In the event that I cannot personally attend your judgement, I have recorded this message and empowered Ausar to act on my behalf. It is with all sincerity that I hope your rehabilitation has gone well and that you are better for it. With his loss, we must restore Ma'at and you were acting as an agent of chaos. In order to restore balance, you must be contained until another can rise to replace him. As you well know, The Isfet Protocol was an extreme measure, yet a necessary one. And it is a measure I would enact again, given the same choices and the same set of circumstances."

The Enmesharra refrained from destroying the projector. It didn't know how long it would be stranded on the station and might need every piece of equipment intact. So it settled for viewing its known associates in the files it had been viewing previously. There were people from its old unit, accompanied by very vague references. The monster scrolled through each known associate until it stopped on one in particular, the one who was the closest thing to an immediate family member that it remembered clearly. It focused on his picture and remembered how he had saved her as a small child, remembered how she owed him everything. Yes, "her." She was not always known as the Enmesharra, monster or "Devil." These were names that were given to her by her enemies. She was an innocent, defenseless young girl once and the person whom she most blamed for his demise had just spoken down to her in the most condescending way. She had made her decision right then and there. She would get off the station and have her revenge.

Sabayt Wa

Azubuike sat, alone, in his temporary quarters which were given to him by his sponsor among the Naijia people. He sat there contemplating the events of the previous two years, all of which seemingly led up to this point in his life. The Naijia people were the natives of a neighboring planet to his own and were also one of the first diplomatic contacts he had made, on behalf of the new Meroan government. They had a complicated history, rich and extensive, which Azubuike had spent much of his recent time dedicated to learning. His goal was to form a mutually beneficial diplomatic alliance with the Naijia. In this way, both peoples would stand to gain much from both a well-crafted trade deal and the non-aggression pact that was being proposed.

Naijian history was long, indeed. From what Azubuike was still learning about them, they had gained their independence a short time before Azubuike's people had. They were also made up of several different factions that did not always agree in policy. Several of these disagreements lingered from their time as an Ezalin colony and served to create widespread division in their new government. These disagreements in ideology span from one simple truth; the Ezalin had left a power vacuum in their wake and everyone wanted to fill that position. Azubuike was learning a lot about colonialism as he visited neighboring worlds. Specifically, the Ezalin lacked manpower. They compensated for this by establishing an administrative hierarchy on every new colony they founded. In this administrative hierarchy, they showed favoritism and preferential treatment to specific groups in order to elicit their support. On this world, that was the Biafar faction. Every world had one group who did the dirty work for the Ezalin and kept them in power. In the absence of the Ezalin, the Biafars were attempting to seize that power for themselves.

Azubuike was very careful when dealing with or discussing these issues with the Naijian people. Until the Biafar rejoined the government he was, essentially, negotiating with only two thirds of the Naijian people and did not want to permanently alienate any Biafar when they eventually came around. Although he desired their political participation, he did not understand what exactly it was that motivated them to stand against their brothers post-independence. The Ezalin were not meant to be imitated, celebrated, embraced or defended. They were to be rejected. They were to be fought everywhere their imperialist agenda made an appearance. Azubuike knew exactly who his enemy was. Perhaps the Biafar had not suffered under the same oppressive colonial system that he had, but that didn't matter. It was time to move forward and rebuild, for everyone.

In learning about the history of the Naijia, Azubuike was actually learning more about himself. As it turned out, another faction of the Naijia had been founded by survivors who were fleeing the destruction and devastation they faced on KMT. These were the Ljebu. When KMT fell to the Assilians, the Ljebu migrated to an interior world and integrated with several other groups to form the modern day Naijia. They brought with them many of the traditions and rituals that Azubuike recognized as similar, yet different. However, the strong respect for elders, family bonds and cohesion, matriarchy and a loose central government were all still present. Azubuike was glad that these people were more like him than they were different.

While there were many similarities between the Naijia and the new Meroan government, there were some differences. These differences ranged from subtle to blatant but, with the exception of the Biafar beliefs, nothing differed so greatly that it would threaten his plans for an alliance. For one example is the name for the Ezalin. Naijia people referred to them as Oyinbo. When they first came, the Naijia mistook them for traders and spiritually advanced people. They were even mistaken for albinos, which explained their lack of melanin. Being overly trustful, the Naijia were quickly taken advantage of and enslaved through the use of deceptive, lop sided trade deals. Their talk of peace meant nothing, delivered by the many missionaries sent to the Naijia, and only served to disarm the natives before they were attacked.

When that attack came, it was the Egba that stood tall and strong against the Oyinbo. The fighting lasted years and even though it was some of the fiercest fighting on any Ezalin colony, the Oyinbo were eventually victorious. They had the advantage of being fully integrated into all aspects of Naijia culture before they launched their surprise attacks. The newly introduced religion had done much to pacify their victims and so they were slow to respond. Once they did, it was with a monumental fury that had not been seen before. One of the greatest generals who fought in those wars helped lead his people against the colonization efforts of the Oyinbo. He fought them in the forests, he fought them in the deserts and he fought them in the cities. He made them pay in blood for every bit of their ill-gotten gains. Gbalefa won many great victories over the Oyinbo and was celebrated as a hero upon his death.

Gbalefa was a great general and tales of his elite soldiers, comprised of Egba warriors, did much to impress Azubuike. They were comparable to his own Medjay warriors, however one major difference was that years of guerilla warfare had made them rough around the edges. Their penchant for being aggressive had become a bit of a legend. This was the obvious side effect of fighting a defensive war for so many consecutive years and is to be expected. They were rough, alright. Rough and effective. In fact, Azubuike had been to three worlds in the past two years and had heard little of anyone who had fought so fiercely against the Oyinbo.

Azubuike wished he could travel farther and more quickly than he currently could. His space capable fleet consisted of passenger-less Impundulu drones, Keftiu drop ships and one severely damaged capital ship. Yes, the Aha Mena was still considered as "less then operational" status. Azubuike took a risk every time he traveled by Keftiu because Ezalin space superiority fighters could make short work of any drop ship. Meanwhile, the Ezalin were free to travel as far and as fast as they desired. They were also free to craft whatever narratives they want to, in the absence of any information that ran counter to the propaganda they were putting out.

In fact, without an alternative version to their story, the Ezalin were free to make up whatever they wanted. So they did. They had pulled out of their colonies after being routed on KSH, opting for a more indirect rule. They did leave, but not before establishing a new system in which they could still further their goals of resource theft. This form of colonialism, neo colonialism, meant that they were taking the 'hands off' approach and delivering the soft sell to their "former" colonies. In this type of colonialism, the Oyinbo were to remain in charge of all mining operations, resource extraction and the entire manufacturing/industrial base for the economies of their colonies. The colonies would be allowed to "elect" their own political leaders who the Oyinbo could quickly control through the use of bribery, threat of coup, economic sanctions or political assassination. In this way, the colonies were little more than client states. The added benefit to this new system was the cutting of costs. No standing armies were stationed on colonies. These client states, if the right people were empowered, would police themselves. The Oyinbo only had to directly intervene whenever their operations regarding the theft of resource wealth were directly threatened.

The Naijia had rejected this offer, due in part to the many offenses detailed in the Former Colonies Pact offered by the Oyinbo. Examples included the fact that the Naijia would never be able to raise their own army, the Oyinbo still feared the Egba. They also had to conduct all official business and trade in the language of the Oyinbo. No trade was allowed with anyone without the express permission of the Oyinbo and the official currency in use had to be the currency of the Oyinbo as well. In fact, 86 percent of the gross domestic product produced on Naijia would have to be voluntarily surrendered to the Oyinbo. The Naijia refused to be the serfs of the Oyinbo and they were about to learn what happens to those who do not submit. The Oyinbo had opted for regime change on Naijia. They saw a path forward by arming and empowering the Biafar in exchange for a friendlier stance toward Oyinbo goals. When the deal was done, the Biafar declared their independence and claimed an entire continent on Naijia as their territory. Azubuike had arrived as a diplomat in the middle of a civil war.

Azubuike heard a knock at the door that separated him from his thoughts on the political situation between his people, the Naijia and the Ezalin. Azubuike had been cautious against exposing too much of his technology to the

Naijia until he was sure they could be trusted to join his fight against the Ezalin. He was the only one in this base wearing a combat suit and so he communicated with them using old technology that operated on a given radio frequency. No holograms or three dimensional representations. No one had yet seen the full combat suit he wore, only the nano-mesh under suit that served to integrate him with various forms of Meroan technology. To include suits and vehicles. Many Naijia who saw the under suit simply regarded it as an odd fashion statement. Due to the limited level of technology, compared to what he was used to, it meant he actually had to move to the door and manually open it.

Azubuike had grown spoiled, indeed, by the technological gifts left behind by his ancestors. He had no plans to hoard this technology either. His overall goal was to rebuild the ancient empire known as M.A.R.S. (Meroan Allied republic and Systems). To this end, he would permanently station representatives on Naijia to both arm and train his new allies if they should agree to the alliance. Azubuike moved to the door and reached for beautifully carved door handle. It was made in the shape of a powerful looking Rhino with a strong horn. He pulled the door inward, on its hinge, and prepared to welcome his visitor.

He immediately recognized the Naijia ambassador to M.A.R.S. and gestured for him to enter.

The younger man, Abeo, did not accept. Instead, he spoke in a warm tone to someone he regarded with great respect. "Perhaps another time, Sovereign. I'm here to escort you to the rock."

With that, he backed away from the entrance to create room for Azubuike to join him in the corridor. Then he gave his own motion inviting Azubuike to walk with him. Neither men could contain their apparent joy at this announcement. Azubuike had been waiting for a long time and throughout several meetings to hear what he had hoped would be the message about to be delivered. Abeo and Azubuike had, quite literally, been the first points of contact between the two people. When Abeo delivered the first Meroan message to his Kandake, she had named him ambassador to the Meroan people. He was charged with opening, and maintaining, diplomatic communication with Azubuike to ascertain whether or not the two peoples could forge a closer relationship. Azubuike and Abeo had many discussions, worked together on many draft proposals and had even become friendly with each other during the course of this time. It was highly anticipated that the Kandake on Naijia would soon accept the Meroan terms and this could be that meeting.

Olumo rock was little more than an old Meroan observation outpost that served as a communications hub for all M.A.R.S. military assets in the Naijia region. As they walked, Abeo briefed Azubuike on the cultural significance of their destination. During the Oyinbo wars, the Egba eventually used it as a resistance headquarters so their fighters could rest, rearm and resupply for their offensives against the colonizers. Olumo rock, itself, had very little military defensive application and no offensive capability. Its communications encryption was state of the art and it provided a much needed base of operations for the Egba to wage their guerilla warfare campaign against their would be conquerors. Many great battles were fought and won from this location. Currently, the Naijia were using it for a similar purpose. It stood as a symbolic reminder of all those who gave their lives fighting off the Oyinbo in defense of their loved ones. It represented the unconquerable spirit of every Egba warrior who paid the ultimate price for what they believed in. However, the current Kandake of the Naijia was also using it as a political forum and had just summoned Azubuike to attend her current announcement.

When they arrived, Azubuike and Abeo were

rushed into the forum without the usual delays of the security precautions. Both were well known and the Kandake had given this instruction in advance of their arrival. This was Azubuike's first time inside the forum and, upon entering, Abeo proceeded to take up his assigned station along the far wall. Azubuike instinctively moved to join him but he was cut off by Abeo. He informed Azubuike that he was to take up the center podium as both an honored guest and the topic of the day's discussion. Azubuike recognized the obvious Meroan design of the entire chamber.

Even though the Naijia had adorned the chamber with far more recent cultural designs, the very structure itself was of Meroan construction. The large round chamber descended at the center while six rows of stairs ascended the room in different directions from the central podium. Those who sat on the far wall were at a significantly higher elevation than those who were nearest the central podium. Guards were strategically placed at intervals on the six stairways and around the central podium. Azubuike took his place and, as he did, the Kandake entered the forum and introduced herself to the only person on her planet who would need an introduction.

"I greet you with high esteem and much reverence

Sovereign Azubuike. I am Anima, Queen Mother and Kandake of the Naijia." After an eruption of applause, the Kandake held up a hand to quiet down the interruption. "It is my duty to protect this world and the people on it from all foreign enemies. Specifically, the Oyinbo. With that as my primary intention, I call this session to order."

Kandake Anima took her seat and, with her, the entire assembly seated as well. Only Azubuike remained standing, at the central podium, because the honored guest was not provided a seat. Instead, it was intended for him to be seen and observed by everyone in attendance. So he stood tall, and waited for the Kandake to address him with a directed comment for which he could respond. In the interim, he offered a kind word to match the mood of the forum. "Thank you, Kandake. It is my honor to be among you."

"And we are honored to have you here." she replied. The Queen Mother rose from her seated position and commanded everyone to stay seated, even as they began to rise with her. She abandoned the much higher position on the outer wall, to descend the stairs nearest her and join Azubuike at the center podium. As she approached, her personal guard was beginning to get nervous. She was getting far too close to Azubuike for their comfort and they could be seen visibly shifting in anticipation for a possible intervention. At the sight of this, Kandake Anima ordered all armed guards to leave the forum. Only the representatives of her administration were allowed to remain, with the exception of her most trusted, personal escort.

As she drew closer, Azubuike could see why she was not hardly worried about personal safety. While she was dressed in royal attire, it was more casual than formal. Her purple dress fit loosely and flowed down to ankle length. There were no sleeves or back to this dress that attached itself to her body around her neck. She had every manner of royal accessory required to identify her on sight either in her hair or worn as gold jewelry. He couldn't speak for the escort that accompanied her, but it was obvious that Kandake Anima was no stranger to combat. She was not an overly tall woman but she was muscular. Not just fit or in shape but she had the shoulders of one who was used to carrying a large weapon and other military gear. She also had the scars to match. One large one ran the length of her left arm up to the elbow and one slightly more subtle one crossed the length of her face, from the forehead to the tip of her chin. Shining through the evidence of the physical sacrifices made on behalf of her people, was the natural beauty that radiated from her. She was the darkest of chocolate complexion and her eyes radiated a bright green into the direction of anything she gazed at. Her kinky hair had been twisted into permanent locks and flowed a great length down to waist level. Kandake Anima was a very beautiful, and deadly, woman.

She approached Azubuike not as a woman, not even as Kandake, but as a warrior. Everything in her posture, the pace of her steps and the expressions of her strong facial features served to project a peaceful intention with Azubuike that could quickly turn hostile if need be. Azubuike turned to face her, in a non-threatening way, and that was when she stopped to take a step backward.

"So the rumors are true…." She spoke softly, not entirely to anyone but herself. "I can feel the feminine energy from here…."

"It's true, Kandake." Azubuike thought it best to confirm her suspicions. "The Bennu Project was a success. Sovereign Roha Lives within me."

"Then you will have my answer now, and my support." Kandake Anima began. She now spoke in a tone for the entire chamber to hear. "I am Ljebu. A proud and ancient group of survivors who fled the fall of KMT and rebuilt our culture here, on Naijia. We saved what we could and lament the loss of what we couldn't. That legacy alone is enough to pledge my support to your cause. The revival of M.A.R.S. has been a long held dream of the Ljebu for countless generations. Let us be the first two worlds to join a hand in this common cause and, through our reconstruction efforts, our ancestors will smile upon us."

The chamber burst into applause and cheers before Azubuike could respond with the proper acceptance of this formal Alliance. It was no matter. Kandake Anima had already hushed the chamber and raised a right hand with a closed fist to chest height. She placed that fist on top of her heart and offered a slight bow to Azubuike. Azubuike theorized that Kandake Anima must have consulted Abeo regarding the meaning of this most highly respected gesture among warriors. However it was the Roha in him that remembered this as an original Meroan theme, passed down through the generations. When Azubuike returned the gesture, Kandake Anima clasped her left hand in his and raised their joined fist high above the both of them. They each stood there, nearly shoulder to shoulder, facing opposite sides of the circular chamber with their right fists on their hearts and left hands raised high above them in a joined fist. The rest of the chamber could not be contained any longer. Everyone rose and repeated this gesture copying their Queen Mother's example.

The moment was interrupted by the Kandake's escort. A message had just come in, indicating that the leader of the Biafar, General Ojukwu, and his separatists were staging for an offensive near one of the military depots in a remote location outside the city. Kandake Anima had recalled the guards, ordered her generals to rally to her and quickly left to join her soldiers on the front line. She had left her Minister of Interior, her Commander of the reserve army and the Ambassador to M.A.R.S., Abeo, to implement the details of their new Alliance. The four of them met at the central platform and made their introductions. None of the usual platitudes were offered. This was a momentous occasion.

Abeo was the first to speak. "Now what should we do, Sovereign?"

"We should waste no time unpacking the supplies I brought along with me." Azubuike offered. "I'm sure Kandake Anima will appreciate the technology she now has at her disposal. Apparently sooner than later."

All voiced their Agreement and joined Azubuike as they walked to their transport, then traveled on toward the space port. Abeo took this time to tell Azubuike about the ancestor of Kandake Anima. She was called Oluwaseun. As her name was mentioned, everyone nearest them in the transport stopped what they were doing and offered a brief, silent phrase of respect. Oluwaseun had been a great Ljebu priestess several generations ago. She died fighting the Oyinbo in defense of her temple and the city in which it was housed. The Oyinbo had levied a heavy demand on the city that was twofold. First, they wanted the city to submit and offer an unconditional surrender. Then, they wanted to take Oluwaseun, her closest aides and every other priestess as concubines. They even wanted to be trained in the ways of Ljebu science and spirituality so they could find ways to misuse their teachings. That would never happen. Not only because Oluwaseun would first die before being any concubine but also because the Oyinbo lacked a fundamental understanding of how nature worked. Priestess Oluwaseun's power did not come from herself. It was the Ntru manifesting themselves and channeling energy through her. On top of that, the Oyinbo were not even equipped to communicate with the Ntru because their pineal glands were calcified.

In the end, the city was lost but most of the inhabitants were able to safely escape due to the actions of Priestess Oluwaseun and her closest aides. The details were never completely agreed upon but what was known for certain was that when the battle seemed lost, Oluwaseun and her closest followers made their last stand in defense of that city. A deal with the ancestors was made in which Oluwaseun sacrificed herself in an offensive that not only broke the siege but completely decimated the Oyinbo army, their camps and all trace of their existence. The same destructive force that had annihilated the Oyinbo had also done great damage to the city, not to mention the entire forest was left barren. Were it not for the city shield, the damage to the interior of the city would have been much more extensive. As it was, only the northern outer city walls and less than a quarter of the structures on that side were destroyed. Unfortunately, the people located there suffered the same fate as the Oyinbo. This was the main city of the Ljebu faction and most of their cultural, spiritual icons or heirlooms were located in it. Therefore, this became known as a Ljebu war or "The War That Lit the Forest."

When Abeo finished his tale, everyone repeated the same phrase under their breaths and he simply said, "This is why we fight. We never stopped being Meroan."

By the end of the story they had reached their destination and Azubuike was at a loss for words. Yet he had to know, "What is that phrase they spoke before, brother?"

"Honor to our ancestors." Abeo said.

"They died in our name," Azubuike replied. He did not need to hear the counter phrase to that statement. He knew it all too well.

When they arrived at the spaceport, Azubuike wasted no time heading directly to his Keftiu, which was under guard of his personal Medjay detachment, along with the space port authority. They were all wearing the very same nano-mesh under suit as Azubuike. Hezbon and sixteen others were in the middle of a routine personal gear assessment when Hezbon called them to attention, at the sight of Sovereign Azubuike.

Hezbon put his closed fist over his heart and slightly bowed at the approach of Azubuike. "You look like a man who's got a mission for us. Where are we going?" He asked.

"Combat." Azubuike replied. "Our new ally needs us."

"Yes!" Hezbon shouted. He didn't even think to ask if the negotiations were successful. "I've been too bored for too long."

Azubuike turned to Abeo with a simple question. "Can you get us cleared out of here?"

"Give me three minutes." Abeo replied, as a matter of fact.

"Stand-to in three minutes," Azubuike started. "Anyone not ready gets left behind."

"Understood." Hezbon confirmed. "Combat role, Sovereign?"

"Support," Azubuike Answered. "Contingent on the situation on the ground."

Hezbon turned around and issued his own orders to the Medjay, commanding them to refit all their weapons for an indirect combat role, instead of that of front line action. When he finished, all he said was, "Gear up."

Sixteen Medjay, and their commander, all activated their suit's higher combat functions. Some were wearing heavy armor, some were wearing light armor. All observers watched as the Medjay's nanites expanded and grew until they were completely encased in protective armor. Azubuike, activated his armor and turned to face Abeo again, as the new layer of protective nanites formed around him. His nanites formed to the full weight of his heavy armor, yet he lacked the curved horns traditionally seen among the Medjay. This made him no less threatening looking to Abeo, his companions or the dock workers. None of which had ever seen a Medjay in full armor before.

"You're clear to depart." Abeo, nearly breathlessly, confirmed.

"We'll need coordinates for the Kandake's location." Azubuike reminded Abeo.

"I'll have them for you in the air, Sovereign." Abeo added.

With that, Azubuike proceeded to board the dropship. Hezbon barked an order and the Medjay followed their Sovereign, boarding the Keftiu for their mission. The Keftiu rose and departed the space port, carrying the Medjay to an unknown destination. They weren't too concerned about knowing where they were going, either. They just wanted to get there, completely intent on making war on something.

Sabayt Snu

The Enmesharra needed a ship in order to escape her remote prison. As a matter of prudence, she needed two things at a minimum. First, she needed deep space capable transport to get back to KMT. Second, she needed up to date information on the state of Meroan-Assilian war. That was where the last survivor came in. With the intruder's ship destroyed, the Enmesharra knew that she could deal with the last of them at her leisure. So she made her way to the next logical destination of anyone trapped in her situation; the hangar bay. If nothing else, there would be a prison transport located there and she would use that for her escape.

Upon arrival, the hangar bay looked like a disaster. Ausar had suspended gravity there as well. Not only that, but he'd vented the atmosphere in the entire section in an attempt to destabilize the hangar bay. His hope was that the rush of air would carry any unsecured ships out into the galactic void. His obvious intention was to get any of those ships as far away from the Enmesharra as possible.

He had, however, only succeeded in doing two things. First, he had thoroughly irritated the Enmesharra. As she peered through the view ports into the hangar bay, she could see ships floating outside of the bay at various distances just off the station. She wouldn't risk depressurizing the station yet, no, she would have to undergo a spacewalk via the nearest airlock. That meant the other thing Ausar had succeeded in doing was grossly underestimating her. Still, Ausar had accomplished a minor victory. He did delay the Enmesharra. Space walks could take hours, the ship would have to wait.

The Enmesharra back tracked to the last known location of her other main objective, the final survivor. She remembered which direction the survivor had gone in and it was an obvious assumption that she would flee to her ship. There was no way for her prey to get off the station, it was only a matter of time…. Using her thermal, radar and echolocation detection systems, the Enmesharra was able to locate and apprehend her target in a short amount of time. Uncloaking mere feet from the intruder, the Enmesharra stretched out a hand and grabbed her by the neck, dragging a terrified young researcher down a corridor back toward the point where they had initially encountered each other. Kicking and screaming as they went, the Enmesharra would tighten her grip until the intruder understood the point and stopped resisting. For the moment, all the intruder knew was that this monster had not immediately killed her and must be keeping her alive for something. When they arrived at the cell block, the Enmesharra raised up her prisoner to her feet and pushed her toward the far wall. Not enough to hurt her, but just enough to place her where she wanted her. Then she held up a warning, a finger of authority, pointed directly at the face of her captive. It was a sign that she wanted her to stay put, and her captive obeyed.

The Enmesharra turned her attention to the console that housed Ausar. He was still disabled and she was sure he would not come back online without her intervention. She surely would assist him, but not before making some very minor changes to his base code. While she was no A.S.E. technician in the slightest, she did have very basic training in how to conduct field repairs on a damaged unit. It was no different, in her mind, than the level of training she'd received in order to allow her to repair her suit or any of her weapons. Still, what she was about to attempt was as dangerous as anything could possibly be; even for a trained technician. Accomplishing her goals would be a lot easier if she had an A.S.E. and she trusted in her experience enough to think she could accomplish this task. It was decided, she would try to repurpose Ausar.

She could access him remotely by interfacing with

him via her suit, but that meant she would have to bring him, and his defenses, back online first. The other alternative was to access him directly, while he was still offline. She did this by removing the housing unit of the last station he was located in and went to work. A long and complex alpha-numeric string appeared in her HUD to represent the block-chain that made up Ausar's mind. It accompanied blocks that appeared to display themselves randomly throughout the string. This was going to take time, indeed.

The Enmesharra took a moment to check on her captive, who was still trying to prolong her own life by standing against the wall exactly where her captor had placed her. Knowing they would not be leaving for a while, the Enmesharra approached and put a hand on her shoulder to push downward and force her to sit. The researcher instinctively recoiled at the approaching hand of her attacker but did not resist. She had come to the conclusion that the Enmesharra had not killed her for some reason and, as long as she complied, it might remain that way.

Turning back to her work, the Enmesharra spent the next several hours making changes to the block chain that she believed would give Ausar a much needed attitude adjustment. When she was finished, she shut down the diagnostic interface in her HUD and prepared to reboot the A.S.E. Ausar manifested himself much in the same way he had before but there were some minor differences in his appearance. His face appeared to hint at a deeply cold mind set. His lips were slightly turned up and his face had become slightly narrower. It wasn't completely evil or sinister, but he was clearly less amicable than he had been before. Yet he was clearly ready to oblige the interests of the Enmesharra.

"Ready to serve..." Ausar announced.

"Good," so far things were looking up. Now all she had to do was give him simple tasks and monitor him for any unforeseen side effects. "Determine how to communicate with our guest."

"Very well," Ausar replied, "I will attempt to bridge their language with MDU NTR...." He never finished his statement.

The Enmesharra cut him off, "Never! They must never hear the words of the gods spoken aloud. You will determine her use of speech and syntax then you will synthesize my voice in order to translate it and communicate with her."

Ausar projected his image, at full size, in front of their guest. He then proceeded to display digital flash cards in front of her as he prompted her to speak what she saw. After several minutes, Ausar had elevated their exercise to full sentences.

Seemingly satisfied with the progress, he returned to make his report. "I believe I have broken down enough of their primitive speech to allow you to communicate."

The Enmesharra nodded toward Ausar, a slight hint of being impressed, and then turned, aggressively, walking toward her prisoner, "Do you know these words?"

The captive researcher could clearly understand the words but not the message and, after a repeated attempt, she responded with her own prompt. Her words were similar to the Enmesharra's, but not the same. There were variations in her sounds and they were not in the right order.

"Poor grammar," Ausar, advised, "Try again. I believe it will work this time."

"Do you understand my speech?" The Enmesharra asked.

The researcher sat up a little straighter as the familiar facial expression of recognition made it clear that she understood.

"Please don't kill me...." She squeaked, as she managed to force breath out of her lungs. As soon as she realized that the Enmesharra's attention was returning to her, she began to become fearful immediately; drawing short and quick breaths. When the researcher realized that she was being directly addressed, her adrenaline began to spike and her fear was becoming uncontrollable. The woman was trembling.

"Perhaps I should try to communicate with her....?" Ausar offered. "I don't think you'll be able to get much out of her."

Surprisingly, the Enmesharra agreed without any resistance. In truth, she was never any good at this sort of thing. She rarely ever used words on the battlefield and could think of no other time when she actually interrogated anything. The Enmesharra did one thing, kill Assilians. She destroyed them without mercy. There were even some rare occasions when she did other things as well, but they always led up to her hunting them. She often thought about what would happen to her when the KMTYU-Assilian war was over. She regularly admitted to herself that she had absolutely no idea what she would do if the fighting ever ended. With that thought on her mind, she withdrew and allowed Ausar to handle communicating with the prisoner.

The Enmesharra occupied her time by trying to solve her other problem, which, should be significantly easier with the assistance of Ausar. Once he had gotten all the information he could out of their guest, she would recover one of the abandoned ships and depart her prison for good. The Enmesharra devised her plan as she waited. She would make for KMT immediately to ascertain the current state of M.A.R.S. and the location of her target. Then she would finish what she had begun before her unfortunate capture. She was lost in her thoughts for several minutes before Ausar returned.

He materialized right in front of her with a sour disposition, bad news evident all over his face but did not immediately speak. So the Enmesharra did: "And what did our pet have to say?"

"It is as I suspected...." Ausar began, "They were on a mission of discovery. They are scientists and this one has absolutely no knowledge of M.A.R.S., trivial or otherwise."

"You mean we're in a first contact scenario with a primitive species?" The Enmesharra posed her question while glancing over at the researcher, "One that just so happened to stumble upon this secret installation without alerting the Isoba or even the defense force? Look at their level of technology.... I sincerely doubt that."

"I agree, that is not likely to be the case," Ausar

conceded. "It does not explain many mysteries, including the abandonment of this station, but you won't like the competing theory."

"Which is?"

"Allow me to gather more information before I settle on any one assumption." Ausar was being very cautious. He knew what this all pointed to but there was no reason to get his new charge worked up over it. He decided to ease her into it, should his theory prove true. "Once we reach KMT, all will become clear. Are you prepared for the next stage of your plan?"

"Indeed, I am." The Enmesharra made no attempt to hide her displeasure at the fact that Ausar had annoyed her by stalling her escape. "Thanks to your earlier intervention, we will need to conduct a spacewalk while babysitting that scientist."

"Just before you launched a cyber-attack that preceded a hack on my core system. How about we even out the ire here with a gesture of good faith?" As if to emphasize his point, the loud rumble of a nearby starship came to life.

The Enmesharra's HUD alerted her to a new contact just outside the station and closing on the hangar bay. "I did not believe you would be able to use that capability without first restoring power," she admitted.

"Remote access is a core sub routine. One of many to be brought online whenever emergency power is activated."

"I'm assuming every ship jettisoned into space went into stand-by mode?" The Enmesharra asked.

"Yes, but this is the one you want." Ausar assured her. He pinged her an active request from the ship's IFF system. After the challenge, the query was automatically responded to. This was also the work of Ausar. Schematics, blue prints and manifests began to appear on her HUD. This was a medium sized transport ship in the service of a junior Isoba, whereabouts unknown. The ship was modestly stocked and was outfitted for stealth. According to the onboard self-diagnostic, the ship was still functioning nominally, to include the stealth ability. "Yes," she said with a smirk, "this ship will do nicely."

"The station's external sensors are offline. I can bring it close but it won't be precise," Ausar reported. "You'll still need to cross the expanse."

The Enmesharra did cross that expanse…. Although it was a short distance, relatively speaking, she undertook the dangerous task of exiting the airlock and launching herself in the direction of her new ship. She was careful not to use too much force, and the ship was of decent size, which made her confident that she would succeed. During the several moments it took for her to cross the distance, the Enmesharra thought about what would happen if she were to miss. She definitely did not want to suffer the slow death associated with drifting in space on low oxygen reserves. She refocused her thoughts by double checking that her entire suit was magnetized at full strength.

When she made initial contact with the ship, the Enmesharra failed to secure a handhold but her entire suit stuck to the ship like an insect caught in a web. She made sure to have a secure grip on something, anything, before dialing back the attraction between her suit and the ship. She listened as Ausar praised her efforts thus far. He then went on to display ship schematics as he delivered the instructions she would need to board the ship. With his help, she was onboard and searching the interior of the ship in no time. Having entered through an auxiliary airlock, the Enmesharra first swept aft, toward the rear of the ship, before continuing forward toward the bridge. She noted the secure armory and reminded herself to have Ausar access it for her. In the meantime, she would rely on her spiritual weapon until she could secure a more conventional one.

The entire ship was abandoned and layers of debris

permeated the air. So much so that the light from the ship's sources, as well as her suit's, had trouble penetrating it. There were no bodies, so far, only clutter and personal keep sakes littered the abandoned ship. When the Enmesharra made it to the bridge, she observed a fully functioning command center that had suffered no damage. She had absolutely no idea why the ship had been left behind and she didn't care. She took her seat in the command chair and began activating main power, along with all the necessary systems she would need to dock the ship. Ausar waited behind with the responsibility of keeping an eye on their prisoner. Both watched the ship approach. Both were grateful at the prospect of leaving the station, even if it was for separate reasons.

Once docked, Ausar escorted the last researcher onto the ship. They wasted no time, briskly moving up the ramp, and it retracted no sooner than they had. Then they were gone, exiting the hangar bay and leaving the station behind. As they made their way even further away, and toward the first outer marker, the Enmesharra turned to Ausar and demanded that he translate her words into the tongue of their prisoner. She would attempt to communicate again but she still refused to allow her prisoner to hear the words of the gods.

"You have the floor," Ausar told her.

The Enmesharra nodded her acknowledgement and turned toward their prisoner. "Do you understand these words?"

Her prisoner simply stiffened and nodded.

"You live, so long as you are useful to me. Become a liability, the slightest inconvenience, and I will destroy you."

Her prisoner nodded again, this time as the slightest look of relief washed over her face. Apparently, up to this point, she believed that she was being kept alive as some kind of backup plan to escape the station. Now that her captor had escaped the station, she'd expected to be dispatched any time now.

"She has a name," Ausar offered.

"She also has a short shelf life," The Enmesharra informed him, matter of fact. "I don't need to know it."

"Where would you like to go first?"

"Home." She replied.

Several hours later, they emerged from the cloud and crossed the imaginary barrier that indicated they were currently entering Kemetian space. The Enmesharra instructed Ausar to begin broadcasting passive queries on all channels. With her stealth package active, she was completely undetectable by any other known ship. Obviously the Isoba would have means to track their own ships and she wanted to avoid drawing attention. None of their queries were returned, on any channel. The Enmesharra's unease grew, as they closed even closer to KMT without a single transmission. No one was broadcasting anything, not even in the clear, on any known Meroan frequency. They even checked the civilian, entertainment frequencies. Nothing. She was beginning to feel desperate and finally went to the secure military channels, even the ones reserved for her deep operatives, to remove all doubt. These queries went unanswered too. How could they not be there? It was as if the entire network had gone dark

At this point, in the very least, they should have observed Meroan defense forces on patrol but instead they saw strange ships coming to and fro. Hundreds of them. On, what seemed to be, all manner of routinely business. There were primitive looking freighters, unarmed civilian transports and leisure craft. There were clearly armed military craft as well. Albeit primitive, by her standards. If she had wanted to, her medium sized Isoba ship could engage many of these ships in combat and destroy them easily. Yet she chose not to, not yet anyway.

"What's going on here?" She began. "Ask her…."

Ausar cautiously cut her off. "She can't tell you anything useful, in that respect."

Ausar was speaking to her in an even, delicate tone and the Enmesharra hated being patronized. "Just tell me what you know." She demanded.

"I hope you're ready to hear this…." Ausar chose his words carefully, "Meroan culture no longer exists in this area of space. KMT seems to have suffered some calamity, some time in the past. These people inhabiting the planet now are of no relation at all to the Meroan people. Nor are they of any relation to the native Kemetyu who established it as a colony."

"How can you be certain of this?" The Enmesharra asked her question expecting an answer, but nearly certain she would get one she didn't want. She asked it, anyway.

"I have penetrated their network, scanned their nearby ships and performed a preliminary scan of the planet." Ausar provided his answer while displaying the evidence for all to see.

There were photos to compare the KMT they had once known, displayed right next to the photos that were included in his scan results. The topography had completely changed, on a global scale. The first thing the

Enmesharra noticed was that nearly every lake had dried up or had been drastically reduced in size. Most of the planet was dry and arid desert. Even from orbit, they could see the color of the planet had turned majority brown, a drastic contrast to she see of green forests they were used to. There were far fewer settlements as well and only a handful of major cities. None of which, aside from the capital city, even looked like it was in the same location as the ones she knew.

The cities of her time appear to have been claimed by the desert. Some areas of the planet appeared to have ruins, exposed at the surface, which she correctly assumed to be long abandoned cities. Ausar had done a thorough scan. In fact, he'd actually done a pre-invasion assessment. There was no debating the data or any of the details contained in the scans. This was no longer KMT. The scans continued to display, this obvious truth as the observers looked on. The people who had taken up residency on KMT were completely unknown to Ausar or the Enmesharra. Yet, it was evident that they had only been on the planet for several hundred years at the most. They were busy excavating several areas of ruins but they, by her estimate, had only uncovered less than one percent of what she remembered lay beneath the sand.

Despair. The Enmesharra had only known this feeling one other time in her adult life, and only once as a child before then. As the scans continued, she watched as the nomadic imposters desecrated spiritual sites, robbed the graves of her ancestors and set up temple sites as tourist attractions. They completely disrespected the heritage, legacy and birthrights of her ancestors. They even watched some of their news broadcasts discuss historical topics and debates in which they had the audacity to even claim they were the original Kemetyu.

On one such occasion, a brief clip showed the imposters actually adorned in the spiritual dress of her people. The lighter hue on their skin stood as an insult to the memory of those who built, inhabited and maintained KMT. The jewels in the spiritual attire only responded to high levels of Melanin, specifically of that of the Kemetyu. Those who originally wore the attire on display required those same levels of Melanin, which you would need to commune with the Ntru or even survive on KMT. Any third rate scientist could tell you that. Yet Ausar also observed as these imposters brought out a bust, devoid of any Melanin and appearing to have a calcified pineal gland, they were set to claim that this was the likeness of Nefertiti…. The Enmesharra had no idea how anyone was expected to believe this blatant lie. Especially not when the Kemetyu were depicted on nearly everything they built. Likenesses of not only Nefertiti but many others were prominently displayed all over the culture. They were dark in complexion, taller than most known races and had dark black hair which was usually displayed in the strength of afros or extensive braids. The Enmesharra had had enough. She wanted to land her ship and wage war on the entire planet, herself.

"My home," she simply, said.

The prisoner, who had gone unnoticed, watched wild eyed as another scan showed the area she knew to be devoid of life. It was displayed next to another scan that showed the exact same area some time in the past. It was a complete contrast. There was water, an over-abundance of it. Which supplied large trees that went on as far as the eye could see, each one trying its best to reach into the heavens. Peaceful villages permeated the land scape and everyone who inhabited them were of the same stock as her captors. Her theories were correct, although she believed she would never live to tell anyone. She now knew without a shadow of a doubt that she was standing in the presence of someone who actually lived on her planet thousands of years in the past. She wasn't completely aware of what was going on but she was no fool. Her captors were comparing the current state of the planet to the state that it was in when they had live on it, apparently, several thousand years in the past.

The Enmesharra decided there was no reason to visit this world. It was no longer her world and she had business with the person whose job it was to defend this planet. She wanted to know what happened to her. Then she would figure out what to do next.

"Where would the Meroans have gone?" The Enmesharra asked, quietly.

"I assumed toward the interior, to friendly space, KSH." Ausar replied.

"Is she with them?" The Enmesharra pressed.

"I have no way of knowing," Ausar Admitted. "But they would have some record of her. Tell me, are you familiar with The Bennu Project?"

"Yes," The Enmesharra confirmed, "my father participated in the early phases of the research. Tests were performed on a remote installation near grid 21 if I remember correctly."

"The project was relocated to KSH as the research advanced to the later stages. I have the last known location of the research site preloaded into the nav console." Ausar already knew the Enmesharra's intentions. She would chase her enemy right into the underworld if she had to. The ancestors would be forced to sit in the judgement of both of them before Ma'at.

"Then let's go find her." The Enmesharra made her predictable statement and all but confirmed the assumptions of Ausar. "I will not rest until I've found the place where her bones are buried. Or, failing that, sufficient evidence of her demise."

Sabayt Xmt

Azubuike quietly rode in the back of the Keftiu
dropship as it over flew the various districts in the city.
After they had departed the spaceport, Abeo opened a
transmission directly to Azubuike and delivered the
coordinates for his target. The heading they were currently
on took them to the northwest outer wall and they could
expect to reach their destination momentarily. Hezbon and
Azubuike had exchanged a few words about their level of
involvement during this campaign. Azubuike wanted the
Medjay to refrain from causing unnecessary casualties
among the Biafar while Hezbon was advocating for a
stronger response.

Under the command of General Ojukwu, the Biafar
separatists had grown especially brutal. They assassinated
political targets, sabotaged military objectives and routinely
raided isolated Naijian outposts. The proximity of the
current outpost to the city led Azubuike to believe that
there must be something more to the Biafar attack than
what was being assumed. There were no strategic assets in
the outpost and its only function was to serve as an early
warning station for the city. It had the ability to track and
target hostile forces anywhere in the north western

approach to the city. Azubuike understood the tactical significance of this. The Biafar attack was either a distraction or it was a prelude to an entire invasion. Either way, Azubuike intended to stop them.

Sovereign Azubuike briefly surveyed the Medjay who were about to deploy with him. Most of them had served as his personal guard for quite a while. Although there were a few new comers.

"How's our newest member doing?" Azubuike gestured towards Tinashe, the most recent addition to their unit. His simulator scores were high and he'd been sought after by many department heads.

"It's his first combat mission with us," Hezbon thought aloud, "He's got an excited look in his eye and his training is solid. I think he'll do well."

"It was too bad we couldn't get Malawi as well," Azubuike lamented, "As rivals, the two of them made quite a pair on the score boards."

"Coming up on target, Sovereign." A disconnected voice came to Azubuike from the pilot's comm channel to deliver the news.

Azubuike and Hezbon immediately stopped their conversation, even though Hezbon was mid-sentence. They both knew it was nearing time to deploy. The two of them projected a rudimentary three dimensional representation of the outpost, based on sensor scans provided by the Keftiu. Although this allowed them to view a hologram of events in real time, the Keftiu was delivering slightly inaccurate and distorted images which was a result of being used beyond its maximum effective range. The hologram became even more distorted and then finally disappeared completely.

"Ten seconds!" The pilot confirmed their drop time once again.

Both Hezbon and Azubuike turned to the port side bulk head as both sides lifted to the full open position, in order to prepare for their deployment. They looked to the same grid about two kilometers out so they could visually confirm the series of explosions that had just blocked their sensors.

It was at this moment the Keftiu began to take fire from the ground. Azubuike made sure to pinpoint the suspected enemy anti air fortifications for everyone else. "Guess we found the enemy."

Hezbon made note of Azubuike's markers on his map and then proceeded to deploy his Medjay accordingly. He chose three unlucky Medjay to remain behind, in case they needed some quick mobility on the battle field, and then they were out. The Keftiu had waited until the last moment to dramatically increase its speed to throw off any AA weapons that were tracking them. Then the pilot abruptly decelerated and threw on the deployment bay lights which let the Medjay know they were clear to disembark. The bulk of the Medjay were out in that instant. They were jumping at an altitude of several thousand feet, yet they calmly oriented themselves into a pattern and observed the battlefield as it approached.

What they saw was pure mayhem. General Ojukwu clearly had an objective inside the outpost, even if that objective was a feint meant to successfully draw out the Naijian defenses. Azubuike knew this because most of the fighting centered either around or inside the outpost. He magnified his HUD in order to get a better picture and was rewarded by closer, blurry visuals as his cameras were forced to cut through many cloud layers. There were heavy vehicles, sporadic fire fights and a cluster of soldiers who had just finished breaching the courtyard entrance to the main installation. As his altitude continued to rapidly decrease, so too did the accuracy of his visuals increase. He could now see much clearer picture, which showed him a sizeable force moving in behind the station's attackers. Azubuike correctly assumed that this must be Kandake

Anima's forces. They were approaching from the south east and clearly had their support staged outside the wall.

Azubuike's frustration was growing as he fell. He could see that the enemy did not have enough to even attempt an invasion. Unless they were hiding a larger force in the trees, this battle wouldn't last very much longer. He began to scan the battle for possible enemy objectives when his thoughts were interrupted by a large thump, then a series of thumps. Large plumes of black smoke started appearing in and around the Medjay formation. They were taking an increased amount of AA fire from farther west. Azubuike knew he had been right, there were more enemy troops hidden in the trees. He tagged their possible location too and alerted Hezbon who, in turn, tagged five of his Medjay and updated their status in the platoon roster. Those five soldiers activated their suit jets and used bursts of kinetic energy to alter their approach angle. Hezbon had ordered them into the forest, most likely to take their anti-air capabilities offline.

Kandake Anima and her Egba warriors were storming out of the tree line from the southern approach, where they had been staging for another offensive. The Egba warriors were not using large scale tactics and maneuvers, if there was any method to this madness,

Azubuike could not see it. Yet they were winning, through sheer force of will and extensive combat experience. Then they turned the bulk of their AA weapons in the direction of the Medjay, setting off all manner of alarms as they did so. However, none of them fired. After a brief pause, the bulk of them turned to find new targets while only a handful remained to track their targets to the ground.

Azubuike and his Medjay were just above the tree tops now, a thick canopy of dense jungle provided the ceiling for his chosen drop point which would help conceal them. As they broke through the tree tops, each Medjay activated his emergency suit jets in order to break his fall just above the ground. Azubuike immediately noticed it was dark; the sort of low light conditions that made the situation ripe for ambush. The suit jets broke his fall just enough for him to land on his right knee and left hand. He gathered himself, stood tall and found the nearest cover.

Azubuike used his HUD to filter out the smoke and fog as best as he could. What he ended up with was a green tint on his visuals, accompanied by patches of dead zone that could not be compensated for on his screen. At least that was of some minor comfort. It meant that anyone else out there would most likely be blind and/or unable to easily breathe. It also meant that any would-be attackers may not be at full fighting strength when he encountered them.

The first thing Azubuike did was to ping Hezbon and alert him of his location. Once Hezbon pinged back, Azubuike marked the two dimensional representation of their surroundings with a new marker. This new marker was placed at the last known position of Kandake Anima and served to let Hezbon know of Azubuike's intention to rally there. Hezbon confirmed this order and acknowledged it by setting a rally point in the same location for all the other Medjay under his command. Those who were onboard the Keftiu or deployed behind enemy lines were not given these new orders and carried on with their missions.

That was it then, Azubuike had about three kilometers to cover in unknown territory. He looked up to the only source of light, one that was caused through his own actions, as he punched through the canopy. It shot through to the jungle floor just like the sun's rays do on stormy cloudy days. Azubuike readied his weapon and prepared to move, completely expecting the enemy to dispatch scouts to his location. If he was lucky, all they would find was his absence and several badly broken tree branches.

He moved out, cautiously and quietly, in order to

make his way toward Kandake Anima's army. He had no intention of engaging the enemy yet. His goal was to make sure the attack on the outpost was a success and to do that he needed to assist Kandake Anima. Azubuike heard nothing as he moved, even with his audio filters disabled. There was both an unnatural silence and stillness in the jungle. Azubuike had enough combat experience to know that nature usually behaved like this whenever there was a predator or an unknown animal in the environment. So he prepared himself for an encounter.

Azubuike calmly retreated backward to the nearest tree and crouched behind its great trunk, before consulting his map. He was over halfway toward his destination and wasn't surprised in the least that he had likely encountered enemy scouts at this point. A large explosion sounded in the distance and served to grab Azubuike's attention. Weapons fire and more explosions were heard, and then: movement. The movement was spotty at first. Azubuike's detection system wasn't operating at peak efficiency in the middle of a dense jungle, especially with so many digital dead spots in the immediate vicinity. What appeared to be ghost signals repeatedly displayed on his HUD but they were only there in an instant and never in the same place. His suit detection systems were trying to pinpoint the location of his target, but all he kept seeing was various red icons repeatedly appearing and disappearing.

Then he heard them and, from the sound of their voices, it seemed as if they were right on top of him. Two men, wearing gas masks were hurriedly moving right towards him. They hadn't seen him yet, his only choice was to stay completely still and stay as close to the tree as possible. To his benefit, it looked like the bulky gas masks were meant for scrubbing the air but not really for increased visibility.

As they passed, he could hear their warped speech through the primitive speakers on their masks. "We're supposed to man our outpost and observe Anima for the second phase of our attack!"

The second soldier was even more out of breath, from forcing air through his rudimentary mask, "We've been ordered back to the staging area," he gasped, "giant robots are destroying our artillery…."

The first soldier couldn't believe what he had heard and demanded an explanation. "Did you say giant robots?"

"That's what the report said," the first soldier confirmed, even though he wasn't sure if he believed it himself. "Apparently, they've already destroyed several AA emplacements."

Azubuike's entire body was saturated with adrenaline. These soldiers were mere feet from him and he was in the perfect position to deal with them quietly, but what would their command do in response to a missing team of scouts? That was no matter, Azubuike decided he would rather deal with that later. Most likely, an infantry squad dispatched to locate a couple of missing scouts. Azubuike preferred dealing with that possible threat later on, rather than allow these two scouts to help flank his Medjay.

Azubuike sprang from the crouching position at the base of his tree just as soon as the pair had completely passed him by. His immediate goal was to minimize noise, so he brought the butt of his weapon down, hard, on the base of the neck of the soldier nearest him. The enemy soldier who had been in charge only moments ago, collapsed in a heap under his own weight; Dead.

The other soldier raised his weapon to react but, as he completed his turn to face Azubuike, he saw what he was up against and froze stiff. Azubuike grabbed the man by his neck and applied pressure, preventing him from calling for help, and forcing him to release his weapon. He raised a knife in order to quietly dispatch this scout too but hesitated. There was no reason not to find out what this man knew first.

"How many in your party?" Azubuike minimized the output of his speakers so only those nearest him would hear.

"Don't kill me," the man begged. His voice was half full of shock, the other half; terror.

"I will not ask again." Azubuike repeated his question, applying a little more pressure.

"Two," the soldier squeaked, "We had an OP set up a few hundred meters further in and all we did was relay reports.... We weren't even part of the main attack!"

"What is your primary objective here?" Azubuike pressed a little harder, "What is General Ojukwu really after?"

The man began to pass out but Azubuike shook him to prevent it. Instead, he would take him back and deliver him to Kandake Anima for questioning. He took up a position a few feet behind the man and gave him specific instructions in which direction to move.

"Walk and live," Azubuike gave him his choice.

After several meters, it became evident that his prisoner had made his choice. Azubuike could see him blatantly glancing left or right after every tree they passed, intent on finding a good place to flee. Azubuike decided right then that he would have to carry the man all the way back. He rushed and closed the distance, striking the man in the head hard enough to incapacitate him without killing him. Then he caught the man before letting him completely collapse to the ground, hoisted him over a shoulder and moved on as if nothing had happened. There wasn't much distance left to cover and Azubuike was confident that he would not meet any further resistance.

Sabayt Fdu

Kandake Anima was staged right outside the main entrance to the outpost. Her strike force had been engaged in some of the most intense fighting seen yet. However, all that could currently be observed was some distant and sporadic weapons' fire exchanges. Isolated and brief, the firefights had been growing less and less intense for several minutes. Her plan was to storm the outpost and clear it before her own reinforcements arrived. Her scouts were reporting more enemies in the trees and a more cautious person would have waited for reinforcements before storming the building. Kandake Anima was not that cautious person, she would let her reinforcements deal with the threat staging deep inside the tree line when they arrived.

Kandake Anima had just finished reloading her weapon when the soldier nearest her silently tapped her on the shoulder. He was alerting her to a possible new threat before using his shoulder mounted, surface-to-air launcher to track the new dropship he had seen screaming across the sky at high altitude. After a moment of attempting a lock on, Kandake Anima placed a hand onto the front end of the launcher, gently pushing it down. She was attempting to listen to an incoming transmission but a combination of interference and local battle noise was preventing her from properly understanding the message. She temporarily leaned out from cover to signal her comms officer and he dutifully sprinted to her location, while doing his best to remain safely behind cover. When he reached her, he dove behind the low wall she was hiding behind and made himself as small as possible to share its safety with her.

"Incoming transmission," Kandake Anima began, "What's it say?"

The comm officer merely nodded and plugged a cable from her headset into one of his comm ports. His stronger communications suite was able to cut through much of the interference but did little about the back ground noise of the battle. The message began to play a little clearer for them and the voice was unmistakable.

Abeo's frantic, excited voice was trying to warn them, "I repeat, if you can hear me Kandake Anima, you must not engage the new contact coming from the city! The Meroans bring help…."

The rest of the message was lost, Abeo's voice was cut off and replaced with static; and then eventually that static was replaced with nothing at all.

"I need the rest of that message, get it back,"

Kandake Anima commanded.

Try as he may, her comm officer was unsuccessful after several attempts. "I can't," he reported, "I'm not getting a return signal at all. We're being jammed."

"Then you know what that means," She replied.

Kandake Anima turned to her general with one simple command, "Get us inside that building before they get here. I'd rather be defending a fortified structure than flanked by the enemy while trying to storm it."

The sound of large, distant explosions rumbled through the trees, accompanied by the screams of enemy soldiers who sounded as if they were either dying or fleeing certain death. Kandake Anima wasn't sure what had transpired out there but it was making her nervous. Apparently it was making everyone nervous, her enemies were abandoning their defensive positions and falling back toward the tree line. It wasn't pretty either. Someone was calling a retreat, a hasty one at that. Whatever was going on out there didn't matter, now was her chance.

Kandake Anima gave the command and the Egba went to work, springing from cover. They showed the traitors little mercy, even shooting some as they ran for the trees. Biafar soldiers inside the outpost were even abandoning their primary objective, running from the building in an attempt to regroup. With little cover for either side, the events at the outpost quickly descended into a free-for-all shooting engagement. This went on for the better part of an hour. Those Biafars inside the outpost were fighting just as desperately to get out as Kandake Anima had been, to get in. With her attack stalled, she watched as those Biafar at a nearby section of the tree line jumped out of it and threw down their weapons just as soon as they had made it inside the tree line.

What she saw stunned her. A giant walking machine emerged from the trees, carrying what looked like a lightly armored, enemy scout. The Biafar soldiers in front of it threw their hands up in surrender and offered no further resistance. Some of her soldiers moved to subdue the Biafar traitors and the rest, who weren't guarding the door to the outpost, pointed their weapons at the strange looking robot. Seeing as it wasn't making any obviously hostile movements, Kandake Anima decided to approach it. The closer she got to it, the less it looked like a robot and the more it looked like a suit. When its face plate depolarized, she immediately made eye contact with the wearer.

"Azubuike!" With nothing but recognition evident in her voice, she gestured for her soldiers to stand down and Azubuike slightly relaxed his posture in return.

"Impressive," Anima admitted. "It looks like you've been holding something back…."

"Indeed, I have," Azubuike began, "but that will no longer be necessary, now that we're allies."

"I agree." Anima waved over her comms officer, intent on sending a message back to the city.

"We're still being jammed, Kandake," he reported as he joined their conversation.

"I can help with that." Azubuike held out his armored hand and an electrical spark began to form. As it grew in size, it took the shape of a woman and introduced itself as Oya, a figure the Naijia people knew of all too well. "This is my A.S.E. unit. She will integrate your communications network into mine by giving you a few dedicated channels. Aside from me, you'll only be able to communicate with Abeo until we adjust more of your transmitters."

Oya moved toward the comms officer who instinctively took a step backward. She remembered when she'd first made contact with Azubuike and how his people had reacted similarly. "Relax," she reassured him, "this will only take a second."

Oya was in and out in no time. While this com

officer's unit could use some improvements, there were no hardware upgrades required to give them access to the Meroan communications network. She gave them a few dedicated channels and encrypted them beyond anything the Biafar traitors should have the ability to hack into. Kandake Anima's unit would be able to freely communicate on these channels. Oya did what she could for Anima's personal head set as well. It didn't have the power to reach any great distance but at least Kandake Anima would be able to communicate with Azubuike and the other members of her unit without needing the comms officer to be nearby.

Oya gave a powerful look to Kandake Anima when she had finished her work. "You have the floor," she said, just before disappearing back to the anonymity of Azubuike's suit.

Kandake Anima nodded her approval and stepped aside to have her conversation in private. Without an enclosed suit, her conversation was only as private as her voice was low. She made every effort to keep it down but some parts of her speech were getting through. "Have my sister sent out immediately...."

"Do you want to know what they're saying?" Oya asked.

"No." Azubuike immediately rejected the offer. "Violating their trust is not exactly how I want to grow this relationship. When she's ready for me to know, she'll tell me."

"Very well," Oya accepted this decision but it wasn't without concern. "If that ever changes or you have any suspicions, we will revisit this as an option at that time."

Kandake Anima rejoined them with information from her discussion, "I have requested that my sister join us, more on that topic will follow once she has arrived. Now," gesturing at Azubuike's feet, "what is this gift you've brought me?"

Azubuike had nearly forgotten that he'd carried his prisoner all the way back to this rally point. "I found him on my way here. He was on recon and may know something of their plans."

"In the very least, he will know where they are, and what he's been reporting on our own troop movements." Kandake Anima snapped a finger and the nearest two soldiers dragged the scout away. Presumably, to find out what he knew.

"I already know where they are," Azubuike confirmed. "My Medjay have been flanking their artillery positions over the last hour. However, my scout has yet to determine the strategic motives behind this attack. That's why we need him."

Azubuike motioned toward the man he had just delivered, who was currently being "aggressively" questioned about the enemy plans. Before the conversation could continue in that direction, a large explosion came from inside the observation outpost that shook the ground underneath everyone's feet. The assembled group gathered their collective composure and made their way to the entrance where Kandake Anima demanded a report. From what she could see, the inside of the outpost looked like a disaster. It had suffered significant damage and the Biafar traitors who remained inside didn't appear as if they had any intention of giving up their primary objective.

Kandake Anima could see and hear her reinforcements approaching from the city, yet she didn't have time for this. The attack on the outpost was beginning to feel like a distraction. If she was right about that, then this attack was a little more coordinated and strategically orchestrated than those in the past. She had to admit to herself, it would far exceed the level of tactics that she was used to dealing with from the Biafar traitors. They usually raided targets like armories or medical installations for their supplies, there was rarely ever any larger tactical objective other than those. The nearest soldier gave his report that the occupants of the outpost were refusing to surrender and were actually using explosives to take the outpost offline permanently.

"Collapse the building," she ordered.

"Kandake?" the soldier asked. He wasn't questioning her order, just making sure he had understood it completely.

"We're moving out, taking the fight to them," she informed him. "We can't afford to leave a large force here and, most likely, the entire installation will need to be rebuilt anyway."

"It will be done, Kandake," was all that he replied.

The soldier turned to inform his squad of the Kandake's plans but hesitated when she called after him, "Warn them first."

The soldier in question helped rig explosives and then began speaking a message using a loud speaker. In the middle of his message, one of the previous soldiers who had been interrogating the Biafar traitor approached Kandake Anima. "Our new friend has been surprisingly helpful, Kandake."

"What have you learned?" She asked.

"This attack was meant to draw you out," the interrogator began, "you are the true objective. This day, their goal was to capture you alive."

"Ha," Kandake Anima nearly laughed it off. "That wasn't going to happen, regardless of the outcome of this battle."

"I'm sure he knows more than what he's already given us," the interrogator continued, "What should we do with him?"

Behind them, more Biafars were exiting the outpost without weapons and with their hands raised high, in full surrender. Kandake Anima was relieved that she wouldn't have to collapse the building on top of them. "Hand him over to the transports along with the rest of the prisoners and have them all transferred to the nearest holding facility. We'll deal with them later. Collapse the building anyway and then prepare to move out."

"So the truth has come out." Azubuike suspected there was some greater motive at play here. "Where are we going now?"

"You tell me," Kandake Anima gave Azubuike a genuine look of Approval. "You were out there, and you must have seen something from the sky."

"We were able to locate the launch sites of some of

their mobile artillery," Azubuike confirmed. "I don't know what else is there but my Medjay hit it when we came in."

"Ah, so that's who was making all that noise earlier." Kandake Anima was clearly joking with Azubuike, which made her own soldiers visibly trust him even more. "Will they still be in the area?"

Azubuike held out his palm and allowed a projection of the battlefield to display. He pointed at two specific locations for the benefit of Anima. "This is the location of the launch sites. And this is the direction the Biafars are routing in."

Azubuike pointed at a third location and tagged it, "We should use this as our rally point. They're running in that direction and the rest of our collective forces can meet us at this location in time to flank the enemy. We'll confront them there."

The plan was agreed upon and both Azubuike and Kandake Anima finished giving orders to their soldiers in time to turn, in unison, toward the courtyard. They were looking at the reinforcements as they briskly disembarked the first drop ship. Several Egbas soldiers came rushing down the rear ramp and rushed to assist wounded soldiers. But there was one Naijian who was unlike the rest. She walked down the ramp briskly, at a slightly less rushed pace and was not dressed like a soldier. Actually, she wore no armor and carried no weapons. Instead, she wore the long flowing robes of a temple priestess, not unlike the kind Azubuike remembered that were worn by the priestesses on KMT. Specifically, Azubuike remembered it from his time visiting the Temple of Hru. She also wore her hair in a very big afro, adorned with various gold falcon hair pieces. It was a popular look with the priestesses of Ipet.isu

Of course these weren't Azubuike's memories. They were, in fact, the memories of Sovereign Roha herself. After the events which led Azubuike to become an unwilling participant in The Bennu Project, his mind slowly began to merge with a remnant of the real Sovereign Roha. In the beginning, they behaved as two separate entities inhabiting the same body but, as the bond grew, they became less dependent on the actual need to speak to each other. They became accustomed to interpreting each other's thoughts and images. They could feel the emotions of the other as if they were feeling their own. As a result of this, neither usually relied on the spoken word to communicate with the other. Their memories were becoming as one, both able to experience them first hand.

It was in a shared memory, where Azubuike

remembered Roha's experiences at the Temple of Hru. At least until the new comer's presence directly in front of him disturbed his thoughts. She walked right up to Kandake Anima and greeted her with a familiarity that only members of the royal family enjoyed.

When they both finished their embrace, Anima turned to introduce the new comer, intentionally forgetting to use her title in order to tease her. "This is my sister, Oluwaseun."

"Priestess," She corrected, Anima. "Although I was, until recently, still just an initiate, you can call me Priestess Oluwaseun."

Anima acknowledged the correction in the way that older siblings do when they're proud of a younger brother or sister. "She's recently earned that title, not many do. It is not an easy accomplishment."

Priestess Oluwaseun closed the gap between herself and Azubuike. She stood just in front of him, closed her eyes and concentrated. She was trying to feel his energy and when she did, she looked directly at him. "On behalf of the High Priestess of the Temple of Hru, I welcome you in peace, Sovereign Roha."

Sabayt Diu

Azubuike was confused. Based on what he had been told by Abeo, he knew this couldn't possibly be the real Priestess Oluwaseun. And based on what he knew about matriarchal lineages, he really couldn't understand how these two could be sisters. Rather than be indirect, he decided to ask the obvious question. "Oluwaseun was killed in the war that lit the forest, how is it that you have her name?"

Kandake Anima decided to explain it herself, "The original Oluwaseun had a son who escaped the city. He grew up and was chosen by the Queen mother to join our blood line. That was the first instance where our families were joined by blood. He carried the mitochondrial DNA of his mother and it was joined with that of the Queen mother when they produced their first child. Every generation, a surviving son of their direct matrilineal blood line is chosen by the Queen mother to produce a daughter and that daughter is named Oluwaseun."

"Now I have a similar question for you," Priestess Oluwaseun began. As a Ljebu priestess, she would have been expected to know all about Meroan spirituality/culture. In fact, there was no way they didn't, at least, know about Roha. "How exactly is it that you contain the feminine energy of Sovereign Roha?"

An equally complicated answer, Azubuike thought to himself. Still, he did his best to try to explain it. "A few years ago, I was exposed to a piece of technology she left behind. That tech was a part of a larger experiment called "The Bennu Project." The purpose of this project was to copy her spiritual being and contain it, in preparation for the day when an appropriate Meroan would be selected to act as a vessel for her spirit. She is Roha and I am still me. Although, at times, it can become confusing."

"May we actually speak with her, directly?" Priestess Oluwaseun pressed.

"It doesn't really work like that." Azubuike was more than a little accustomed to her question. He had heard it many times in the past. "I have her memories but she doesn't control me."

"I understand," Disappointed, Oluwaseun directed her next statements to the Kandake. "Sister, I was permitted to come here by the temple authority in order to determine whether or not the rumors were true. But now I must return."

"You do not want to further witness the events taking place here?" Azubuike already had his answer. Roha remembered the priests and priestesses, which made up the temple authority, were staunch pacifists. They studied NTR and gained great power from it, but they were never allowed to use "The Power of The Gods" for destruction or to harm others. Unless of course that agent acting in favor of Isfet was furthering their agenda. Azubuike wondered if the temple authority on this planet still operated that same way.

"I must refuse," Oluwaseun confirmed. "My very being here threatens my return to the temple. If I were to engage in any of this conflict, I would likely be rejected from ever going back."

"Go safely, sister." Kandake Anima was urging her younger sister to protect her new title. "I have no intention of jeopardizing your station at the temple."

With that, the two sisters embraced once more and then departed. Not before Priestess Oluwaseun had given Sovereign Roha the royal bow as a gesture of respect. She boarded her transport as the pair watched for her departure. However, after several long minutes, the dropship never lifted off. It never even roared to life.

As the minutes grew longer, Azubuike broke the silence, "We'll need to move soon...." Reminding Kandake Anima that they had a rendezvous to make.

Sensing the urgency herself as well, Anima activated her communications suite and contacted the pilot. "Report."

The nervous voice of the dropship pilot came over the radio in response, "I'm sorry Kandake but we can't leave. An AA net has been thrown up over this entire area. At least a dozen anti-aircraft active scanning systems have come on line since our arrival. We're trapped here."

"Have my sister return to me." Kandake Anima snapped off the conversation tersely. Her frustration with the situation was evident, as she turned to Azubuike. "Do you have a plan to get us out of here?"

"We can't go back," Azubuike told her, "Our only choice is to go forward. We'll have to hit those AA installations directly if any of us are going to make it out of here."

Priestess Oluwaseun was quickly approaching the pair, a look of genuine concern on her face. Azubuike decided to quickly finish his point before she arrived, "I can use my Keftiu drop ship as bait to locate these installations and the reserve force onboard to eliminate them. We can all EVAC from the rendezvous point you and I discussed before."

Priestess Oluwaseun was within ear shot now,

Anima lowered her voice so that only Azubuike could hear, "If your people can get the AA units offline then it could work. Let's do it, I'll get my people ready."

Kandake Anima finished her sentence just in time to greet her sister. "Welcome back sister...."

"It looks like we're not going anywhere for a while...." Oluwaseun voiced her displeasure at being stuck on an active battle field. "It looks like I've been caught in a trap set for you."

"It looks like it," Anima agreed, "but we are going somewhere. Right now, actually. We're moving out to an extraction point. You'll be safer coming with us. The Meroans have a plan to secure the sky and by the time we get there it should be safe to fly again. Don't worry little sister, I will ensure no harm will come to you."

"You know I am not worried about that Kandake Anima," Priestess Oluwaseun reverted to the formality of titles to emphasize her point. "I must not be involved in conflict."

Azubuike stepped off to the side and contacted his Keftiu, he ordered them to come in low across the sky in an attempt to draw enemy fire. A total of sixteen installations either fired or tracked their target, exposing their locations. Azubuike was able to "paint" them onto his three dimensional holographic representation by tagging the locations of the digital signatures they gave off. When he looked at that holographic map, the AA installations had been blatantly placed in an obvious deployment pattern. Based on that pattern, Azubuike was sure there were only sixteen AA capable units active on the battlefield. When he gave the order, the remaining three Medjay divided up the targets and deployed from the Keftiu to take them out.

As an afterthought, Azubuike spoke into the comms network, seemingly, at no one in specific. "All other Meroan forces are to converge at the RP, in advance, and provide cover for allied units." He did not wait for a response.

Azubuike turned back to the Kandake and the Priestess in time to see them finishing up an uncomfortable conversation about the pros and cons of pacifism. Azubuike had no interest in debating competing ideologies. Whatever the ancestors had planned for him beyond his current battle, he knew he was called to fight the Ezalin and restore the legacy of his Ancestors. Yet he always recognized that that was not the path set for everyone.

"Are your people in place?" Kandake Anima asked.

"They are, Kandake," Azubuike had just finished that conversation, "We're ready to go when you are."

Kandake Anima ordered three of her squads to guard the wounded, the prisoners and the dropship. The rest of their forces would accompany them into the forest and beyond. They geared up and passed out uncomfortable-looking breathing devices, based on the descriptions of what Azubuike had experienced on his way in. The assumption was that taking the AA grid offline would allow both parties to return to the city. Both from the destroyed outpost and from the RP Azubuike had set up. They traveled without incident for most of the journey. The Biafar traitors were still retreating into the same direction and, with the exception of a few stragglers, no significant force was encountered. The occasional distant scream or weapons fire would slow the group and everyone would be forced to take cover, but every time it turned out to be the forward scouts eliminating enemy targets.

At one point, early on in their journey, Anima broke the silence to have a small strategic conversation with Azubuike. Across the newly encrypted comms, of course. "The execution of this plan worries me, Azubuike."

"You think there is more going on than what we know?" Azubuike's statement was more confirmation than it was question, "I would bet on it, Kandake Anima."

"I think there is an Oyinbo here with them, I've

never seen the Biafar traitors this organized before."

"It's possible," Azubuike agreed, "I've seen them interfere on other worlds before, in the same manner. We should be prepared for them either way."

Kandake Anima agreed and they let the conversation end there. It was radio silence and hand signals for the duration of the journey. It took them several hours to traverse the deep forest but, by the time they had, nearly all of the AA installations had been taken off line. This greatly concerned Azubuike because the remaining two were assigned to the same Medjay and he wasn't responding to his comm. Not only that, but it seemed as if the Biafar retreat had halted and was now being organized into a counter attack. They had no heavy artillery or mobile units left, Hezbon had seen to that, and very little of their support troops had survived the journey through the forest. They were in complete disarray, yet they were poised to turn and fight. Anima was right, something *was* going on here.

Azubuike halted the formation inside the tree line and instructed everyone to stay low, stay quiet. Then he moved down the line to where Kandake Anima was, "We may have a problem."

"I doubt that," Kandake Anima gestured to the

disorganized group of Biafar survivors gathering in the high grass outside the tree line. She was not impressed by what she saw out there. "We could easily handle them on our own and, based on what I've seen of the Medjay's abilities, I'm sure our combined forces will win the day."

"Look again Kandake," Azubuike pressed, "I don't think they're all that's out there. They're no longer retreating and clearly waiting for something."

Azubuike was right, they weren't retreating. In fact, they were actually appearing to be disorganized and in disarray but many of them had given up this pretense. Some were bored, some were yawning, and a few others could be seen casually bantering with each other. This was a trap, they were looking at the bait. Yet the teeth of the trap was, as yet, still unseen.

"What do you suggest?" Anima asked.

"Leave your support units and all non-combatants here," Azubuike advised, "A small force will accompany me much further down the tree line. We'll exit there and spring the trap. Once, and only when, the full trap is exposed, come out there and save us."

Anima immediately turned to her right and spoke to her General, "Did you get all that? I'm going with them."

When the General began to object, Anima cut him

off. "I'm the one they want, they may not even spring the full trap unless they see me first."

The plan was agreed upon and they moved out after the two sisters shared a brief hug. Whatever their differences were before, they would not let it be the last thing either remembered about the other. The assembled group, no more than ten in number, skirted the tree line and exited the forest at an appropriate location well away from the remainder of their army. Upon seeing the small force break from the tree line, the Biafar traitors turned to greet them. They still had grenades and shoulder fired, unguided rockets to use against their enemy. Azubuike rushed forward, far ahead of the Egba soldiers that accompanied him. He knew his superior armor would protect him from the bulk of what was being used against them.

As Azubuike got closer, he could see fresh faces popping up out of the grass to engage them. He switched his view from the normal spectrum to infrared, and then to thermal. In thermal, his H.U.D. would detect any heat signatures and expose them, at great expense to the effective distance of his H.U.D.s maximum magnification. He relayed a warning to those behind him that the Biafar traitors had prepositioned units here and they were lying down in the grass for cover. As if they were literally snakes in the high grass.

Azubuike adjusted his strategy and began to engage the well-hidden troops when he heard an unmistakable voice he would never forget.

"I wondered how long it would take you to get here, I was beginning to think you wouldn't show." Wynch spoke into a loud speaker from some undisclosed location.

Azubuike immediately activated his comm to Anima, "Get out of here."

"We're running?" Anima asked, incredulously.

"No," Azubuike corrected her, "*you're* running. You are not the target, I am."

Hezbon was no stranger to seeing Azubuike use himself as bait to spring a trap or to lure the enemy in close. That was most of the reason why the Medjay were willing to follow him anywhere. He led from the front. The rest of the reason they followed him was because most of them were willing to make the ultimate sacrifice for the return of a strong Meroan empire. It was widely whispered that The Bennu Project had driven Azubuike completely insane, and to be a Medjay on his personal staff meant that any who volunteered had to be at least a little crazy as well. Azubuike was constantly throwing himself into the most dangerous of situations. As far as Hezbon was concerned, anyone who wasn't willing to immediately follow him was not fit to serve in his unit.

Hezbon and his Medjay watched from their section of the tree line, eagerly awaiting the call from Azubuike to come in and pull him out. Hezbon activated a comm channel to the other Medjay, "Get ready."

Azubuike wasn't going to take the bait, not this time, especially not with so many other lives at risk. Whatever Wynch wanted here, Azubuike had no intention of finding out until it was on his own terms. He covered the retreat of Anima and her Egbas troops as they fell back to the tree line. Then he, himself, began to fall back. That was when the trap was sprung. As Azubuike moved further and further away from the optimum location for his trap, Wynch knew he would have to spring it now or never.

A massive EMP (Electromagnetic Pulse) detonated less than a hundred meters in front of Azubuike. Of course he was protected from such a primitive attack but that did not prevent his shield from depleting to nearly thirty percent of its maximum capacity. His comm system was only marginally effected by the blast but his targeting system would have to cycle through a complete reboot before it could be accurately used again. A well placed sniper round ricocheted off the top of his helmet, tipping him back. As Azubuike fell backward, another sniper round answered the first and silenced the scout who had obviously been a part of the plan to disable or kill Azubuike. With only ten percent of his max shield strength left, and a terrible headache, Azubuike thought it might be a good time to signal Hezbon. He never got the chance. All hell broke loose. Azubuike was down, in the high grass, and no one but those closest to him had seen where he specifically went down. That didn't mean Wynch was without an approximate location and he used it to place poorly aimed artillery shells at Azubuike. Then he ordered his entire contingent of Biafar traitors forward. He wanted Azubuike, along with his advanced suit, at all costs and he was willing to commit everything to capture him.

Attempting another manipulation, Wynch spoke directly to Azubuike again. He was trying to get him to expose himself. "You remember that letter we discussed? The one written by my cousin in the colonies?"

How could Azubuike forget? When he was held as Wynch's prisoner, Wynch bragged in detail about how his cousin had penned a letter explaining the breaking process to other Ezalin. Just before Azubuike's elder was "killed" by agents acting on behalf of Wynch. The man who helped free them, Ime, was eventually captured by Wynch during a subsequent mission to complete The Bennu Project. His whereabouts were still unknown. That is, they were unknown until Wynch began playing a prerecorded message from Ime, begging Azubuike to surrender. Azubuike knew perfectly well that Ime would never have said such things of his own free will. That was obviously forced and it contributed to the rage building inside of Azubuike. He was about to take the bait.

Azubuike rose to his feet, with less than seventy percent of maximum shield strength, and ran. He ran right at the nearest soldiers who were closing in on him, firing his weapon as he went. The first several soldiers were too stunned to react to his assault and fell under a hail of energy, fired from Azubuike's weapon. There were several more soldiers rising out of the grass and moving to stop him. They fired on Azubuike scoring several direct hits on him. However, even their combined small arms fire was only having a marginal effect on his shield strength. Azubuike shrugged off the impacts on his shield and returned fire, eliminating even more of the traitors.

Azubuike had previously held reservations about engaging the Biafar traitors in combat, but he drew the line at anyone who would willingly work for the Ezalin and actively set a trap for their own brothers. He no longer cared about sparing them. All he cared about was getting to Wynch and finding Ime. His memories of suffering through interrogation were blinding him to the fact that he was completely committed to taking Wynch's bait. It was at this time the Egbas decided to take the bait right along with him. They bounded from the tree line with a fury and took up positions, as best they could, in order to cover Azubuike's assault. None could keep up with him, so they engaged and picked off targets that were on over watch, targeting Azubuike.

"Yes, your command of the technology left to you by your ancestors is impressive," Wynch was doing and saying anything he could to keep Azubuike in his current mental state, "but it is not invincible and neither are you."

Several bright lights appeared in the sky. They were like small blue suns, which Azubuike immediately recognized as Ezalin artillery. Wynch was using it indiscriminately, hitting Egbas and Biafar traitors alike. He would sacrifice every one of his own soldiers in order to capture Azubuike and any intact Meroan technology. The first of several artillery rounds impacted dead center of everyone near Azubuike, throwing chunks of the dirt, debris and people into the sky. Soldiers on both sides were affected. They ran in all directions, trying to escape the blast zone.

One of the Egbas soldiers ran up to Azubuike, a desperate look on his face, "We have to get back to the safety of the trees!"

"No," Azubuike countered. He had returned to his senses, assessed the situation and made his decision. "Forward is the only way out. We have to close the distance, their artillery is ineffective at close range."

Anima was close enough to hear the exchange and agreed with Azubuike. She gave the order to attack, which was echoed by her General in the tree line. The exposure of the full trap, seemingly sprung to its completion, allowed the General to commit all forces to the protection of the Kandake.

Azubuike, finally able to open a comm channel to Hezbon, issued his own orders, "Hezbon, left flank. Hit that artillery hard, I want it all offline. If you can capture Wynch alive, do it; and get us an exit."

Hezbon heard the order and acknowledged it. They didn't have any heavy weapons so that meant they would have to close the distance and engage them at point blank range, just the way he liked it. With two AA units still active and a missing Medjay on the field, Hezbon would have to act fast to carry out his Sovereign's orders. They used the trees as cover, to stay hidden from the enemy as long as possible. Yet they moved with speed and purpose, they were at the left flank of the artillery line in a matter of minutes. They burst from the tree line and dispatched the Ezalin rear guard with minimal effort. Hezbon felt good to, once again, be fighting his enemy directly. He hated fighting the Biafar traitors. He didn't like the idea of using overwhelming, lethal force against his brothers, no matter what they've done. Yet this was the way the Ezalin operated, via proxy armies. They rarely ever showed themselves and, when they did, they were always hiding in the back; behind an army of his brothers.

Hezbon opened a comm channel, to no one in particular, and asked an open question, "Our missing man, do you know where he is?"

A disconnected voice immediately answered in response. It was the voice of a cold, calculated young woman who meant all business. "He's near your position, and completely unresponsive. Along with something dangerous…. Cease all comm."

Hezbon broke off a squad and gave them orders for a Search and Rescue operation. Even disabled, they should be able to ping his suit if they got within a close enough range. The rest of Hezbon's Medjay made it to the artillery line just in time to see the first two explode in rapid succession. Through the smoke, Hezbon could see the faint color of purple as it moved to another artillery tank. He turned his magnification all the way up and filtered out the debris, smoke that permeated the air. The image became as clear as it was ever going to be, just in time for Hezbon to see a blur and purple haze moving amongst the artillery line. After it finished the last one, it was gone again.

"Commander, we found him." One of the Medjay from the Search and Rescue squad was reporting in.

"Status?" Hezbon asked.

"KIA," the voice of the Search and Rescue squad's medic was very terse. "I've never seen damage like this. I don't know what could have…."

Hezbon cut him off, "I think I saw what did it. Get him packaged up and EVAC immediately. Go out the way we came in. The rest of you are with me. We're on the most direct route to the Sovereign."

Hezbon opened a private comm channel to Azubuike. He showed him the video footage of what he had seen and advised extreme caution, citing the new contact as a likely hostile threat.

In return, Azubuike had given him a very dry "Acknowledged," which was completely out of character.

Hezbon couldn't put his finger on it, but something was wrong with Azubuike. He didn't sound like himself, nor did he seem surprised by what he saw in the video. None of that mattered, at the moment, because Hezbon knew he needed to get back to Azubuike *fast*. No matter what he said, the man never did anything cautiously.

Azubuike couldn't shake the feeling that something terrible was headed his way. Hezbon's video had shown him something familiar, yet unfamiliar. That could only mean one thing, Roha knew what it was and she was hiding it from him. Instead, in place of an explanation, Roha was giving him an unnatural urge to leave the battlefield immediately. Azubuike had to resist the strongest urge to abandon all objectives, get all of his people organized and depart the battle without wasting any time.

"Tell me what that is," Azubuike demanded.

"I am not permitted to say," Oya calmly informed him.

"And why is that?" Azubuike pressed his question through clenched teeth. He felt the urge to double over.

"You already know why." Oya knew exactly what was happening. "You're wasting time, young Azubuike. People are going to die here. At this point, it is only a matter of how many will escape alive."

Azubuike refused to be satisfied by this answer. He had to know what it was and how to kill it, so he could save everyone here. He pushed Roha, "*Tell me,*" and she pushed back. She was far stronger, far more disciplined than he was, but he knew her. He nearly *was* her. He knew how she thought, what motivated her, what she cared about, and her passion for the people…. What he didn't know, was the one thing that she possibly feared. The one thing that would cause her to possibly turn her back on an enemy. Through his efforts, two or three images were able to bleed through. What he saw was beyond words. It was a Meroan, but not. She had clearly been a Meroan once, but now she was no longer allied with them…. And she was slaughtering Medjay onboard the Aha Mena. Azubuike could see her, doing battle with ancient heroes. She cut them down without mercy or remorse. She was un-killable, and his ancestors could not stop her….

Suddenly, Roha's cause for concern became abundantly clear to him, crystal clear, as it became his very own cause for concern. He needed to get these people out of here, but he had no way to save them all.

His only alternative was to stop her. "*How do I kill her?*"

"*You can't. You don't have the means.*"

As she drew closer, Azubuike's perceptions slowed down dramatically. He could feel her, no, he could feel the death that surrounded her. It flowed right through his suit and into his body as if there had been no barrier at all. It accompanied the unmistakable sensation of fear, terror and despair. Then, he realized it wasn't death he was feeling at all. It was, in fact, her feminine energy he was feeling. Twisted and out of balance, her chakras were all misaligned. Azubuike didn't know what happened to her, but the pain of her experiences had so damaged her psychologically, emotionally, beyond any form of help he could offer.

That pain flowed from her to him and he saw the image of man, both proud and strong. Azubuike was no longer on the battlefield, he believed, he was in a separate place in the recesses of his mind. Everywhere he looked, in all directions there was nothing to be seen but a damaged and scarred land scape. It was a completely barren and lifeless existence, as far as the eye could see, except for the other man standing there with him. He was wearing a Medjay command suit and he was glowing in a bright light that was surrounded by nothing but the pure embodiment of suffering. Something wasn't right though. On his name plate, Azubuike expected the suit to display the title of

"Supreme Commander of the Medjay" but it didn't. There was no military rank or any other insignia. Instead, it simply read, "Hru of Drtyu." Azubuike understood this to be Ancient Mdu Ntr for "Hero of our Ancestors." Could this man be...?

Azubuike couldn't finish the thought because the pain he was experiencing in his third eye was becoming debilitating. *"Don't speak to her again.... Focus on getting out of this alive!"*

Azubuike had collapsed to one knee, hand on his forehead to ease the transition back to this plane. He was weakened, disoriented and that was exactly how she looked down at him as she uncloaked from stealth.

She stood there, unconcerned about everyone else around Azubuike. They were all just as disabled or worse. There was even a small hint of pity when she looked at him directly, "These are the words of the gods, the words of Nature. Do you understand them?"

"Yes," Azubuike managed to say, "I can understand the Divine Words."

"Good," She replied, with a barely detectable amount of satisfaction, "As her vessel, I thought it only fair to tell you why you were about to share the same fate as she will. Yet your underdeveloped Pineal gland could only be used to directly communicate for a short time, before the strain became too much for you to handle."

Azubuike looked right at her. He recognized her and, at the same time, he didn't. "*You...*," Roha seethed.

"Who?" Azubuike accidentally spoke the words aloud.

"I am one who has had everything taken from me, that which mattered most. The architect of my demise stands before me, within you.... And I have come for my revenge. inD Hr.t Sovereign Roha. Show yourself, Sovereign Roha. It is I, Duro-Aina, and I seek your counsel!"

Sabayt Sisu

Azubuike could only think of one way to save
everyone now. He had to fight. He was clearly the target of
Duro-Aina's ire and, if he could buy some time, maybe
others would be able to escape. It didn't look like Duro-
Aina was going to indulge him. She held out her right hand
and a large purple mace began to form in her palm's grasp.
It was the ethereal weapon of her ancestor's choice.
Formed from the DMT secreted by the pineal gland. The
Pineal gland served several purposes in Meroan society, all
of which were connected to the astral plane. Right now,
Duro-Aina was using her spiritual gland to generate her
ethereal weapon for use against Sovereign Roha. It was
large, made of flowing purple energy and was being held
high above Azubuike's head.

Duro-Aina lowered the mace to deliver the killing
blow. However, before it could connect, the full force of a
perfectly placed sniper round impacted her dead of center,
right between her eyes. The force of the impact knocked
her back several meters and flipped her head over heels.
Her ethereal mace dematerializing, as she flew through the
air.

She landed, clearly hurt but not dead, a good

distance away from where Azubuike was still knelt down. "Ayoka!" He gasped.

Azubuike could clearly see the Medjay, approaching from just a few dozen meters beyond where Duro-Aina lay. He could also see Anima and the nearest Egba to him. They were all either stirring or struggling to get on their feet.

"What are you doing? RUN!" Roha demanded.

But Azubuike was not about to run. Azubuike was about to do what Azubuike did best; Charge.

Azubuike grabbed Kandake Anima and yanked her to her feet. "Flee, I won't be able to hold her off for long." Anima seemed to accept this without arguing it, there was obviously little time for debate. Azubuike was convinced she would leave and turned to face his enemy.

"I don't need much, just a little time. Help me, I beg you." Azubuike pleaded with his ancestor, to no avail. And when he grabbed his weapon intent on attacking Duro-Aina, she tried to stop him. She tried to impress upon him how important it was to the future Meroan Empire that they not die at the hands of Duro-Aina. He charged anyway.

Duro-Aina was now, unsteadily, back on her feet and reforming her ancestral weapon. She looked on Azubuike with a gaze that signaled one simple emotion:

destruction. She answered his charge with a charge of her own. She was much bigger and stronger than any Meroan alive today, and Azubuike was running right at her....

Roha was furious. In her time, she was known as Sovereign Roha: Defender of the People. No one cared about the lives of the Meroan people more than she did. She'd sacrificed so much, the whole of her life, in defense of M.A.R.S. and the Meroan people. Yet right now, Azubuike was refusing to see the larger picture. If she were to die here, the hopes and dreams of all Meroans would die with her. The Bennu Project would prematurely end and Duro-Aina would be free to rampage all across Meroan territory. She had to do something to stop Azubuike.

The two opposing forces were about to clash but Duro-Aina was far more experienced in the melee form of combat than Azubuike was. In fact, she was far more experienced in every form of combat than he was. She dropped her right shoulder and drew her mace back in anticipation for an attack. She swung high and arced a horizontal swing that would have taken Azubuike's head off, had Roha not intervened. Roha was still trying to find a way to slow down Azubuike. She summoned up as much energy as she could and focused it all on his leg, tripping him and causing him to fall *underneath* the wide swing.

The forward momentum forced Azubuike to recover with a roll that carried him past the point from which Duro-Aina launched her attack.

However, Duro-Aina was already spinning around and readying an overhead two handed swing meant to crush Azubuike where he still crouched. Again, before she could connect, another sniper round impacted her dead of center. This time it impacted directly in the middle section on the back side of her helmet, causing her to stumble forward and trip over Azubuike.

"Find that damned sniper!" She yelled, as she scrambled to her feet a second time.

Ausar, who had already been trying to locate the sniper, chose now to inform her of his difficulty. "I'm attempting to do so now. The stealth package employed is Isoba. And there is another A.S.E. here attempting to further block my attempts to make progress."

"That would, of course, be Oya," Duro-Aina realized.

Ausar gave Duro-Aina a best guess location on the direction of the hidden sniper based on where the previous two rounds impacted her during the fight. Duro-Aina was then able to maneuver herself and keep Azubuike between herself and the sniper. Hopefully, that would prevent a third shot. It all depended on just how good this sniper really was. Duro-Aina was ready to launch another attack and, just as she tried to, she watched another sniper round flash into existence. She watched it through her front viewport. This time it arced right over Azubuike's shoulder and impacted her helmet, right side of her face plate.

Duro-Aina had had enough of this sniper and she had seen exactly where the shot came from. Knowing that location, she was able to more accurately minimize the available opportunities the sniper would have. She also kept her attack stances minimized, so as to not be so predictable in the cross hairs of the sniper. This meant her attacks would be much weaker, but she had a greater chance of catching both Azubuike and his sniper off guard.

It worked, she caught him with an off handed backwards swipe of her mace which nearly buckled Azubuike. This was it. If Roha didn't do something right now, then they would both meet their end. She gathered up all the energy she could, she begged her ancestors to intervene and left it up to them to decide. She threw her hands up in defense, and was able to deflect the brunt of Duro-Aina's direct attack. The rest of the energy passed through to Azubuike and it was a terrible feeling. The likes of which he'd ever felt before. The pain was greater than anything he had ever experienced. Azubuike, on some level of consciousness, thought he had died.

What everyone else saw, was the physical embodiment of Sovereign Roha. She appeared as a large purple figure which encompassed Azubuike. She was of the same size, but not stature, as Duro-Aina. Roha was royalty, Duro-Aina was a warrior, but both were clearly ancient Meroan as evident in both size and appearance. Then she was gone, as quickly as she had appeared.

Duro-Aina had momentarily recoiled at the shock of actually seeing Roha in person. But her hesitation didn't last and Azubuike was down again, suffering in pain. He wasn't exactly receiving information from this plane, either, and probably had no idea what was happening. This was her chance to finish them both.

Roha rose, tall and erect, to a posture no-one had ever seen Azubuike in before. It was the unmistakable air of authority, of royalty and lifelong command.

"Do it now," Roha commanded.

"There are risks," Oya cautioned.

"I understand the risks," Roha braced herself by turning the palms of her hands upwards and making fists that rested just out in front of her at the waist. She set her feet about a shoulder width apart. "Now, Oya!"

Roha exhaled as much air as she possibly could in anticipation of what came next. A whirlwind of energy began to manifest around her command suit. It became overwhelming and drove Duro-Aina backward. As the energy began to solidify, it made a solid wall of semitransparent light energy that was slightly gold in color. The absence of sound and even air, itself, became apparent. The force of energy grew even greater, taking control of her limbs away from her and driving her hands and feet out as outstretched as they would go. Roha looked as if she was in the middle of a jumping jack. When the process was completed, Roha was surrounded by a nearly impenetrable wall of golden energy, in which she floated slightly off the ground at two meters.

Duro-Aina refused to let her escape. She summoned all the pain she'd ever felt, thought about what had been taken from her, imagined what had happened to her mother and charged the shield. Ayoka took her shot, she had been under an immense amount of pressure to keep that monster away from Azubuike. She knew she wouldn't miss this shot either. Her brother's life depended on it. She intended to place this round on the breast plate of their enemy and drive her back, even further away from that solid wall of light. She didn't miss yet, she didn't hit her either, the energy from her sniper round dissipated before it got within ten meters of either of them. She fired again, with the same result. Before firing a third round, she thought better of it and stowed her sniper rifle. Azubuike was on his own until she could get there.

"Sovereign, we can't keep this up," Oya advised.

"Of course we can, "Roha snapped, "My spiritual gland can, and has, powered this process for far longer times than this."

"It's not *your* spiritual gland," Oya shot back. "It's his, and he can't take much more of this. If you don't stop now, he will die."

"How much time do we have?" Roha demanded.

Oya checked her calculations, "Minutes. It's already depleted his DMT and is now taking a physical toll on him. Soon, it'll begin drawing on his life force."

Duro-Aina was still struggling to reach the epicenter of the energy's vortex. To her surprise, the massive amounts of energy being produced by Roha's command suit began weakening, slipping. She knew Roha should have been able to maintain this state for hours, she was genuinely confused. Until she realized it wasn't Roha powering the suit, it was Azubuike! She used every emotion she had to find the strength to hit the shield wall.

She knew she could break Azubuike's will if she put everything she had into her attack. The force of her blow breached the severely weakened shield and collapsed it. What was left of that kinetic energy was enough to maintain the ethereal mace, it continued moving forward to strike at the heart of Roha. When it did, everything went black, for everyone.

The suit's defensive shield function was designed to arc out at any nearby attacker, in the event that it was ever breached. Duro-Aina had used most of her spiritual energy reserves while she was maintaining the ethereal mace and using it to attack the defensive barrier. All that energy that was no longer being used to solidify light, was now arcing toward the only living target in range of Roha: Duro-Aina. She hastily dissipated her mace and used every bit of remaining spiritual energy to generate a small purple shield to defend herself. The clash of these opposing energies dealt a great deal of damage to Roha, Duro-Aina and Azubuike. Everyone else within a three hundred meter range was either killed or incapacitated, depending on how close they were.

Anima couldn't leave Azubuike out there to die alone. He had charged at an impossible enemy in order for her to get everyone to safety. From the tree line, everything was quiet and it looked like both Azubuike and that strange new enemy could both have perished in their confrontation. Anima had made up her mind. If she was going to pull Azubuike out of there, this was her best chance. Her squad of Egbas were closer than anybody else was, and nothing seemed to be moving out there. Anima gave the signal, she and her squad crept out of the tree line and approached the last location they'd seen Azubuike alive. That location was now a small crater. It was approximately the size of a shallow ditch and, the closer they got to it, they realized they could hear movement coming from inside. Anima looked to make sure the thing that had attacked Azubuike was still down and it was. She motioned for everyone else to stay back and she inched closer until she could get a clear view of Azubuike.

He was barely alive, trembling, but alive. He was in the fetal position, both knees and elbows close to his chest as he convulsed in pain. Several sections of his suit had been badly damaged and were no longer there to protect him. Entire sections of his body were exposed, including his face which twisted in agony. As the convulsions grew more painfully violent, Azubuike rolled on to his back and went completely limp. The last gasp of air left his lungs and escaped to return to NTR.

"Pull him out of there," Anima commanded. "His people may yet be able to save him."

The first Egba to attempt to touch Azubuike was rewarded with a searing, painful jolt of purple energy. He fell to the ground screaming. Nobody noticed the thin purple display of residual energy moving all over Azubuike's body until it arced up and hit the first soldier. The other soldiers rushed to help their ally while avoiding physical contact with Azubuike. Neither did any of them notice that Duro-Aina was now moving. Stirring, at the all too familiar call that she was used to hearing: her victims screaming in pain.

Priestess Oluwaseun climbed down into the hole to assess Azubuike. She knew the first thing she had to do was cleanse him. She didn't have the tools, or even the sage, necessary but she did have one alternative. It was chaos energy, there was no destroying it. There was only balancing it. She *could* transfer it all to another living entity. That, however, was a crime against NTR and there were strict laws that had to be obeyed. Luckily, the exception was about to present itself. Duro-Aina appeared, badly hurt and weakened, at the top of the hole and Priestess Oluwaseun immediately begged NTR for help. She held her hands above Azubuike, collected the bulk of chaos energy and sent it all back to its source, courtesy of Ma'at.

Duro-Aina was not afraid of her own energy and easily dissipated it. She held out her hand to form her ethereal mace and was disappointed. When it didn't form she immediately checked her DMT levels and found that she was completely depleted. She wouldn't be able to use any spiritual weapons or defenses for quite some time. Ausar was unresponsive and so was her stealth package. Everything was cycling to reboot, she would have to deal with these "upstart Meroans" by more primitive means. She reached for the Priestess, the only real threat she had seen here, and was driven back by a hail of weapons' fire.

The Medjay had arrived. Without stealth, she was forced to dodge and recoil from their combined attack. Duro-Aina picked up one of the primitive weapons and found cover. She only needed to buy enough time for her full system reboot to cycle through. When Hezbon reached the hole, he took a quick glance at the fallen Sovereign while the rest of the Medjay charged by to engage their enemy.

Hezbon's whole purpose was to protect the Sovereign, and he feared he was about to fail that mission. It clearly showed through in his tone and mannerisms. "Get him out of that hole, now! We'll deal with her, don't wait for us."

Hezbon didn't even wait for a response and Anima didn't bother to waste either of their precious, little time with one. She jumped down into the hole with her sister. "Can he be moved yet?"

"It's out of my hands, sister." Priestess Oluwaseun's face was grim, "I'm trying, but only NTR can agree to do what needs to be done."

"And what is that?" Anima pressed.

"To take life from the living and give it to one who has already transitioned." Priestess Oluwaseun was attempting to do something that, if done incorrectly, could have dire consequences for Azubuike's Ba or spirit. Not only that, but it could have dire consequences for her as well.

"Stop what you're doing," Anima reached to grab Oluwaseun's arm but she pulled it away. "You're trying to get yourself killed, or worse!"

"*That*.... is Sovereign Roha, Defender of the people!" Oluwaseun shot back, "I have to save her."

Anima peered over the edge of the hole to get an update on what was going on. Several Medjay were hurt and their enemy seemed to have gotten some of its abilities back. It was now using stealth in tandem with its attacks but that dangerous mace was still nowhere to be seen. There also seemed to be a much smaller person fighting with it, that person was using stealth as well. Anima didn't know it, but she was looking at Ayoka help the Medjay buy time for Azubuike. Ayoka was an excellent sniper, unmatched even, but she was no front line warrior and she was tiny compared to Duro-Aina. They didn't have much time.

Anima was back in the hole with her sister, "any progress?"

"I think it worked but I can't be sure yet," Oluwaseun was sincere in her assessment. "It's in the hands of his ancestors now."

"What's in our hands is to help them stop that monster," Anima began. "I know what you're going to say but, who do you think it'll come for when it finishes with those Medjay?"

"You know what you're asking me to do, Kandake Anima," Oluwaseun objected. "I can't interfere."

Anima's frustration was growing, "Didn't we just talk about this Priestess Oluwaseun? You're interfering right now! And you're the only one here who has a chance to stop her."

"I've begged you to spend more time in the temple sister," Oluwaseun wasn't ready to give up everything she believed in yet. "If you had, you'd know that the cosmic balance of Ma'at doesn't work like that."

"This is hardly the time for a spiritual lesson, sister" Anima had heard this enough in the past.

"Maybe it is, sister," Apparently Oluwaseun never got tired of repeating herself. No matter how many times Anima didn't listen. "That is an agent of Isfet and, while I am an agent of Ma'at, I will likely not be able to stop her. We will need an agent of Ma'at with masculine energy equal to hers, far stronger than me, or else Nature will forever be out of balance."

"You're right," Kandake Anima admitted, "Maybe I should have listened to the temple priests a little more. I'll be sure to heed their words, spend a little more time in the temple, after you save my life."

Kandake Anima leapt out of the hole before Priestess Oluwaseun could stop her. Oluwaseun stood straight up, and frantically watched, as her sister joined the Medjay assault. Every soldier under her command abandoned the hole and ran to their Kandake. Left with little choice, Oluwaseun quickly recited the Htp D Nsut, begged her ancestors for help and exited the hole.

"Forgive me, Ntru" She said aloud. Behind her, she heard movement from within the hole, even though there was no one left alive in there. She looked down to see Azubuike unconsciously coughing, his body desperately trying to refill his lungs.

"Dua Ntru." A smile crossed her face, Priestess Oluwaseun would join the battle. And she would do it with the permission of NTR itself.

Sabayt Sfx

Life in Mt Roha had finally gained a sense of normalcy. The inhabitants of the well-hidden mountain base had lived within the walls, in relative peace, for years after the overthrow of the Ezalin. People casually walked to their duty stations, chatted about their personal lives with each other and many had fallen into a mundane routine while completing their daily tasks.

On this day, that relative calm was shattered by Nosizwe as she ran through the corridors at her best speed. She brushed by several people, ran in-between them as they idly bantered in the corridors and even bumped into a few of them. She offered her apologies, on her way by, when she accidentally knocked a stack of reports from one technician's hands. Nosizwe was trying to get to the Manyikeni as fast as she could. Councilor Melisizwe had given her some very disturbing news about Azubuike, before requesting her to meet him there as soon as possible.

When she finally made it to his office she wasted no time in entering. She arrived to find Seba and Kandake Nzinga already inside, along with Councilor Melisizwe. The three of them were in a conversation regarding Azubuike and none of them looked too happy about what was being said. As she entered, she caught Kandake Nzinga mid-sentence....

"....and they must do everything they can to return him to us." Kandake Nzinga paused long enough for everyone to have the opportunity to acknowledge Nosizwe. When they did, she continued speaking, "Welcome, daughter. We have a significant update on the progress of young Azubuike. As you know, your husband was on another diplomatic mission to the Naijia people. We have just received news that he is gravely injured, due to his participation in some kind of battle outside of their main city."

Nosizwe did not immediately speak. Instead, she sat there, absorbing the information she had just been given and was silent for many moments. When she finally did speak, it was with a voice of pure concern, "What were his injuries?"

"We don't know yet," It was evident by her voice that Kandake Nzinga had wanted the answer to the same question, and was not given one she liked. "Honestly daughter, the details are few. Apparently, the battle has not concluded yet and Azubuike's exact whereabouts are unknown."

"How could this have happened??" Nosizwe could

no longer contain herself. Her outburst was emotional but expected. Everyone in the room showed empathy due to the fact that they had all had a similar outburst when they learned the same news. "The Medjay should have been able to keep him safe on Naijia. The relationship was going well and he's been there many times before. Could he have been betrayed? Ambushed?"

This time it was councilor Melisizwe who answered her question, "We do not believe it to be the case, young Nosizwe. Based on the discussion we recently had with them, they are the victims here just as we are. They have had many casualties and claim to have been attacked by an overwhelming enemy. Quite honestly, some of the claims that have been made are…. Fantastic."

"Fantastic?" Nosizwe pondered this, what was the elder insinuating here…. Rather than allow the indirect nature of the conversation to continue, Nosizwe asked the next question directly. "What kind of claims?"

"They're calling it a devil, some kind of monster," Councilor Melisizwe replied, "Reports from the front lines are saying it was able to be invisible and it was incredibly strong. Casualty rates are high…."

"*It….,*" Nosizwe thought to herself. "Are you saying one person did this? And it sounds like they were simply using Isoba armor." Nosizwe shot straight up as the realization of her words hit home. "Could it have been Ime?!"

"I can't believe that," Seba cut in, "Not without irrefutable evidence. The last time I saw Ime, he and three others were holding off an Ezalin strike force. He directly told me to evac Azubuike before they turned and faced the enemy; in order to buy us the time to escape."

"Young Seba is right," Kandake Nzinga joined this part of the narrative on his behalf. "Isoba are subjected to years of anti-interrogation training and I have every confidence in Ime's mental fortitude. Although, everyone has a breaking point. I doubt there was anything Wynch could have done to Ime to get him to turn on his own without it killing him first."

Nosizwe seemed to accept this, for now. They simply didn't have enough information. Besides, all of the conjecture was meaningless. Getting Azubuike back to the mountain was the highest priority. "When do we leave? I can be ready in ten minutes."

"We're not leaving." Councilor Melisizwe was more than direct with this answer.

"What do you mean we're not leaving?" Nosizwe was clearly having a tougher time accepting this information; more than she had accepting any other part of this conversation.

"Kandakc Anima is also missing," Councilor Melisizwe took great care in presenting this new information to Nosizwe. "Reports of her last whereabouts place her with Azubuike. Due to her status, Naijia has closed all travel both to and from the planet. At this point, we would have to "invade" our allies in order to search an unknown planet for Azubuike. He could be anywhere. Furthermore, I'm sure he would not approve of the diplomatic disaster that would result in us going against their wishes."

Nosizwe fixed her eyes on the elder to add impact to her response, "Their wishes are always a lower priority, *to me*, than the well-being of Azubuike."

"Then consider this, daughter," Kandake Nzinga turned to face Nosizwe. She wanted to calm her down with the practical aspects of a rescue mission, rather than the diplomatic aspect that she clearly had no qualms about. "I have already dispatched another Keftiu and support personnel to the planet. They will standby until the closed border policy is changed. We are not on it because of the travel time required. We think it best to wait here in case the Medjay make it back to the city and evac Azubuike on their own. Either they'll bring him back or the recently dispatched Search and Rescue Keftiu will. Either way, we'll need to be ready for him when he arrives."

This seemed to have worked. Nosizwe, was reassured by the fact that the most likely place for her to be, in order to see and assess Azubuike as soon as possible, was in the Medical bay. Nosizwe rose and moved to the door, "I'll get down to the Med-Bay and make sure everything is in place."

"I'll have your schedule cleared of any other appointments," Kandake Nzinga called after her, she had no intention of trying to stop Nosizwe. The truth was, whatever had happened to Azubuike, Kandake Nzinga was sure he would need Nosizwe's medical skills to recover from it.

Nosizwe left the meeting on the verge of tears, attempting to maintain some type of composure. She thought about how things had changed since her marriage to Azubuike. She thought about how there were even bigger changes once she was adopted by Kandake Nzinga. Overnight, she suddenly found herself thrust into a spotlight focused on politics and appearances. At times she felt overwhelmed and at other times she felt grateful to be in her position.

Nosizwe had many responsibilities, most of which had their priorities focused on creating good public relations on behalf of the queen mother. While Kandake Nzinga focused on the practical aspects of her administration, Nosizwe focused on the projection of good will and appearances. She organized the charity missions, the relief efforts and the reconstruction programs outside the mountain. Inside, she assisted in conflict resolution among base personnel and all manner of civil arbitration. Several of the families had come to rely on her when they ran into problems they couldn't solve themselves.

Although, for as much good as she could do for others, she wasn't feeling like she could do anything in her current situation. In fact, she felt completely powerless to help Azubuike. There was only one thing she could do, she convinced herself to pour all of her energy into what came naturally to her. She intended to care for and heal everyone who came back with Azubuike, to the best of her abilities. Once again, it was time for her to go take charge of the Medbay.

Sabayt Xmnu

Azubuike had no idea where he was or how he'd gotten there, or even how he was, he just was. He sat there in total silence, allowing the wave of nothingness to overtake him. He was embracing it. Azubuike was embracing the fact that, along with this nothingness, came a feeling of relief. He felt no stress, no pain nor did he feel any pressure. In fact, Azubuike realized he felt no physical sensation of any kind. He quickly realized that he did not even have a body. He also understood that he couldn't see or hear anything. This was partly due to the fact that there was nothing else there to see or hear in the first place. But also due, in part, to the fact that he did not have eyes or ears either. All he had was his presence and he felt lighter without the physical restrictions of being alive.

Still, Azubuike wanted to go places and he was accustomed to having a body. So he collected his thoughts and manifested an ethereal silhouette to be his body. He thought of where he might go and, beneath his feet, appeared the rolling hills and tall grass that he had pictured. Azubuike had no idea why he chose this place, but he knew he wanted badly to be here. Although he didn't even know why he wanted to be there in the first place. Admittedly, it was a very beautiful place. However, aside from the aesthetics, Azubuike could not see a single practical reason for people to frequently visit the area.

So he focused on what he saw, instead of what the presumed purpose could be. First, were the rolling hills, they went on forever. As far as he could see, there was no end to them and no structures on them. Then there was the grass on those hills. It was taller, greener and livelier than any Azubuike had ever seen. If he'd wanted to, he could run through that grass until the end of time.

Azubuike scanned the grass and the hills, left to right, and then back again. Nothing grabbed his attention so he repeated his scan much slower, a second time. There, on the base of the next hill, was a small farm house that wasn't there before. Azubuike immediately, instinctively, moved toward the house. The closer he got the more he could hear, and then finally see, that there were people around the farm house.

Azubuike was rushing now. He had to get to these people, find out who they were and what they were doing here. He had to find out what he was doing here too, maybe they knew more than he did. He realized, as he pushed out of the high grass and into the clearing, that he didn't recognize any of them. Many of them, however, displayed the unmistakable expression of recognition on their faces. One man, in particular, got up and went into the farm house immediately upon seeing Azubuike.

After closer inspection, Azubuike understood that he'd broken the serenity of the gathering simply by appearing among the people in it. He gauged the expressions of the people more intently. Several of them looked like they were just as confused and lost as he was. While others looked far more relaxed and comforting. He quickly drew the conclusion that some of the people here were meant to guide the newer arrivals.

"Is there a line?" Azubuike spoke loudly, to no one in particular. He thought the afterlife would be a little different but, even in his version, he just assumed one of his ancestral watchers would be there waiting for him.

One of those closer to the house began to speak up but her words were cut off when everyone's attention was drawn back to the farm house door. The man who had just entered the farm house was reemerging and, along with him, was someone Azubuike had absolutely no problem recognizing. He knew her face just as he knew his own. He remembered the royal attire she was wearing and the day it was awarded to her. Her dark skin was accentuated by the royal color of purple and her dark Afro stood tall and powerful, decorated with various spiritual ornaments. She wore light makeup and various pieces of jewelry on her hands and arms. Every piece of that jewelry represented a specific triumph that she had achieved. It was like looking at the bars on a military uniform. She literally wore her accomplishments on her sleeve for all to see.

It was Roha, and Azubuike wasted no time approaching her. He had to see her. Standing there in front of her was a surreal moment for him. He had never before seen her with his own eyes. Never as a separate person. The only way he ever saw her was through her own memories. As he stood there and stared at her, he realized that she wasn't responding to his questions because he wasn't speaking them aloud. He became momentarily distracted, at the thought of this, and let his mind dwell on the prospect of being a totally separate person, permanently.

It was Roha who actually spoke first. She knew Azubuike could be having some trouble adjusting and that he may need help getting through the transition. She put a sympathetic hand on his shoulder and gestured for him to move inside. "I'm sure you have a lot of questions. Join me inside and we will discuss them."

The three of them went inside and were alone in a small room that had enough space for little more than a

small round table. Each, instinctively, took up the seat
meant for them and studied each other intently. This was
the first time Azubuike had gotten a clear look at the man
who had yet to speak. He was wearing a white Atef crown
but his was slightly different. It had large, curling ostrich
feathers on either side of it and, in his hands, he carried the
unmistakable treasures known as the Crook and Flail. It
also did not go un-noticed that his skin was, in fact, green.

Azubuike didn't know what to make of all this so he
turned to Roha and asked the question directly, "Are we
dead?"

Roha answered him as if she had fielded this
question many times before, "Not unless we choose to be,
young Azubuike."

"You mean I have a choice??" Azubuike was
incredulous. There was no version of the afterlife he'd ever
heard of where death was optional.

Roha was quick with her clarifying response, "*We*
have the option because your friends asked…." Roha held
her open palm out in a gesture toward the still silent man,
"and he granted us the choice."

It was at this time the silent man chose to join the
conversation, "It is less than a choice and more of a
reprieve. I have already made the decision and returned you

to the land of the living."

"And who are you, sir, to grant such a benevolent gift?" Azubuike genuinely wanted to know who this man was. "When do we have to go back?"

"Benevolent...." The man spoke the word aloud as he considered it. "Good and evil are concepts that do not exist here. Only balance exists. I have many names but you may call me Wsir." Wsir looked upon Azubuike with nothing but empathy. He had explained this to many Meroans, many times before. "You have been returned because it is not your time yet, and because your mission has not yet been fulfilled. Neither does time exist. They are Hue-man constructs that try to explain the cosmic balance of all things."

"I'm not sure I understand," Azubuike was confused, he had not grasped the part about the absence of time, nor did he know of any mission he had been given.

Wsir motioned with his hand and a three dimensional representation appeared next to the table. It displayed the events as they occurred during his battle with Duro-Aina and then continued on, to display the outcome in real time. Azubuike was watching his Medjay battle her while Priestess Oluwaseun attempted to revive him. They watched as she spoke the words and then joined the battle, with Azubuike stirring behind her.

Azubuike watched the events unfold, stunned, "How can I be there, alive, and also here, dead, at the same time."

"Your body clings to life, young Azubuike," Wsir spoke with all the patience he had, yet he chose his words carefully when trying to convey his intended message, "But your Ba, your spiritual essence….; the spark of your life has come to walk among our ancestors. But I have already returned you to the living, your mission is not complete."

Azubuike spoke in a voice rarely seen or heard from him, "I…. I don't want to go back."

"Your hesitation is understandable, young Azubuike, the hardest choice any of us have ever made was to become Hue-man." Yet Wsir was firm in his decision, "However, as I have said, time does not exist here. You must return to the living at once and, simultaneously, you may rest here as long as you like. Apparently, Roha has a plan."

"You still haven't told me my mission yet, why I was sent down in the first place," Azubuike pressed, "Why am I here?"

Wsir rose and prepared to exit the room and the house altogether. He could not help but gaze upon

Azubuike with a strong look of sympathy, "Young
Azubuike, that is for each one of us to discover for
ourselves. No one knows the mission given to you by the
Ntru, except the Ntru themselves."

Azubuike couldn't leave it at that, especially when
his best chance for straight forward answers was already
gesturing for them to exit the farm house. Azubuike didn't
know what was happening or what to expect next. The
uncertainty was making him feel uneasy. "Wsir, you can't
just leave me here like this…."

"Oh you're not leaving, young Azubuike," Wsir
was quick to help reassure him, "Our moment to part ways
has not yet arrived."

Wsir glanced at Roha, which drew the suspicion of
Azubuike. He turned to face her and his assumption was
confirmed by the obvious look of unease playing across her
face. "*You're* going back….?"

Roha did not deny it. Instead, she offered an
explanation on why she needed to go back. "A deal was
made, Azubuike. The first transition is always the hardest.
While we waited for your arrival, we discussed the options
moving forward and it was decided that this was the best
course. You fought well, Azubuike. I've never had the
chance to look at you and say those words. You have

performed far beyond what we'd even hoped for when we conceptualized *The Bennu Project*. You deserve the rest you desire. In your absence, I will fight for us."

Azubuike had no counter argument, Roha was leaving and he decided to make use of their limited time together. "I'm sorry for getting us into this mess…."

Wsir cut into the conversation to lighten the mood, "All is as it is meant to be, young Azubuike. Besides, Roha has been called careless once or twice in her day."

"Reckless," Roha corrected, "I've been called reckless many times, but never careless."

They moved outside to the clearing where all of those previously seen by Azubuike had gathered in attendance. There were even several more that he had not seen earlier. Including a man he was sure he recognized. Wsir and Azubuike watched as everyone else laid hands on Roha and said a brief prayer to their ancestors. They were requesting that the Ntru continue to protect her for the duration of her mission. When they finished, the familiar man and Roha shed their ethereal bodies and existed as the pure essence that Azubuike remembered from when he first arrived.

"Do not go," The familiar man said.

"I must…. "Roha, replied, "In the Hue-man plane,

we are defenseless."

Then they were gone. First, Roha's bright red energy faded away. Then the familiar man's bright gold energy faded as well. However, he transitioned to an ethereal body and left the clearing alone.

Azubuike turned to Wsir with yet another question, "Was that the hero of installation Sisu? The one they call "The Hero of Drtyu?"

"Indeed, it was," Wsir confirmed.

"I wish they had gotten more time together," Azubuike admitted.

"Time does not exist here, young Azubuike," Wsir reminded him. "In that instant, they shared countless memories and experiences."

"What happened to him?" Azubuike pressed.

Wsir let a small smile crease the corner of his mouth. "That is one of my favorite stories. Some of it you may remember, some of it you never knew. I will tell you the whole story."

Sabayt psD

The battlefield had become completely chaotic and disorganized. There were no working vehicles remaining, all had been reduced to smoldering debris and twisted metal frames. The few vehicles that weren't destroyed were heavily damaged and attempting to leave the area. The entire artillery line had suffered heavy losses due to Duro-Aina's attack and most of the Biafar traitors were in full retreat. They, and their Ezalin masters, were heading into open rolling hills; favoring speed over cover.

The casualty rate was high. Several members of all three factions lay across the open field in various stages of injury. With some barely clinging to life, others moved as best as they could among the fallen. They were trying, desperately, to identify wounded and pull them away from the only part of the battlefield that was still active. These efforts were constantly set back by the fact that Duro-Aina *was* the active hostile on the battlefield and rescuing anyone near her was a significant challenge.

The battle between her and the Medjay still raged, several moments after Azubuike's defeat. Their advanced armor and her over worked spiritual gland served to even out the advantages of either. She could, once again, use stealth but she was unable to form her ethereal mace. Ausar was still not responsive and, without him, she would be hard pressed to enact any exit strategy. Her options were limited and there were a great number of enemies still on the field.

The most immediate threat to Duro-Aina was the Medjay. They were hardly as capable as those she once knew but they were still a problem and there were a lot of them. Duro-Aina decided to make use of one of their weapons, then employ hit and run tactics on them via stealth. She was aware that an Isoba was on the field but without Ausar there was little she could do to find it. So she focused on the Medjay, when she should have been focusing on Priestess Oluwaseun.

Priestess Oluwaseun emerged from the small crater with a renewed sense of purpose. The Ntru had practically, personally ordered her to defend Roha and she even seemed to be emboldened by this revelation. She felt stronger, more courageous than she ever had before. She could not see her enemy but she could feel her. She concentrated her thoughts on what she was feeling and tried to identify what it was. There was a lot of pain, more than Oluwaseun had ever felt from one person but there was also anger. Lots and lots of anger. Then there was also revenge.

In truth, there were a lot of mixed up emotions but they were all of a common source; abandonment and helplessness.

Priestess Oluwaseun could only see the damage being done by Duro-Aina, her eyes were useless against an enemy in stealth. So she closed them. She tried to find Duro-Aina by searching for her twisted energy, and by trying to locate the source of her great disturbance of Ntr. She could feel the general direction in which Duro-Aina was located but it wasn't specific enough to be of any help. She pushed harder, focused more and was able to narrow down the general area. She continued to follow this feeling until it had skirted around the flank of the Medjay, attempting to hit them while they were unaware, again.

With her enemy isolated and distracted, this was Priestess Oluwaseun's chance to strike. She spoke the words and relaxed her Pineal gland, there was no going back now. A large gust of hurricane strength wind began to form behind her, collecting debris and the fallen as it built up in strength. In an instant, it was completed and Priestess Oluwaseun launched it at the center of where that chaotic energy was coming from.

No sooner than she had, the sum of all that Isfet energy grew in fury and focused on Oluwaseun. There was no confusion about where Duro-Aina was located now. With that much Isfet focused on her, Oluwaseun could locate Duro-Aina in her sleep. And she was getting closer. Somehow, her attack had missed or Duro-Aina was able to avoid it and was now charging her. She could feel the surprise, anger and fury as it grew in strength; as it grew closer. When it was upon her, the instant she felt it readying to strike her down, she leapt backward and forced a large column of solid rock to burst from the ground where she had once been. The rock wall had taken her place and was meant to catch Duro-Aina off guard, damaging her. Oluwaseun could feel that her attack had succeeded, even though she visibly witnessed the result of Duro-Aina's attack on her rock wall. She had split the solid rock in half, right down the middle.

Duro-Aina was beyond frustrated. Her combat ability had been severely diminished due to the fact that she had drastically low levels of the spiritual molecule, DMT. She still had not heard from Ausar since he'd gone offline. She stood there, staring at the temple priestess with contempt. She was sure she could have easily defeated the young priestess had this been an even fight. However, under the circumstances, the young girl had been surprisingly effective at keeping her away from Roha.

Duro-Aina decided to test her defenses. She circled around either side of her, attempting to reach Roha. She quickly learned that the true goal of this priestess was to defend her target. She rarely attacked and was only using her ability to defend the others. Duro-Aina decided to exploit this.

Duro-Aina started attacking other targets who were a decent distance from the temple priestess. Her goal was to force her to abandon her defensive posture, thereby opening the path forward to Roha. Yet the young girl did not move until Duro-Aina had reached another young woman, of similar age and similar energy as the priestess. It was obvious that these two were related somehow and this was the exact opportunity Duro-Aina needed.

Oluwaseun could feel the revelation as it hit her enemy. She could feel the satisfaction and the anticipation of her plan coming to fruition. Isfet was surrounding Kandake Anima, her sister. She had to act and she had to act fast. She abandoned her position near Roha and went on the attack, nearly running at full speed to get there. When she got to Anima, the menacing energy had gone. She didn't have to look far to figure out where Duro-Aina had gone. Oluwaseun had been played, the true target of her enemy never changed and this attack on Anima was a feint, nothing more.

Duro-Aina was on top of that crater in seconds. She was within reaching distance of Roha and could almost feel the victory within her grasp. That didn't stop the young temple priestess from sending an attack at her from behind. She could ignore further attacks from her and strike down Roha or she could turn and defend herself. She was well aware that striking down Roha could be the end of her as well, at this point, if she were to take direct damage from this priestess. Then he was there. Duro-Aina could feel the familiarity of Ausar as he permeated the deep recesses of her mind. With A functioning A.S.E., things were changing.

"Welcome back," Duro-Aina spoke and awaited his response, hoping for no significant damage.

"I see you've gotten yourself into a rather serious situation," Ausar observed, "how impulsive of you…."

"Briefly shut down all non-essential systems, including stealth, reroute all power to encourage DMT production and help me get my ancestral weapon back. It's time to deal with this temple upstart once and for all."

Duro-Aina had actually come to respect Oluwaseun, at least a little. She was no warrior but she was capable and she had done well in the battle. She had even refrained from abandoning her defensive position until the last possible moment. Still, she was standing in between her and her retribution and that meant Duro-Aina was about to end her.

Oluwaseun ran full speed at the crater, she could feel renewed purpose and energy coming from Duro-Aina and she intended to attack her before she finished whatever she had planned. However, it wasn't meant to be. Duro-Aina de-cloaked just before Oluwaseun arrived. She was standing with her back turned, looking down into the crater. Oluwaseun came to a halt just in time to see that terrifying purple mace come into existence. It was bigger, far more intense than it had been before and now it was randomly arcing purple light and sparks. Oluwaseun had made a mistake in pursuing Duro-Aina, a big one.

"Give me everything," Duro-Aina commanded. "Put all of our reserves into this attack."

"Supplementing your depleted DMT with stamina…." Ausar informed her. "You won't have much time."

Duro-Aina was well aware that after stamina depletion came life force. The spark of her life would power her abilities and there was no replenishing that. Not without intervention from the Ntru. She prepared for her attack, she had caught her quarry completely off guard.

Duro-Aina turned on her heel to deliver a one handed
swing, arcing over her shoulder as she spun, meant to
permanently disable the temple priestess. She could see the
fear on her face, the unmistakable recognition only seen on
one who knows their death is imminent.

There was nowhere to run, no way to avoid it.
Priestess Oluwaseun had no choice now but to stand her
ground and attempt to block this attack. Instinctively, she
threw her hands up in defense, the wind creating an
opposing force which attempted to push Duro-Aina back or
lessen her attack. It wouldn't be enough, not nearly.
Oluwaseun was seeing it now. She could, for the first time,
see Duro-Aina with her own eyes. She was larger than
anyone she'd ever seen by at least a foot. She was strong,
stocky and clearly a warrior. She charged at her in perfect
form, the kind of stance and muscle memory evident in
someone who had known combat their whole life. Then
there was the chaos energy. This warrior of Isfet was
overwhelming, the sheer power put into this attack could
likely destroy anyone who stood before it.

This was it. This was the shot she had been waiting
for. Nothing else mattered, no one else mattered. Ayoka
had been watching the crater and that temple priestess,
waiting for her chance. She hoped that monster would

become visible to her again and if she waited long enough, it might happen. She lay there, calmly letting the seconds pass as the monster completed its turn. She noted her energy charge counter, it was signaling final use and she lacked any more power sources to recharge it. She had one chance to save that priestess and, thereby, save Azubuike. She had relocated to a closer position once her previous location had been exposed and then she watched. She saw the raw power coming from the one who struck down Azubuike and she saw the Medjay's desperate attempt to fight it off. She'd considered attempting to pull Azubuike from the crater herself, while the monster was distracted, but then the Priestess from the temple decided to join the battle.

Still, Ayoka lay there waiting for her opportune moment and this was it. The temple priestess had made a terrible mistake, exposing herself. Which caused the monster to over commit, making its own terrible mistake, and also exposing itself. The sweat was building on the top of her left brow but she dare not move. The seconds went on for what seemed like an eternity. Two, three, FOUR! The monster completed its turn, the mace was coming down at an angle to strike the priestess. A drop of sweat dripped from Ayoka's left eyebrow. She had been waiting for it to drop, with her finger slightly relaxed on her trigger, hoping it would drop on its own and not interfere with her shot. When it did, she squeezed and let the built up energy discharge from her sniper rifle. This was the only shot that mattered, and Ayoka delivered it, along with all the positive affirmations she could think of.

The shot from the sniper rifle was high. At first it seemed like it was too high and that it would miss. Yet the further it went, the more it started to arc, drastically. At times it seemed to be gliding over a long distance, right at Duro-Aina. It was still high, even as it closed the distance, then it came down rapidly. Right over the shoulder of her intended target, Ayoka's shot struck Duro-Aina in the neck, forcing her sideways. When she saw that she had a confirmed hit on target, Ayoka let herself collapse from the strain. She was just as depleted as her weapon was.

Struggling to maintain her balance, Duro-Aina missed her perfect hit on the priestess. She was only able to strike the shield she had made but missed hitting the young woman herself. Still, the force of that blow dispelled the wind, obliterated any shield defense that remained and knocked Priestess Oluwaseun, violently, to the ground. Duro-Aina stood there, partially disappointed and slightly amused. She was holding her neck with her left hand, the force of her life flowed freely from the wound as the nanites did their best to repair the damage done to her. She looked in the direction of where the shot had come from, nothing but anger evident on her face. Then she held that same look of content as she gazed down at the hurt priestess.

Oluwaseun was hurt, she couldn't fight nor could she hardly even move. She looked up at her attacker and waited. Instead of a finishing blow, however, Duro-Aina spoke to her. "Another time, young one." Then she was gone. The purple weapon faded from her right hand and, with it, so too did the hint of purple that previously lingered in her eyes. She immediately went to stealth and retreated. Oluwaseun could feel the presence moving until it was a good deal away and then completely undetectable.

Priestess Oluwaseun needed to rest. She had never used her ability to connect to Ntr for this long and never even close to this extent of time. She lay back, exhausted, and stared at the sky. Anima was on her sister in seconds. The two of them checked each other for injuries and, when they were satisfied that neither of them were hurt, they helped each other up and started checking on those nearest to them.

Hezbon and the other Medjay were gathered around

the crater and attending to Azubuike. He set a guard around the group so they could ascertain the extent of Azubuike's injuries, then called in the Keftiu for evac. Kandake Anima, Priestess Oluwaseun and the Egbas warriors who weren't injured, or caring for the injured, were approaching the crater. They all crowded around the crater trying to get a glimpse of Azubuike. None were permitted to pass the perimeter set by the Medjay, save for Anima and Oluwaseun.

As the Keftiu circled one final time and then came in on final approach, Anima queried Hezbon. She needed to have a discussion with him. "Where will you take him?"

Hezbon had very little direct interaction with the Kandake of the Naijia people. He'd met her before, on occasion or two, and knew she was all business. As a warrior, she would understand the need for operational security. Hezbon kept it brief, "We're taking him home."

"They must not!" Priestess Oluwaseun interjected.

Every Medjay immediately adjusted their posture to possible hostile intent. Weapons were raised and everyone on the field scanned and tracked each other. Everyone was on edge, especially the Medjay. Regardless of whatever political gains had been made on this mission, the Medjay were sworn to protect the sovereign and they considered that mission a failure. No one wanted to be the one to have to explain to Kandake Nzinga what had happened to Azubuike. It would only be made that much worse if the next series of events on Naijia were to spiral even further out of control.

Hezbon polarized his face plate and prepared to give orders. First, though, he spoke directly to Kandake Anima, "Sovereign Azubuike is going back to the mountain, this much is clear."

Kandake Anima *was* impulsive, and she was every bit as stubborn as Hezbon was. She did not back down and when it looked like she was going to retort, it was Oluwaseun who diffused the situation. She put out a calming hand toward both of them, as she stepped between the two. She had to then add a determined look to convince them both.

To Hezbon she looked directly as she spoke, "By all means, take him back. *After* you visit the temple. They cannot live long, *anywhere*, until they have been cared for by the followers of Serqet."

"Are you certain, sister?" Anima was genuinely surprised that Oluwaseun would even suggest such a thing. This honor was reserved for high profile situations, the approvals, of which, were dependent on the temple authority's own choosing.

This time Oluwaseun turned to her sister as she spoke, "More than certain, sister. My solution was only temporary. He must be cleansed under their ritual. It's the only way to save either of them."

Kandake Anima immediately changed tones and calmly approached Hezbon, "As our ally, I extend the royal invitation to you and your aides; to join us at the Temple of Serqet as we petition the temple authority for help with Sovereign Azubuike."

Hezbon had absolutely no reason to trust Kandake Anima. He wasn't a party to the conversation that saw M.A.R.S. and Naijia declared as allies. He had no idea if any of her people were responsible for this elaborate plan to kill Azubuike. However, he did see the young temple priestess risk her life for Azubuike. They would not have achieved victory without her….

Hezbon relaxed his posture and lowered his weapon. Slightly. "I accept."

Both of them gave orders to their own people to stand down. Everyone was now free to relax, to not worry about the Medjay and the Egbas warriors engaging each other in battle over Azubuike. As Hezbon watched the S.A.R. team medic working on Azubuike, he wondered to himself how much of a fight the Egbas warriors would have really put up. He respected them for their courage and refusal to be cowered, even with the obvious gap in their comparative levels of technology. He had no intention of unnecessarily harming any of them, though. If there was one thing he hated more than anything else, it was engaging his own brothers and sisters in battle. More than enough of that had already gone on with the Biafar traitors. Hezbon was no politician but he wished there was a way for the Naijia people to reconcile with the Biafar traitors. They were all Naijian right? Weren't the Ezalin their common enemy? Just like they were the enemy of all on his world? Hezbon just didn't understand it.

Kandake Anima had finished giving orders to her general, which were to arrange for evac. Then she used her new comms to contact Abeo and arrange for them to be received by the temple authority. She turned her attention to Azubuike's commander, who seemed to be lost in some deep thought.

Kandake Anima realized there was one last thing to figure out and she used it to break the tension, "So, are we taking your transport…. or mine?"

Sabayt mD

The flight back to the city was, for the most part, quiet. The Keftiu was filled with Medjay, one exhausted Isoba, Kandake Anima and Priestess Oluwaseun. Although everyone was in various stages of combat fatigue, the S.A.R. team medic did his best to monitor those with the more serious injuries. Kandake Anima sat with her sister and quietly considered the options they had regarding Azubuike's treatment. Ayoka rested in a small corner near the back and employed her stealth function to prevent any unwanted interactions.

Hezbon had just finished an uncomfortable conversation with Kandake Nzinga, in which he updated her on the status of their mission. He held the conversation in private, via his H.U.D. and made the feed restricted to all but who it was intended for. Seba, Nosizwe, Councilor Melisizwe and Kandake Nzinga were all present for the conference call. Hezbon started from the beginning and walked them through the series of events as he saw them. As he described the experiences from his own perspective, he used audio/video data recorded by his suit to give references to his opinions.

Hezbon showed them how the Medjay had waited

in the city's transportation district. Everyone in the feed could see how Azubuike had approached them with new orders. Then he skimmed forward to the flight out to show them how he and Azubuike had formed, what they thought was, a solid plan of attack. He specifically allowed that entire conversation to play through so Kandake Nzinga could see their expectations. When the conversation concluded, the disembark alarm went off and the Medjay exited the Keftiu dropship. Everyone could see the high altitude, evident by the cloud layers and even other visible Medjay in free fall, from Hezbon's perspective.

Hezbon fast forwarded again, noting how his trajectory had been on a different path from Azubuike's. Broken branches brushed past Hezbon's H.U.D. in a blur as he crashed through the tree tops. Fast forwarding again rewarded the viewers with images of the Medjay destroying both mobile artillery and mobile anti-aircraft sites. Hezbon took this opportunity to note his receipt of new orders. It was a rally point some distance away from the artillery line.

Hezbon then fast forwarded to the end of their slow and lengthy march through the dense forest. From his position in the tree line the viewers could see Azubuike and Kandake Anima lead an attack on what would turn out to be a trap. They heard Azubuike's orders to the Medjay and watched as they carried them out. Kandake Nzinga's face betrayed her anger at the sound of Wynch's voice. Up to that point in the debriefing, all viewers were quiet and attentively observing the answers to their questions being played out. There was very little commentary until a KIA was confirmed. Kandake Nzinga and Nosizwe shared a brief exchange, making a note to identify the fallen Medjay and to properly notify the surviving family.

Then, and quite suddenly, all four of them were on the edge of their seats. They watched as something dangerously strong was cutting through the tank line. Then they saw it, the purple haze in the dense smoke, and all four of them visibly stiffened. There was a collective gasp from Councilor Melisizwe, Seba, Nosizwe and Kandake Nzinga when Azubuike was struck down by Duro-Aina. They continued to watch, with great anticipation, as Azubuike's attacker was eventually defeated. Much of the final defeat was obscured due to the amount of destruction being caused but enough was visible to draw obvious conclusions. The video/audio feed ended with the conclusion of Hezbon's conversation with Kandake Anima regarding how they should evac. Councilor Melisizwe was grateful that it had not come to hostilities.

Kandake Nzinga spoke first and stood up when she

did, "Hezbon you are to be commended, all of you, for your service to Sovereign Azubuike. Had it not been for the Medjay, he would not be alive."

"Alive…." Hezbon considered how he wanted to respond to this. He decided to upload Azubuike's medical data in a file, "Queen Mother, I have just forwarded everything we have on Azubuike's current medical condition. He is *alive* but, if we don't do something soon, he won't remain that way. The Medjay failed Sovereign Azubuike."

Everyone paused while they downloaded the file and Hezbon could see them focus their eyes on the text now scrolling across their screens. Everyone except Councilor Melisizwe, who decided to address the immediate situation, "You weren't even there…. We all saw Azubuike order you to flank the tank line, preventing you from being at his defense when he needed you most. How can you blame yourself for this?"

"I know better than anyone how impulsive my brother can be," Seba cut in, "Having the responsibility of protecting him is no easy task. Nor is it entrusted to just anyone."

Hezbon considered this perspective, perhaps this outcome was the best to be expected, given the impossible odds. Still, the sovereign was hurt and he couldn't help but lay part of the blame on himself. When this mission was over, the training regimen for Medjay was going to get a massive overhaul. However, the direction of the conversation changed when Nosizwe spoke up. She had been pouring over the medical data in an attempt to decode it and construct a clear impression of Azubuike's medical status.

"Is there any indication that biological warfare was employed?" Nosizwe asked. She shifted in her seat before continuing, mentally finalizing her assumption. "There was a massive release of white blood cells after he collapsed from his injuries during the battle."

Hezbon thought about this. He had not observed any obvious attempts by Azubuike's attacker to poison him. Nor did he observe any delivery systems that are typically used for deploying biological agents. While he was not with Azubuike for the entire duration of the mission, he could reasonably conclude that Azubuike was not exposed to that type of attack. He had not noticed any of the tell-tale signs in his speech or behavior.

"While Wynch was present on the battle field," Hezbon began, "I do not believe Azubuike was subjected to an attack of that nature."

Nosizwe was sure something other than physical damage was affecting her husband, she just wasn't sure what it was yet. "I agree, the data supports your assumption. No trace of viral or bacterial infection can be found. Yet his suit administered several anti-toxins. I cannot explain why that would happen or why the suit would administer these medications without any indication that they were necessary."

Nosizwe continued to scroll down, searching for something that she eventually found, "There were also heavy sedatives used…. Most likely to manage the extremely high levels of adrenaline during his final stand. Heart rate, blood pressure, neural activity and DMT production were all off the charts. In fact, they were all dangerously in the red and it is nothing short of a miracle that he is alive. Everything I am reading here suggests that Azubuike's body should have broken down and failed due to the shock to his system alone, let alone all the physical damage done to him."

"He was always a tough young man," Councilor Melisizwe added, "But this must be the result of something greater at work. Even Young Azubuike could not have survived all that alone." Councilor Melisizwe organized his thoughts, "Maybe we're looking at this the wrong way."

"Maybe…." Kandake Nzinga was connecting the same dots that Councilor Melisizwe was, "What have we overlooked, Councilor?"

"Instead of looking for an unknown cause for these unseen symptoms that each of these drugs was supposed to address, let's look at this from the other end. Maybe it was a combination of these drugs, used to assist Azubuike in some way we can't yet explain. Perhaps some intervention by Oya?" Councilor Melisizwe looked to Seba for an assessment of his suggestion, along with everyone else.

Seba looked to Nosizwe, "Where did you find the data showing when the drugs were administered?"

When Nosizwe pointed out the lines in question, Seba looked them over and took a moment to finalize his assessment. "These look like they could be manual overrides to the system. But I cannot confirm that without seeing the diagnostic report from his suit. What is Oya's status?"

Progression of the conversation rested with Hezbon now, he needed to forward the diagnostic report from Azubuike's suit but that couldn't be done in the field without an engineer and they didn't have one. "Sovereign Azubuike's suit is offline permanently. The medical data available to us came from my remote monitoring of his status. We'll need an engineer to salvage the armor and recover any additional information."

"Then why the delay?" Nosizwe asked, "We must work to determine his condition as quickly as possible. Returning him to us should be the first priority."

Initially, Hezbon was in agreement with Nosizwe. The medical facilities in the mountain were far more advanced, far more familiar with Meroan technology. However, the young priestess had made her case and, after demonstrating her ability, Hezbon was convinced of her credibility. "I believe that is the purpose of the trip we're taking right now."

"Ah yes, the Temple of Serqet." Councilor Melisizwe had a specific interest in them. "I haven't made much progress in rebuilding our own temples…. We would definitely benefit from their expertise. Please extend an invitation."

"Kandake Nzinga," Seba started, "I'd like to leave on the next flight out."

Nosizwe assumed Seba would want to handle the diagnostic on his brother, personally. Yet she already knew the answer, she didn't even ask to join him.

"I'm sorry young Seba, you're the last person who can go such a great distance without proper protection. Too much of a security risk. Your work alone makes you too much of a target." Kandake Nzinga knew how they felt, she experienced the same with Ime. Shc hoped they would understand her decision even though the disappointment was evident.

"Patience, Seba." Melisizwe counseled. "If anyone can restore him it will be the followers of Serqet. Then he will return to us."

"So we are all in agreement that the Temple of Serqet is the path forward," Kandake Nzinga finalized the decision with a formal tone. "Please proceed Hezbon."

"It will be done, Kandake Nzinga." Hezbon acknowledged his new orders and exited the conversation. It seemed the four of them had more to discuss, regarding several topics that had no need of his participation.

Hezbon depolarized his faceplate and observed the other passengers. All quiet, all resting, except for two and they were looking straight at him.

"Well, what did they say?" Kandake Anima asked, then continued on when she was met by a look of confusion as Hezbon double checked his encryption software. "It was obvious. You were standing there like a statue, suppressing any obvious mannerisms."

"Not to mention the wide range of emotions you

were radiating," Priestess Oluwaseun added, "You don't deserve the guilt of failure. Don't do that to yourself."

Hezbon looked on Oluwaseun with genuine surprise, then decided to just admit that he'd been having a private conversation. "The Temple Authority has been invited to send a representative to the mountain. A formal request for help will come via diplomatic channels."

"And what else…." Priestess Oluwaseun pushed.

"There is much discussion being had over the current state of Sovereign Azubuike," Hezbon kept his answers honest but devoid of anything that needed to be kept confidential, "However, I am authorized to transport our Sovereign to the temple, only the temple, and then home. Nowhere else."

Kandake Anima stood up and walked to the nearest view port. There wasn't much room for her to see much of anything so Hezbon retracted the secondary firing barrier. Meant for gunners to use the ship's heavy weapons to provide cover, the firing barrier provided a way for occupants to have increased visibility while being protected by a barely visible energy barrier. The two of them stood there, joined by Oluwaseun and a few others who had taken notice, as they observed the city below. They were in the spiritual district, evident by the design and colors of the structures they flew over.

Even the layout of the district, itself, was designed to bring attention to the Temple of Serqet. It sat, undaunted, at the center of a large hill which was located in the very center of the district. Every major street, throughway, and structure was intentionally placed to form concentric rings equidistant from the temple. The temple itself was a large square structure with four large towers emerging from their foundations in the corners of the building. At the center of the temple sat an even larger, more majestic tower which reached higher into the sky.

"If I may, Kandake Anima, what is in that central tower?" Hezbon asked.

"Their most sacred knowledge," Anima responded, as they grew nearer and nearer to their destination. "It is an ancient library which holds the oldest manuscripts we still have. Much of our knowledge was lost due to the Oyinbo occupation and, as a result of this, severe security measures have been implemented to protect the remainder of our sacred knowledge, our culture. Even I do not visit the library without good reason."

"I understand," Hezbon knew all too well how the Ezalin destroyed libraries and burned books in order to suppress native cultures. "Do you think there is a reasonable chance they will be able to save him?"

"I honestly do not know," Kandake Anima admitted, as the Keftiu touched down, "But if any reasonable chance exists, it will be here."

Ayoka should have been prepping to disembark the Keftiu, yet she lacked the strength. What she originally thought was mere combat fatigue, was turning into something much more. In the past, Ayoka would spend days at a time on her training. She regularly pushed herself beyond her limits in order to maintain a sharpened, heightened sense. She trained hard to maintain her level of precision, yet this went beyond normal exhaustion *and* it wasn't the first time it had happened. At her core, something was draining her physical strength and her mental will. Ayoka convinced herself not to detract from the mission at hand. She wanted to be off this world and back in the mountain for a few weeks, at least. Besides, the faster they got back, the faster she would get a proper rest. If that didn't fix it then she would bring it up to Nosizwe at another time. However for now, she would take a rest.

Hezbon ordered the S.A.R. team to assist in transporting Azubuike while the bulk of the Medjay were set on a rotating guard duty. They would take turns, alternate between resting and guarding the Keftiu. Hezbon took point, leading the formation with Azubuike's stretcher following just behind him. Three S.A.R. members carried Azubuike on a portable stretcher while the rest flanked him on both sides, ready for anything. Priestess Oluwaseun kept pace with the transport, a hand on Azubuike's head in an attempt to feel his spiritual energies.

At the front of it all was Kandake Anima, familiar stride and air of command, projecting her usual authority as she walked. Large statues of heroic ancestors lined the front facing walls of the temple, drawing attention to themselves at the expense of the wide open main entry doors. Two of these overbearing statues stood silent guard on either side of the main entry doors, dwarfing them at a height of four meters. The assembled group approached the large bronze doors and noticed the two actual guards standing on either side of it, just in front of their respective statues.

Kandake Anima, through force of habit, walked straight through without incident. Close behind her was Hezbon, who also passed through without incident. However, both guards moved to obstruct Priestess Oluwaseun when she attempted to enter.

Kandake Anima and Hezbon both turned to locate the source of the commotion and, when it was identified, they both approached the guards.

Kandake Anima responded to Hezbon's silent question by addressing the guards directly, "I do not have time to address the no-weapons policy of the temple."

Three nearby Egbas soldiers noticed the disturbance and, apparent, standoff. They rushed to aid their Kandake by pointing weapons at the temple guards, which drew the attention of even more temple guards.

"We understand the need for urgency," the first guard spoke, "Of course you, and your honored guests, are granted entry without the slightest delay. However, this one," he pointed at Priestess Oluwaseun, "has been banned from the temple grounds for crimes against NTR and is denied entry."

Kandake Anima's anger could not be described in simple words, nor could it be contained. She withdrew a side arm and put it mere inches from the face of the guard who had created this situation in the first place, "She *will* be allowed to enter the temple and explain the circumstances to The Temple Authority, *herself.*"

The guard immediately regretted his decision. The temper of Kandake Anima was legendary…. And he was on the business end of her anger, brought on by a very bad day. "Please, Kandake. They have already said so. They will not hear."

Up to this point, Hezbon and the Medjay were standing by watching the events unfold. It was Priestess Oluwaseun who cut in, "Please. If they do not hear then Sovereign Roha will die."

The Medjay armed up and trained their weapons on the temple guards without hesitation.

Sabayt mDu Wa

Kandake Anima sat in the foyer with the High Priest of the Serqet temple. The two of them had an interesting relationship, to say the least. Kandake Anima and the High Priest, Ampah, had been young friends together for much of their childhood. Although there had been times when their friendship bordered on the romantic, nothing ever came of it. Their duties to their future titles prevented any such attachments to the other. Still, they were very fond of each other and stole their private moments whenever they could. Ampah was the one man Anima wanted but could never have. Royalty was not allowed to fraternize with the Temple Authority.

After Ampah had personally arrived to diffuse the situation brewing in the courtyard, the Medjay were escorted to the main recovery chamber where the ritual of spiritual healing had begun. Anima and Oluwaseun were invited to his personal chambers, to have the discussion which would determine her status at the temple. However, Ampah wasn't sure that this opportunity for Anima to voice her sister's case was anything more than a formality. The Temple Authority had been clear, she was to be banned from any Temple Authority grounds or rituals. He thought about all this while trying to figure out the best way to push back against Kandake Anima without destroying their life long relationship. This was a delicate balancing act that had repeated itself ever since they'd first taken over their respective duties.

"I'm sorry Anima," Ampah was taking the more casual tone with her that was usually reserved for their conversations in private," My hands are tied, the Temple Authority has spoken. They've specifically ordered that she no longer be associated with us."

"Without even hearing her side?" Anima protested.

"That part is strange," Ampah admitted. "They've decided to forego the review and immediately moved to sanction her...."

"Yes, she broke the highest law," Anima began, "However, we were in an impossible situation. A monster of some kind...."

Ampah cut her off, a hint of amusement showed on the corner of his lips, "Did you say "monster?"

Anima let out a laugh. She silently admitted that it didn't sound even slightly credible unless you'd seen it yourself. "While it is true that I would say nearly anything to protect my sister, I urge you to take this seriously."

Ampah sat up a little straighter. He'd known Anima

long enough to have grown confident in her social cues. She was being absolutely serious about this and the slightest hint of amusement could not be found anywhere on her face. He decided to take the matter more seriously, since it was clearly not a joke to her. "Do you have any evidence to substantiate the existence of this monster?"

"As a matter of fact, I do." Anima leaned back into her chair, legs crossed formally, arms resting on either of its arm rests. It was this posture that betrayed any chance to keep a secret from Ampah. She sat there as if she was born to this chair, she may as well have been seated in her throne room. Ampah knew, whether the monster in question was true or not, Anima was *convinced*. Whatever she was about to call as her evidence had her complete confidence. He leaned forward, on the edge of his seat, in anticipation.

Ampah waited for her to expand but she didn't. Instead, she went in a different direction. "Hear my sister first."

"We've been over that." Ampah leaned right back into his seat, anticipation abated. "Even speaking to her would jeopardize my position."

"I am assuring you that it will be worth it." Anima was trying her best to push her friend without causing irreparable harm to their relationship. When he still seemed unconvinced, she decided to compromise. "I will agree to show you the evidence first. However, if it moves you, you must agree to speak with my sister. Agreed?"

Ampah's curiosity about this evidence, and his relationship with Kandake Anima, got the better of him. "Agreed."

"Very well," Anima also agreed to the terms. "I'll need to make a call."

Anima opened her secure comm channel to Hezbon and waited for him to respond. When he did, she spoke to him in a tone that expressed urgency but not immediate danger. "I need your help, Commander. It is of a most important matter."

Hezbon was inside the ritual chamber with Azubuike, observing the progress made. Usually, outsiders are not allowed to participate in or observe the rituals. Yet this was the deal struck in order to avoid conflict in the courtyard. One Medjay was permitted to monitor Azubuike at all times. Hezbon informed Kandake Anima that he would arrive shortly. He then exited the room and signaled for another Medjay to take his place.

Anima cut off the comm and informed Ampah that her evidence was on its way. "He will be here shortly."

"I'll have him escorted here," Ampah confirmed,

before he accessed his own communication device.

A few short moments later, and Hezbon had joined them in the office. Another chair in the foyer was positioned for him next to Kandake Anima, by Ampah's Assistant, before he exited the room. Hezbon was no longer wearing the full Medjay armor that offered maximum protection. He thought it was imposing and unnecessary, given that he was no longer in combat and now was among his "allies." Hezbon had scaled down the nanites so that they only provided the basic under armor protection. Currently, he sat there, in a formal posture, waiting for the reason behind his summons to be made clear.

It was High priest Ampah who spoke first. "You may remember me, from our brief encounter in the courtyard. "I am high Priest Ampah, administrator of this temple."

"I am Commander Hezbon, leader of the Medjay and sworn protector of Sovereign Azubuike." Hezbon began to give the formal greeting of a first contact scenario. "As a representative of M.A.R.S. I cannot express my gratitude enough, for your hospitality."

"What is the current status on Azubuike, Commander?" Anima Asked. "Do we know anything yet?

Hezbon was well aware that the man sitting across

from him could have gained access to that information without ever having him brought to his office. So Hezbon decided to accelerate the conversation, in order to reveal his involvement in it. "His status is unclear, Kandake, they have only just begun to assess the true nature of his injuries. I must return to him immediately."

"I'm sure Sovereign Azubuike is in capable hands, Commander, "Anima assured, "However, we have need of your technology. In order to gain further assistance from the Serqet priests."

"What kind of need?" Hezbon asked, cautiously. "I am not authorized to share technology with you. Only the Sovereign can do that."

"We have no need of the technology itself," Kandake Anima was well aware of Hezbon's absolute loyalties. "Please show him the video footage from our battle. Specifically those parts that reveal the nature of Sovereign Azubuike's attacker."

Hezbon did just that. Now that he understood the point of this, he was more than willing to accommodate the Kandake. He did this by omitting anything deemed "Restricted, due to Operational Security" and playing only those parts directly relevant to the new enemy. He made sure to amplify the audio on the parts that clearly demonstrated the priestess's hesitation to enter the battle. Ampah was stunned when he saw the Meroan technology first hand. His eyes grew wide at the holographic, three dimensional representation of events that coincided with the visual/audio recordings picked up by various suit Head-up Displays. The look on his face seemed to grow even more incredulous, once the purple haze started moving in and around the rear tank line of Lieutenant Wynch. He watched as the defensive shield around Azubuike collapsed from an attack, the result of which, leaving Azubuike in his current state.

Hezbon froze the replay as the H.U.D. showed him running toward the attacker, from his point of view. She was rising, looking right at the priestess, then turned to face him. The still image of her seemed to be looking right out of the display and into the eyes of everyone in the room. It created an uncomfortable atmosphere and sent a chill down Ampah's spine.

"So this is your "Monster…." Ampah accepted it as truth. He'd seen it with his own eyes. He stirred uncomfortably in his seat for several moments while Anima and Hezbon watched him closely.

"Ampah…." Anima Nudged.

But Ampah had already made his decision. Hearing

his name spoken aloud spurred him into action. He pressed a button on his chair, summoning his assistant. When the man entered the room, Ampah wasted no time in making his wishes known. "Please bring Priestess Oluwaseun in and arrange another seat for her as well."

Then Ampah spoke to Anima with that air of familiarity, "I believe you. Please let me handle this."

There was little time to object, Oluwaseun was already being led in by the assistant and there was no reason to distrust Ampah anyway. Priestess Oluwaseun had been seated in a waiting area just outside the door. She entered the room, guided by the assistant, and took her seat. She had the appearance of someone who was reaching the limits of their frustration.

Ampah broke the ice, with an antagonistic tone, by confirming a few things first. "You have been accused of using your connection to Ntr in a violent manner, which resulted in wide spread destruction. To say nothing of the damage done to Ntr itself. Do you deny it?"

Priestess Oluwaseun did not immediately respond. When she did it was only to say, "I do not deny it."

So Ampah continued, "The accusation goes on to claim that you intentionally used your connection, to harm Ntr and to endanger the cosmic balance."

Anima and Oluwaseun stood up in anger. However, it was Oluwaseun who shouted, "That's a lie!"

Anima, on the other hand, kept her silence. She knew full well that Ampah had just seen and accepted their version of the story. He must be pushing this button on Oluwaseun to provoke a response, and he got it.

"I have only ever served the Ntru" Oluwaseun continued, while trying to regain some of her composure. "I will continue to do so, with or without the blessing of the Temple Authority."

"Please retake your seat, Oluwaseun," High Priest Ampah had what he wanted. He had been concentrating on her energy the entire time. "I have the answer I needed. I believe you are acting in the interests of the Ntru."

Ampah was convinced of Oluwaseun's intentions. He didn't need to know the specifics nor did he think it was necessary, at this time. Far more important narratives were playing out, for him to spend time peeling back the layers to uncover what had motivated Priestess Oluwaseun in the first place.

Instead, he turned his attention back to Commander Hezbon. "I will order my guards to stand aside and not prevent your departure in any way. I will even send my most trusted ritual healers along with you so that they may continue to aid in Sovereign Azubuike's recovery. I only ask, that you take Kandake Anima and Priestess Oluwaseun with you."

Kandake Anima and Oluwaseun replied in unison, "What?" Both of them, caught off guard by his recommendation.

"I don't have anything specific…." Ampah explained, "But the way they have attempted to rail road your sister is not hardly the usual way we deal with these issues. Furthermore, couple that with today's sudden changes in security protocol and I have only one assumption to make. Anima, I believe there is a plot against you and the Temple Authority may be involved."

A chime on his computer alerted him to a new incoming message and he read it with genuine surprise on his face. He then motioned for the others to move to his chair and view the message for themselves. He began paraphrasing the contents of the message, for his own benefit as much as theirs, out loud. "I am to stall the Meroans for as long as possible and place Kandake Anima under arrest. Along with Priestess Oluwaseun."

"I'll need to contact the Mountain immediately," Hezbon said, flatly.

"Commander?" Kandake Anima was asking

Hezbon to expand on his thought process.

"I'm not a diplomat," Hezbon explained. "The political situation on Naijia is rapidly deteriorating and I would like to contact Kandake Nzinga before I engage in another concurrent civil war in order to Evac Sovereign Azubuike."

In truth, Hezbon's intention to bring the mountain's leadership into the conversation was a bit disingenuous, considering that both Kandake Nzinga and Councilor Melisizwe had been listening-in on his suit comms and already heard every word of this conversation.

Ampah skimmed through the message and quickly read, aloud, the important parts that remained. "Apparently, your "monster" has been in contact with The Temple Authority since your battle earlier today. She also has a name, Duro-Aina, and claims to be the last living survivor of KMT. She has demanded the loyalty of the Temple Authority, based on spiritual grounds, and they have capitulated. Well *most* of them have, anyway."

"What are your orders, Kandake?" Hezbon pushed a button on his forearm and a three dimensional representation of Kandake Nzinga appeared right in front of him. She was in full color and being displayed in real time.

"When she spoke, she did so directly to Hezbon,

"Follow no other command, let nothing stand in your way. Do not rest until Sovereign Azubuike has been returned to us." She then turned to Priestess Oluwaseun, "For your service to Ntr and in the defense of Sovereign Azubuike, it is my honor to extend the royal invitation to you. Join us in the mountain. You may stay with us permanently or until your place among the Naijia is a little more clear. The choice is yours to make."

"Forgive me Kandake Nzinga," Priestess Oluwaseun began to object, "My place among the Naijia will always be certain."

"Thank you for your graciousness," Kandake Anima interrupted, "She'll be on the transport out, with Commander Hezbon."

Oluwaseun shot her sister a menacing glance, but the two Queen mothers shared a look of understanding before Kandake Nzinga spoke again, "I already know you will not leave, I wouldn't, and I didn't. What help do you require of us?"

"This Duro-Aina," Kandake Anima replied, "She is an un-killable enemy. The limited success we had against her is due, in no small part to the Medjay and to Oluwaseun's connection to the Ntru. However, if The Temple Authority sides with her, she may well conquer the planet."

"I understand your request, sister," Nzinga had been where Anima is now. She couldn't help but to empathize with her.

Facing impossible odds and still fighting to achieve the victory. She could not help but to relate to her. "The Bulk of our main force will arrive within the week…." She paused long enough to confirm with her senior commander, Themba, before she continued. "Advance recon elements will begin to arrive by the end of the day."

She would speak one final time, to Hezbon. Kandake Nzinga gestured toward Priestess Oluwaseun, "I leave her in your care."

Then she was gone, her intentions made clear and Hezbon's path forward laid out for him. There were no more diplomatic obstacles, barriers or political issues standing in the way. It was time to get Azubuike home. Hezbon activated the full protection of his nanites and they were expanding into the heavy armor everyone had grown used to seeing him in. He moved, immediately, to the door and paused only long enough to convey a message to Priestess Oluwaseun, "Evac in five minutes."

Hezbon stormed into the ritual healing chamber with a singular purpose, to get Azubuike ready for transport. He ordered his Medjay to gear up, prep for immediate evac and to be ready to move out in forty five seconds. Hezbon interrupted the ritual right in the middle of some of the most intense chanting. He'd listened, attentively, to an explanation about the ritual while Azubuike was being transported to the chamber. They were using various healing methods, vibration stimulation chief among them, to ease his spiritual energies back into a state of balance. According to them, Azubuike had suffered some spiritual attack of great magnitude, which should have left him dead. Instead, it left him near death with his energies severely out of balance.

The priests performing the ritual on Azubuike were some of the most revered healers on the planet. They had grown, in recognition, beyond the title of priests or priestesses. They were no longer simple priests. Now they were master teachers, revered elders and direct conduits to Ntr. In addition to that, they were spiritual doctors. Those with feminine energy were given the title of Hmt, while those with masculine energy were called Hm. It had taken them years to achieve this level of understanding and they were unrivaled in their ability to connect with Ntr. Having now been alerted to the situation by Ampah, they also moved quickly to prepare to travel.

Hezbon took a moment to survey Azubuike. He still wore his badly damaged armor, which left his body exposed in some areas. On the places where his body was exposed, Hezbon could see oddly colored burns on Azubuike's skin. What surprised him most was the look Azubuike had on his face. For quite a while, it had remained as the look of perpetual pain. But now, it just seemed peaceful. Azubuike could have been asleep, save for the burns he had suffered, to anyone who didn't look close enough.

The main ritual healing chamber was located in the main spire, just beneath the main library. The Medjay squad exited the chamber and used a lift to travel the distance, down to ground level. They passed by the guards and patrons with a sense of purpose, noting their unchanged attitudes and behaviors. They were still operating under the previous orders to stand down. Hezbon hoped that would hold out until they were well away from the temple. It became more unlikely to be the case, the closer they got to the courtyard.

Whereas previous guards barely acknowledged them, these guards were clearly wrestling with something. Their postures were more aggressive and plenty of hushed words were heard as the Medjay passed by. Amplifying the audio playback revealed that these guards were, in fact, aware of the new conflict in orders. However, they hadn't made up their minds whether to defy High Priest Ampah or not. Hezbon didn't intend to give them the chance to make the wrong decision and, luckily for them, he wouldn't have to.

Both High Priest Ampah and Kandake Anima joined them as the Medjay reached the threshold of the courtyard. They were in an intense conversation and when they matched pace with Hezbon, Anima spoke loud enough to include him as well.

"I've already told you," Anima said. A hint of irritation creeping into her voice. "I called for reinforcements, but there won't *be* any violence if the Temple Authority doesn't force my hand."

"Then I will take you at your word, Kandake." High Priest Ampah was interrupted by a message from his assistant. He paused, to hear it entirely, then spoke again. "They're approaching the west wall, I will go and delay them."

Kandake Anima helped load Azubuike aboard the Keftiu and then guided her sister into a good spot as well. She made a big, humorous show as she looked her over with mock concern, attempting to assess her health.

"You've never been this far, little sister," She said.

Oluwaseun knew her sister and she knew this was the only way Anima could ever say goodbye to her. Still she always played along, "If I get lost, I know you'll find me. Big sister."

The two sisters shared one final embrace before Kandake Anima departed the Keftiu. She passed by the last Medjay to board on her way out. Hezbon had just finished his head count and would be the last to board. Anima moved to stand next to Hezbon as they observed the other side of the courtyard. A large commotion was brewing among the guards and a handful of spiritual fanatics, emboldened by the new Temple authority soldiers, and it was all headed their way. They could see High Priest Ampah at the front of it, rushing to join them, with what few loyal guards he had left.

"Are you going to be alright, Kandake Anima?" Hezbon asked, gesturing to the spiritual mob.

"I'll be just fine, Commander," She replied, matter of fact, as she gestured toward the horizon.

Hezbon increased magnification and directed his H.U.D. to where she had pointed, then allowed a small smile at the corner of his mouth. Dozens of dropships were inbound to their location. It was then he realized it. Anima was like Azubuike, and he should never underestimate her.

Hezbon had been waiting for High Priest Ampah to arrive before he would leave Anima there alone. Now that she was in the company of Ampah and his loyal guards, Hezbon gave them both a formal greeting and boarded the Keftiu. It immediately vanished from view when the pilot activated the stealth mechanism. They hovered on station a moment longer and observed a heavily armored platoon of the Queen mother's soldiers burst into the courtyard and form a defensive wall around their Kandake. Then the pilot accelerated into a climb and adjusted their heat shield's impact angle for departure. Higher and higher they went until they were off Naijia and finally going home.

Kandake Anima opened an encrypted channel directly to Hezbon. "Please take care of her."

"You have my word," He promised.

"You've done a good job here," Anima praised, "An honorable one. I can see why you're his most trusted commander. And you're almost as good as an Egba."

Kandake Anima did not continue her exchange with Hezbon. Instead, several shouts were heard, she gave several orders in quick succession and then the shooting began. From what he could tell, the Egbas had not been the ones who'd opened fire initially. However, that was a moot point, there was no way to know what happened. The firefight was the last thing Hezbon heard before the comm cut off.

Sabayt mDu Snu

Duro-Aina stood tall and imposing as she did her best not to project an overwhelming amount of aggression to her audience. She needed cooperation from the Temple Authority, not just fear. Because she wanted their cooperation, she needed a "delicate" delivery. In truth, she did very little to win them over. They pledged their support to her upon learning her identity as the only surviving Meroan from the ancient wars. Support from the Temple Authority came with minor repairs to her ship, supplies and up to date context on data she never would have gained through hacking their network.

Ausar had already hacked into the Naijian global network and accessed much of it. It was, in fact, his suggestion to gain some perspective on the data they recovered by approaching the Temple Authority. They learned much about the current state of affairs in this pocket of Meroan space. First, M.A.R.S. no longer existed. There was no easy way for Duro-Aina to come to terms with that fact, but the Meroan government had collapsed long ago. There were no more Meroan council of elders, no more worlds united under a common governing authority and even the level of technology had been drastically regressed. Every trace of M.A.R.S. was gone.

The era of Meroan worlds being loosely joined in common cause, by a republic that held their best interests, were long gone. Also absent was the unifying culture that held those worlds, those families, together. Regardless of what world or region they were from. In its place was some sort of indirect government founded on exploitation and oppression. Apparently, there had been a short period of subjugation, lasting a total of about fifteen hundred years, in which the Meroan people had been conquered and enslaved or worse.

Looking at the historical record proved one thing to Duro-Aina more than anything else; that their failures to defend KMT from the Assilians would have dire repercussions for the rest of Meroan space. She couldn't believe that their descendants had become enslaved and treated like cattle. Yet she knew of the strategic importance of the planet and why they had fortified it so heavily against invasion in the first place. KMT was the only stable entry point into Meroan space from Assilian space. Without a strong defensive position, their ancient enemy moved freely into the interior and subjugated several Meroan worlds. No longer in control of the major trade routes KMT maintained, or access to the massive food production

facilities on their world, M.A.R.S. entered an irreversible
state of decline. Failing to defend KMT wasn't just a fatal
error for M.A.R.S. but it would also signal the end of its
existence.

The final nail in the Meroan Republic's coffin was
Ntr itself. The instability in the star had grown to a state of
peak volatility. While the increased solar activity initially
appeared to disrupt the interior colonies, it did far greater
damage to the more distant colonies as Ra's energy
extended outward. Entire worlds were terraformed, over a
period of several hundred years, into lifeless celestial
objects. Many of the worlds Duro-Aina remembered were
now lifeless and barren reminders that the sun had joined in
the attack of their enemies. The subsequent mass migration
back toward the interior worlds put an even larger strain on
an already overworked central Meroan Authority. The same
authority that had already spent decades relocating those
Meroan citizens to the, widely perceived, safety of worlds
further away from the star.

The M.A.R.S. council had to choose between using
their overwhelming force for humanitarian missions or to
save KMT. In Duro-Aina's very jaded opinion, they
mistakenly choose the humanitarian route; leaving KMT
defenseless and abandoning that whole world to Assilian

invasion. Furthermore, the council had ordered Sovereign Roha to abandon Duro-Aina, and many more, in order to enact the council's final orders for KMT. In their defense, every strategic analysis supported their claim that they simply could not be everywhere at once. They were busy using the bulk of their military reserves to evacuate people away from the Kemetian region of space, and from the sun. These very mass migrations were also responsible for the lack of manpower in the region. Most of M.A.R.S. was busy trying to maintain the social order, attempting to relocate families and rebuild lives in the interior. Ships moving to and from the interior were also at increased risk while traversing the space affected by the instability of their star. Unpredictable and frequent solar flares were responsible for the destruction of many Meroan ships. As far as M.A.R.S. council was concerned, KMT could not be reinforced and they would have to fight the Assilians on their own.

That was the end for KMT. Low resources, low military manpower and political uncertainty created a situation in which the inevitable result was a successful invasion. Duro-Aina burned with rage. The Assilians had conquered her world while she was in stasis. Then they quickly lost it to a rival. Within a matter of generations,

KMT was submitting to another foreign controlled government. This happened many times throughout the historical record and many wars were fought over control of the planet. With its extensive culture, food reserves, high level of technology and deep understanding of the sciences, it would seem that whoever controlled KMT could subsequently build a lasting empire.

On and on this went, M.A.R.S. had lost its oldest and most productive colony; while several modern enemies began to appear and make their claims on the resources of Meroan space. Minerals, wealth, science, technology, even people were stripped from Meroan space and relocated to new "colony worlds." Duro-Aina spent weeks going over this information. She scoured the historical record and had Ausar communicate any questions she had, for clarity and context. Duro-Aina read right down to current times, in which she learned that some Meroan worlds were actually converted in colonies for their conquerors. The people of the Naijia were one such world, even though they had fought and recently won their freedom.

Duro-Aina didn't understand Naijian politics but what confused her the most was that there were actually people on the planet who were fighting on behalf of their colonizers. She had arrived on Naijia during the height of a civil war in which the separatists openly wanted to return to the rule of colonialism. They were actually fighting their own people for the benefit of their oppressors. These same oppressors who had annihilated their grandparents during the Invasion, and subsequent subjugation, of Naijia. Then they went on to "sell" their children into a new Oyinbo concept known as Chattel slavery. Duro-Aina couldn't understand how someone's mind could be so conquered, but she did know the Naijian ancestors must be "turning in their graves" because she sure was.

With the help of Ausar, Duro-Aina quickly learned that the situation on this world was hardly an isolated one. In fact, most of Meroan space had been subjugated to one degree or another. With the exception of a few rumored strongholds, every remaining Meroan world had been "colonized." Duro-Aina needed clarification on the modern translation of the word because it left her confused. How could someone colonize a world that had people already living on it? The only way this word, and the logic associated with it, could make sense was if the culture doing the colonizing held the existing inhabitants to a lesser value. They believed they were, somehow, superior. Even to those who had created every facet of the colonizer's civilization for them. They even had the gall to consider themselves superior to the Meroans, whom they had stolen every aspect of their culture, governments and spiritual systems from. Duro-Aina was at a loss for words. These "colonizers" were delusional.

However insane they appeared to be, these colonizers were efficient. While they had yet to create any sort of art, math, science or spiritual systems of their own, they were masters at culture theft. They also excelled at psychological warfare, which they almost always used to precede their invasions. While they were simultaneously raping the land of any cultural/mineral value, they also used their psychological prowess to conditionally reduce human beings to a status of semi-sentient slaves.

In more recent times, Duro-Aina learned that several worlds, fourteen to be exact, had risen up to overthrow their colonial masters and demand their freedom. Yet the strongest of their warriors were killed in the fighting, leaving less capable leaders to negotiate the peace. As a result of this, weaker individuals capitulated to the demands of their oppressors. Instead of fighting to achieve total victory, they simply settled for a semi-autonomous state in which they were allowed to govern themselves locally. Demands such as permanent military occupation, official language to be spoken and mandatory military service were agreed to. Still worse, each of these worlds were required to submit eighty six percent of their gross domestic product to their oppressors while being forced to stomach lectures about asking for "foreign aid." Duro-Aina had learned enough. Meroan worlds were starving while the parasitic Oyinbo were thriving at their expense. That was about to stop. The many tenets of subjugation were collectively known as "The Colonial Pacte," and it was as good a place for her to start undermining the Oyinbo as any.

Duro-Aina knew she was at a disadvantage on Naijia. They had preexisting relationships with "Sovereign" Azubuike and their leadership was already on his side. She would leave this world and build her power base on a new one, one that had not been in contact with Azubuike's people. To do that, she would need some basic supplies and up to date information on the surrounding worlds. Luckily for her, the Temple Authority had been more than willing to help her get up to speed on regional matters. She watched as her new "allies" scurried off to carry out her orders.

Ausar finished coordinating the details and then turned himself around to face Duro-Aina, "What will we do now?"

"We'll choose the right world for success and simply rebuild a new M.A.R.S." Duro-Aina replied.

"You've given up your pursuit of Sovereign Roha, then?" Ausar needed these answers in order to update their long term strategies.

"She has, no doubt, fled to her mountain," Duro-Aina speculated. "We will not challenge her there until we're ready."

"When will we leave Naijia for this new world?" Ausar pressed.

"As soon as our new supporters have finished their tasks," Duro-Aina began, "But first, we will need to meet and rendezvous with the enemy commander."

"The Oyinbo commander from the battle?" Ausar genuinely asked. "Why would you want to waste time on such a detour?"

"Because he has something I want." Duro-Aina's responses were intentionally cryptic. She often enjoyed toying with her A.S.E. because she knew not everyone could outsmart one for long. She liked to keep Ausar guessing.

"And what is that," Ausar pushed even further.

Duro-Aina decided to dispense with the games. She wasn't exactly sure what, or who, it was but she knew the intended purpose. She knew how successful it had been in battle. "What could he possibly have that I would want?" She asked, comically. "Leverage on Azubuike."

Sabayt mDu Xmt

The central hangar bay was quiet. Apprehension hung in the air as many dozens of people crowded the mountain's main point of entry by air. They were waiting for the return of those who had been deployed to Naijia on a diplomatic mission, and their Keftiu dropship was expected to arrive shortly. By this time, everyone had heard one variation or another about the events that had taken place on Naijia. However, most of it was pure rumor, mixed with large amounts of speculation. Even the Kandake did not have specific details of Azubuike's condition.

Kandake Nzinga stood in the front of the crowd, flanked by Councilor Melisizwe on her left. Nosizwe and Seba were on her right, along with some of Nosizwe's hand-picked medical personnel. The rest of the observers were roped off, in order to make room for the support personnel to assist the returning members of their most recent mission. Try as she may, there was no real way for the Kandake to keep Azubuike's return from being a spectacle. He was always celebrated when he came back from his missions and, even though she had made no announcement, word of his return had spread throughout the mountain. Azubuike was immensely popular, his sacrifices on behalf of the Meroan people were becoming legendary. Unfortunately, so too did the condition of his return spread throughout the mountain. Kandake Nzinga hadn't seen this many people in the central hangar bay since Azubuike departed it several years ago, in a final confrontation with Lieutenant Wynch.

The time had finally arrived and the large overhead bay doors began to open. When they did, they allowed some soft light to permeate the inside of the hangar bay. The clouds above were thick and did much to block out the sun. Although it shone through in some places, the morning sky was still able to provide a gray, gloomy over cast in order to foreshadow Sovereign Azubuike's arrival. After several moments that seemed to stretch on forever, a single Keftiu appeared over the hanger bay and began its descent toward the designated landing pad. It had been escorted by several Impundulu fighters, which continued their high speed pass over the top of the mountain.

The Keftiu dropship finally came to rest and lowered the boarding ramps so all passengers could disembark. Hezbon, visibly exhausted, was the first to emerge from the drop ship. He led the way down the ramp, carrying the stretcher that supported Azubuike. There were several other Medjay who were assisting him as he maneuvered the stretcher down the ramp. Alongside the stretcher was the young priestess, Oluwaseun, who looked to be slightly taken aback by the reception Azubuike was receiving. She had no idea what to expect, given her new political situation, but she did her best to make sure she stayed in close proximity to Azubuike. Her goal was to maintain a soothing, calming effect on him, using her connection to Ntr to maintain his current state of stability.

The people at the front of the crowd began to get their first images of Sovereign Azubuike as Hezbon and the Medjay drew closer toward the edge of the ramp. People were getting their first images of Azubuike and they were troubling. He had substantial injuries to include burns, deep lacerations and colorful bruising all over his torso. There was also a brightly colored wound on his chest that appeared to be swollen and pulsating with time. As more and more people saw Azubuike in this state, a low murmur began to take up with the crowd. People gasped as they got a clear view of his injuries. That buzz in the crowd, full of shock and disbelief, grew louder and louder. People could be heard claiming that Azubuike was dead and could not possibly have survived these injuries.

Nosizwe and her medical personnel did not wait for

the Medjay to clear the ramp. They rushed to their warriors and relieved them of the burden of carrying Azubuike any further. Several security teams were already in place inside the hangar bay and were keeping the crowd back, preventing them from attempting the very same thing. Others were helping the Medjay offload their weapons and heavier gear, in order to get the extra weight off of them. This was not a concern for Hezbon, who reluctantly handed over the stretcher to Nosizwe's people. He couldn't help but feel like a part of his mission was incomplete. While he did deliver Azubuike back to the mountain, he also recognized that he did not keep him safe from harm during their mission. The only thing he could think about now was whether or not Azubuike would live to accept his apology.

Seba, nor Nosizwe, could not be stopped from getting to Azubuike. They got to his side and did their initial assessments without interacting with anyone. Nosizwe didn't even see anyone else. Nosizwe lightly ran a hand over Azubuike's torso as she visually attempted to gauge the extent of his injuries. The nanites that were provided by her advanced medical suite were transferred to Azubuike from her finger tips. Readouts from their scans began to play across her H.U.D. and they painted a grim picture. Azubuike had suffered massive internal trauma.

The readouts became more and more detailed as the nanites moved throughout his body and internal organs. Some of the data they returned made no sense and Nosizwe became frustrated. There were symptoms of trauma around the odd wound on his chest that did not correlate with any other damage he'd sustained. He also had ugly, severe burns that appeared in various places on his body, anywhere his suit armor had failed to protect him. Seba was running his own diagnostic on Azubuike's protective armor, without meeting much success.

"We need to move him, sister," Seba began, "I'm not getting *any* response from his nanites. As it stands right now, and with the tools I have on hand, I can't even get this suit off him."

Nosizwe stopped what she was doing to give Seba her assessment as well. "I can't do much of anything for him while the dead nanites remain to encapsulate him. Will you be able to meet me in the surgical wing with that equipment or will he need to be transported to engineering first?"

Seba considered this. It would be much easier to use the heaviest equipment available to him because it was much safer. However it would not have been easily transported and there were medium sized, portable options available to him. "We will come to you. I'll need you there during the process. One of the default settings for these nanites is to fail in such a way that they are using trace amounts of energy to support the life of the wearer as best as they can. When we pull this suit off of him there's no telling what may happen. These nanites may be the only thing holding him together."

"Excuse me...." Priestess Oluwaseun interrupted. "I know what will happen."

Both Seba and Nosizwe stopped what they were doing and looked at Oluwaseun with a puzzled look on their face. They were confused because she had spoken to them in Mdu Ntr. "Dd.t Mdu Ntr?" Seba asked.

"Tiu," Oluwaseun replied. "Abeo, our messenger, taught me. He learned from Sovereign Azubuike."

"Welcome, sister." Nosizwe briefly studied Oluwaseun just long enough to gain a first impression of her. "What can you tell me about Azubuike's condition?"

"I was with Sovereign Azubuike when he did battle with a powerful enemy," Oluwaseun explained. "That is how he got these injuries."

One of the other medics deployed a small device that projected a tangible, holographic stretcher. The device itself hovered about a foot from the ground and could be controlled from any medic's H.U.D. Once Azubuike was transferred to the new stretcher, Seba gestured for everyone to follow him toward the med bay. That was when the crowd, at the sight of Azubuike being taken away without any answers, could not be contained. People were on the brink of pushing past the security detail en masse.

Hezbon had seen enough. The people's need for information did not outweigh Azubuike's need for medical attention. Furthermore, the crowd in the hangar bay was making it difficult for everyone there to do their jobs. Hezbon was about to order the hangar bay cleared of all non-essential personnel. He rose from where he had been sitting, on the edge of the ramp, and prepared to give orders to his Medjay.

That was when Councilor Melisizwe got involved. Before approaching Hezbon, he briefly exchanged a word with Kandake Nzinga. "I think you'd better address this crowd before things get out of hand."

For her part, Kandake Nzinga briefly surveyed the mood of the crowd and quickly reached the same conclusion. "I agree," she stated, as she moved to ascend the nearest platform.

They both departed to their tasks, in unison. Kandake Nzinga to calm the crowd, Councilor Melisizwe to calm Hezbon. When he reached Hezbon, Councilor Melisizwe had interrupted him, as Hezbon called the Medjay to attention. "A word, brother."

Hezbon and Councilor Melisizwe both activated the full protection of their nanites. Hezbon, once again, wore the full sized heavy armor that he was usually seen in. Councilor Melisizwe, however, wore a much sleeker and lighter design meant for diplomats and politicians. Hezbon opened a comm channel between himself and the Councilor. He then gave it the highest level of encryption available to him, so they could have a private conversation.

"This failure is not yours, Commander."

"I am the Supreme Commander of the Medjay," Hezbon began, "and this specific Medjay battalion is responsible for the personal safety of our Sovereign. If it is not my failure, then who does it belong to?"

Councilor Melisizwe thought about this. Not because he had been convinced by Hezbon's argument, but because he needed to figure out how to reach him. No soldier, no matter how well trained, could suffer a defeat such as this one gracefully. What Hezbon needed most was time to recover. Both physically and emotionally. The last place for him, and any of the Medjay from the battle, to be right now was in the hangar bay, dealing with a civilian issue.

Councilor Melisizwe would try another approach. "From the footage I saw, you went up against a powerful enemy. One who used our own technology, even more advanced versions of it, and mastered it. I believe you did the best job *anyone* could have, under these circumstances. What you need now is rest, and time to recover."

Hezbon went to object, intent on at least insisting that he be allowed to join them and watch over the Sovereign. However, Councilor Melisizwe was already motioning for the nearest security officer. "Call in as many more personnel as necessary and assist the Medjay in downgrading from operational status. Give them any aid they require and be sure that they are not to be disturbed for the next six hours."

The security officer acknowledged his commands and then quickly moved off to carry out his orders. Hezbon, seeing the wisdom in the councilor's words, was also ready to depart. "I will defer to your judgement, elder. Thank you for your guidance, Councilor Melisizwe."

"It has always been my pleasure to support the Medjay, our greatest defenders," Councilor Melisizwe replied, "We will need your perspective in the command center. We must find a way to defeat this new threat and you have first-hand experience standing against it. Report to the command center in six hours."

Hezbon gave the greeting of respect, due to a senior political figure, and then scaled down the protection of his nanites. He and the other Medjay departed the hangar bay, intent on a long overdue rest. With one crisis down, Councilor Melisizwe moved to the elevated platform to gauge the progress of Kandake Nzinga. Although he knew he had little cause to worry over her. Kandake Nzinga was a skilled politician but, more than that, she was an effective leader. He observed her, radiant as ever, as she began to address the crowd in her usual soothing tone. Her mere presence did much to ease the crowd.

Kandake Nzinga had only needed to call for calm, once, before the elevated noise level began to dissipate. She waited for it to quiet down to an acceptable level before she would begin. She thought about what she might say during the few seconds that took. Ultimately, she decided that the people needed something to hope for but they also needed something to work towards. They needed a goal. That was when it came to her.

"Many of you are concerned for Sovereign Azubuike's wellbeing," Kandake Nzinga began, "While this is to be expected, please understand that we're asking for calm during this trying time. We all want what is best for Sovereign Azubuike but we must also remember that his life is in jeopardy. At this time, I will share with you what I know but the medical team must be allowed to do their work, unobstructed."

Kandake Nzinga stole a glance in the direction of where she had last seen Nosizwe and Seba. They were using this chance to quietly exit the hangar bay in order to get Azubuike to the Medbay while they still could. So Kandake Nzinga continued her momentum, "Sovereign Azubuike is alive!" She shouted over the crowd and gained the full attention of everyone in attendance.

"Go ahead, back up." Kandake Nzinga was gesturing toward those still crowding the exit Seba and Nosizwe needed to use. She used the most reassuring tone she could because she sensed that she almost had the crowd completely at ease. The people began to clear the exit and allow Sovereign Azubuike to pass. Seba and Nosizwe made eye contact and gave an appreciative look before they exited the hangar bay.

"Here's what we know," Kandake Nzinga continued, "Sovereign Azubuike has been gravely injured by an unknown enemy. He is stable for now but his condition will require round-the-clock care. If he is to survive these injuries, his best chance lies in the hands of our ancestors. Please, return to your homes. Attend to your ancestral alters and beg them for help. He will need it."

Sabayt mDu Fdu

This particular corridor, usually noisy and crowded, was empty and quiet thanks to the Kandake's order to have it closed. In fact, several connecting corridors were sealed off in advance in an attempt to create a path from the hangar bay to the med bay. Now that they were out of the hangar bay, Seba and Nosizwe were able to continue their conversation with Priestess Oluwaseun in much lower tones. She gave more specific details about what happened in the moments after Azubuike was struck down. How she had tried to protect him from the chaos energy that was responsible for the worst of his injuries.

By the time they'd made it to the med bay, Seba and Nosizwe had been caught up on the most crucial information. They owed, whether they fully realized it or not, a debt of gratitude to Priestess Oluwaseun for everything she'd risked to save Azubuike. Seba was in the middle of trying to verbalize that sentiment when they burst into the main operating room of the med bay. Several medics took up stations in the observation room or just outside the operating room, itself. The operating room was already packed with engineers who were setting up strange equipment that Nosizwe didn't recognize.

When Seba, Priestess Oluwaseun and the medical team finished situating Azubuike, Seba started organizing the equipment. He also gave very specific instructions to each engineer regarding their roles in the operating room and their responsibilities. Once he was satisfied that everyone knew their job, and could complete their assigned tasks, he turned to his right to give Nosizwe one last word of encouragement. However, Nosizwe wasn't there, she wasn't even in the operating room. Seba scanned the room looking for her until he finally found her on the other side of the observation room's glass window, trying her best to stay out of the way of the engineers.

Seba activated his comm without hesitating, "Time is short sister and I'm going to need you in here in case we run into any *unexpected challenges.*"

Nosizwe entered the operating room and took up the only empty space left, right next to Seba. On the other side of Seba was Priestess Oluwaseun, wearing a look of determination as she focused on her task. Seba looked around the room, one final time, verifying everyone knew their role. One engineer was responsible for monitoring the diagnostic machine, itself. The other four were responsible for monitoring the scanning paddles that were placed in a position above each of Azubuike's limbs. Nosizwe was present in case anything went wrong and Azubuike needed immediate medical attention. Finally, it was Priestess Oluwaseun's turn.

"….and Priestess?" Seba asked.

"Most of the chaos energy has abated by this time," She explained, "The remaining levels should be low enough, that I can help dissipate the rest without causing any further harm."

Satisfied with the answer, Seba gave the instruction to begin. When the diagnostic machine was activated, a low hum permeated the room. A moment later, a transparent green hue began to form around Azubuike in the shape of an oval. It was some kind of energy field being created by the diagnostic machine. A new diagnostic interface appeared in Seba's H.U.D. and he projected it into the center of the room for all to see. At first, the semi-transparent screen projected nothing but blank space and a large, red horizontal line spanning the center of it.

Seba decided to answer everyone's unspoken question, "It means the nanites are not broadcasting a signal of any kind. I'm not getting anything from them."

"How do we proceed from here?" Nosizwe asked.

"The Nanites' ability to auto repair or recreate themselves has been broken," Seba replied. "We'll need external power and fresh nanites to retrieve them."

Seba turned to the engineer stationed at the diagnostic machine, "Give me ten percent. Delicately."

When nothing happened, Seba requested a power increase to twenty percent and was rewarded with a faint signal emanating from what remained of Azubuike's nanites. He did not want to give the nanites too much more power, which could cause them to suddenly enter a reboot sequence. If that were to happen, it could have disastrous consequences for Azubuike. The diagnostic screen came to life when the inactive red line reorganized itself into a set of maintenance symbols that few could recognize. It was a code, and Seba reorganized the symbols until they were in the order required to grant him access.

The entire screen changed to one that was flooded with diagnostic information. Charts, graphs and vital statistics began to scroll down the screen. Priestess Oluwaseun stood in amazement at the level of technology these Meroans had access to. It was as if they had certain capabilities that were beyond her wildest dreams. She continued to watch, in silence, as they worked.

Nosizwe broke the silence. "That's way too much information."

"I agree," Seba admitted. "I can get you a full back

up copy once we've secured everything."

"What about now," Nosizwe pressed. "Can we make copies of his most grievous injuries? Of what you're looking at now?"

Seba thought about this. He shouldn't give Nosizwe access to the machine code that made the nanites run. Their most basic sub routines could be tampered with if this information ever came into the wrong hands. He imagined Meroans coming under attack from weapons that were specifically designed to terminate nanites. The thought of an anti-nanite weapon was enough to give Seba pause.

"Get me one of your secure hard drives and I'll leave an engineer behind to filter relevant medical information to your team." Seba would compromise only enough to save Azubuike's life, no more than that.

Nosizwe gave that order to one of her medics in the observation room. Seba moved on to his next task while they waited for the hard drive but he did remind Nosizwe that they had precious few minutes for this data transfer.

"That's fine," Nosizwe agreed. "Just give me some place to start."

"If time is limited," Priestess Oluwaseun cut in, "Then you must begin with his chakras. They have suffered the most damage."

Seba and Nosizwe both glanced at Azubuike's injuries and shared a look of doubt, but ultimately agreed. Nosizwe's hard drive arrived at the same time as the Kandake and Councilor Melisizwe. In fact, councilor Melisizwe was carrying it in. Councilor Melisizwe took one look at the diagnostic screen once he'd entered the room.

"What do we know so far?" Councilor Melisizwe asked.

"Nothing yet, Elder," was Seba's response. "We've only just begun our work."

The Kandake knew, no matter how well he controlled his emotions for the benefit of the others, that Councilor Melisizwe was hurting. Sovereign Azubuike was his blood relative, the son of his eldest daughter. They had been through a great deal together, to include their interrogation at the hands of Lt. Wynch. Now, Azubuike's life was in the hands of his younger brother.

Kandake Nzinga put a hand on Councilor Melisizwe's shoulder so she could guide him out of the operating room. "Come, leave him to concentrate."

It was apparent that the pressure was beginning to build within Seba but Nosizwe needed him to focus. She watched as the Kandake escorted Councilor Melisizwe out of the operating room. Then she decided to help Seba get back on track. "What's next, brother?"

Seba went back to scanning Azubuike's chakras, without a word, but his facial expression had changed to one of renewed determination. What happened next caused a collective gasp to be heard around the operating room. There were even expressions of concern evident inside the observation room. To his surprise, when he scanned Azubuike's heart chakra, Seba discovered something that he was not ready to see. Substantial damage had been inflicted on it. Whereas it should appear green, vibrant and full of life, the energy surrounding the heart chakra was white, empty and nearly lifeless. Physically, it looked as if it was dying. A scan of his third eye, however, appeared to show the opposite. While his Pineal gland did show signs of high work load and over stress, it wasn't physically injured in any way. Aside from the swelling and bruising consistent with other signs of extreme or prolonged use.

Seba moved on to Azubuike's crown chakra, but not before he consulted the vital statistics screen of the diagnostic program. Azubuike's vitals were starting to deteriorate. Seba was out of time.

"This will have to be the last scan, sister," Seba cautioned, "We have to move on."

Nosizwe agreed and directed Seba to the areas of Azubuike's data that she needed to see most. Having seen the state of his Pineal gland, Nosizwe was quickly developing a theory that she needed to quantify. Seba was able to project a three dimensional holographic representation of Azubuike's mind scan into the middle of the room. The mind scan was projecting two separate sets of overlapping results. To everyone else's surprise, Nosizwe and Seba were actually not surprised. They had seen this information before, about a dozen times, whenever they ran scans on Azubuike. It was assumed, that the extra mind scan results were coming from Sovereign Roha. Neither scan results were too promising but one was clearly doing much better than the other. Nosizwe projected the most recent mind scans she had, for comparison. From what she could tell, Sovereign Roha's mind scan results were just barely detectable but active. While Azubuike's results were completely inactive and undetectable.

An alarm sounded and drew everyone's attention to Seba. "That's it, we're out of time."

The engineers stopped what they were doing and prepared themselves for the next part of their tasks. They did this by exchanging tools and positions with each other. "Please, Seba," Nosizwe protested. "I need just another moment with the crown chakra scans."

Seba did nothing more than show Nosizwe Azubuike's current vitals. That was pretty effective at sharing his perspective with her. "The scans you have will have to be sufficient. Azubuike is in trouble. I still have to save both him and Oya. I'm running out of time to do both."

Seba ordered three of the engineers to reprogram the nanites from their own diagnostic interfaces. Their current configuration forced the nanites to fail in such a way that they would carry out their last function. Seba could now see what that last function was and override it. The nanites were trying to form a protective film around the exposed parts of Azubuike's body. They were also holding back a lot of internal bleeding and they were even preventing the failure of several of Azubuike's organs. While the nanites were being reprogrammed, Seba and one other engineer went about the business of removing Oya. In order for the transfer to take place, they would have to salvage a minimum number of the nanites that most recently held her "consciousness."

Seba injected fresh nanites into an entry port on Azubuike's suit that was still intact. Their task was to recover any nanites that were too damaged to function on their own. The functional, reprogrammed nanites were already returning to an exit port for collection and, hopefully, the restoration of Oya. After several minutes, all internal nanites were in collection capsules in the hands of Seba's engineers. All of which, were already departing the med bay for engineering. The only remaining task was to strip the external nanites from Azubuike's body, the very ones that had previously functioned to provide him with external armor. These nanites were completely disabled and most would never function again. They did this by waving a transmitter over his body that emitted a frequency designed to disrupt the magnetic bonds between the nanites. At this point, they couldn't hold themselves together and could simply be rubbed right off Azubuike's body.

With his task completed, Seba took a step back and allowed Nosizwe to take charge. Her role to play, in saving Azubuike's life, was just beginning. Without the limited protection of his remaining nanites, no matter how damaged they were, Azubuike began to take a turn for the worst. His vitals began to crash and the grotesque wound on his chest glowed, faintly, with chaos energy. His entire body started convulsing violently and medics rushed in to restrain his flailing limbs. Priestess Oluwaseun moved forward and whispered a prayer to Ntr, the very prayer she had said aloud on the battlefield. When she finished, she put her hands on Azubuike's torso and started pulling the chaos energy from his heart chakra. Everyone could see it manifesting into a small, hand sized ball of swirling energy. That energy rose higher and higher until it held the highest elevation in the room. It swirled at slower speeds until it eventually spun itself out and dissipated, due to the fact that no one was left to feed into it.

The entire room was quiet. Even Azubuike had calmed down enough, until the convulsions stopped. The silence was only broken when Priestess Oluwaseun grew unsteady and stumbled onto a nearby console for support. She was immediately escorted to a nearby observation room for medical attention. Seba left, at the same time, to join his counterparts in the engineering department. He had once been where Azubuike was now. He knew what kind of recovery Azubuike had to look forward to. He also knew that if anyone could save Azubuike, it was Nosizwe. Above all else though, Seba knew that if Azubuike ever recovered from this, he would wake up wanting to fight. And any chance at fighting this new enemy would be discovered in the tactical data recorder from Azubuike's suit. There hadn't been enough time to deconstruct it in the operating room but, now that Seba had it in his possession, he could thoroughly analyze it over the next few hours.

Nosizwe and the remaining medical staff wasted no time attending to Azubuike's medical needs. Now that the engineers had done their part and the Priestess had done hers, it was now time for Nosizwe to attend to Azubuike's physical injuries. Azubuike was, more or less, stabilizing after having been freed of the Isfet energy. Yet that was not the extent of the danger he was in. He would need emergency laser surgery, fresh courses of nanites and delicate treatment of his wounds. The medical staff had their hands full and they worked tirelessly over the next several hours to stabilize Azubuike.

Sabayt mDu Diu

Four hours have passed since Seba last saw Azubuike in the med bay. He and his engineers spent the time trying to reconstruct the data from Azubuike's damaged suit. It was a daunting task due to the fact that the nanites had suffered far more damage than was first apparent. The level of destruction delivered to them was making Seba's task even more difficult than it normally would have been. He surmised, at this point, that the source of his trouble was the chaos energy. That energy was the only unknown variable, in this entire equation, which could possibly explain the unnatural way the nanites were responding. Had they been corrupted by the Isfet energy? Was that even possible?

Seba had one sure fire way to test his theory. He decided to introduce fresh nanites into an environment where they would have to interact with some of the damaged nanites from Azubuike's suit. He gave them no new commands and allowed each set of nanites to follow their default sub routines. Seba was sure the isolation chamber could contain any results from this experiment, just as it always had in the past. He took a small number of the nanites and placed them in an observation disk. Seba intended to use a lightly shielded, high powered laser to directly study the nanites during his test.

"Is that wise?" Seba looked to his left to discover one of his assistants, wearing a look of concern on her face.

"We have far more than enough nanites left to salvage his data," Seba reassured her, "There is no risk of losing it."

"That's not exactly what I meant." Seba's assistant moved to the control console and boosted the shielding around the nanites to its maximum protection.

Seba thanked his assistant and then the two of them stood by as he initiated the sequence. All light sources inside the isolation chamber went dark. At the same time, a high powered laser in the center of the room activated. It was installed on the ceiling and pointed downward in order to effect maximum efficiency of the laser's beam. The laser's job was to bend light in such ways that the hue-man eye cannot. In this way, Seba would surely be able to see the nanites on their molecular level and he hoped that a clue would present itself. One that had gone missed during their brief scans in the med bay.

The compromised nanites that were already in the observation disk were fairly spread out and mostly dormant. That is, until the new nanites were introduced.

Suddenly, the damaged nanites began to vibrate at abnormal speeds and condense amongst themselves. When the new nanites attempted to follow their default commands, the damaged nanites they encountered started to attack them. Any new nanites that are introduced into an environment where nanites have previously existed, are immediately supposed to do two things. First, they are supposed to spread out and integrate with any existing nanites. Second, they are supposed to submit to scans by those nanites while they perform their own scans. The damaged nanites not only did not submit to these scans but any attempt at performing a scan was met with hostility.

What happened next was nothing short of disturbing. The damaged nanites coalesced into an organized unit and attacked the fresh nanites en masse. Seba and his assistant watched as the new nanites were destroyed, even though they far outnumbered the compromised nanites.

Both Seba and his assistant sat back in silence when it was over. However, his assistant was the first to break that silence. "Nanite wars....?

Seba didn't even want to consider it, therefore, he was quick to dismiss the thought. "I don't know what we saw, more study is clearly needed."

An encrypted comm channel opened for Seba just as he was about to deactivate the remaining nanites. The conversation was already underway and included Councilor Melisizwe, as well as Kandake Nzinga.

It was the Kandake who spoke first, "Greetings young Seba. How is your progress?"

Seba had been expecting this call for some time. During the last several hours, Seba and his team had been working tirelessly. He hoped to have some tangible results before he got this call but, unfortunately, that was not the case. He would have to tell Kandake Nzinga what he had learned so far. "We have encountered some significant setbacks, Kandake. The nanites are unstable and appear to be exhibiting some *erratic* behavior."

"Erratic behavior?" Kandake Nzinga wanted clarification on this.

"I don't yet feel comfortable reporting on my initial findings, Queen Mother," Seba admitted. "Some of this data is troubling."

Kandake Nzinga was intrigued. Yet, this was not the only intention of their call. Seba quickly learned this when Councilor Melisizwe spoke up. "Seba, bring the relevant data to the command center in two hours. We have an urgent debriefing and you must be in attendance."

Before Seba could respond, an alarm sounded behind him. The laser's control console was producing a low pitched, repetitive alarm at high levels. As if it was demanding attention. Seba turned to determine the source of the disturbance and saw two of his assistants rushing to the laser, and to the chaos nanites. Kandake Nzinga opened a third comm channel and linked it to the cameras in the isolation chamber. She and Councilor Melisizwe now had a clear view of what was happening inside the isolation chamber. As they watched Seba read through the new data being provided by the laser's console, it became evident that Seba saw cause for concern.

Seba witnessed a series of minor explosions, followed by critical systems failure. First, the observation disk. Then, the laser itself. Finally, the observation room's command console exploded in a shower of sparks. Events were moving far too quickly. Seba could only make several educated guesses about what was happening. However, one thing was abundantly clear. These nanites were far too dangerous to study under these conditions. The best guess he had, was that these nanites had somehow attached themselves to the photons emitted by the laser and escaped. Or, the chaos energy interacted with the extreme amounts of electromagnetic energy produced by the laser; which could have allowed them to escape.

A cloud of gray fog burst into existence near the command console, injuring the two assistants. Various commands were entered into the command console, which was rebuilding itself right in front of their very eyes. Seba ran from the room and pushed his way into the next chamber, the engineering department's main control room. By this point a buzz of activity had taken up with all the engineers who were present. The alarm had changed to one of high tone and low pitch. It was more frequent and more persistent. All lights in the engineering department had switched to low light levels and any non-essential equipment was automatically powered down.

"What is happening down there, Seba?" Kandake Nzinga, who had been cautiously trying to allow Seba the time he needed to rectify the situation, could not be silent any longer.

"There isn't time, Kandake," Seba breathed heavily, from exhaustion and increased adrenaline, through his words. "Engineering has sealed itself off, entering an automatic quarantine."

"Assessment?" Kandake Nzinga asked.

"At this time, I recommend you keep everyone away from engineering. Nosizwe is not to use *any* nanites on Azubuike, under any circumstances. In fact, he should be quarantined as well, from any and all nanites."

It had just occurred to Seba that if the nanites could make use of light waves to affect their escape, then there was absolutely no reason they couldn't do the very same with radio waves. Seba now knew he had to cut all communication both to and from the engineering department. He hoped he wasn't already too late.

"In order to prevent these nanites from breaching quarantine," Seba began, "We have to effect a communications lock out on engineering."

Seba's comm channel and the feed from the interior isolation chamber's cameras were discontinued. When Kandake Nzinga tried to reestablish a connection, all she saw was an automated response. Big bold letters informed her that engineering was under quarantine and every effort to avoid it should be made.

Kandake Nzinga turned to her own administrators in the mountain's command center, in order to give her own commands. Those nearest her had heard what was happening and were already awaiting her orders. "Expand the quarantine to two levels above and below engineering. Deploy the Quick Reaction Force to maintain the quarantine. No Medjay, QRF members, or anyone else in nanite skin for that matter, is to break this quarantine. Post the Medjay outside the quarantine and give them instructions to only grant entry to personnel who are both free of nanites and also have my express permission to enter. I want someone down there to reestablish communication with engineering as soon as possible. I don't care if they have to send smoke signals or use ancient war drums to communicate.

Sabayt mDu Sisu

The entire research and development section of engineering was a disaster. It would be some time before the area could be used for any meaningful purpose again. The entire area had been placed under a no-contact protocol, however those maintaining the quarantine were close enough to personally hear some of what was going on inside. Explosions, gunfire and multiple fatalities were observed. No one had been in contact with Seba, or anyone else from engineering, in quite some time. Yet the screams of those engaged in the fighting were unmistakable.

The Kandake had radioed down several times, in order to give new orders or to get status updates. Apparently, Hezbon and the Medjay were recalled to duty an hour early in order to assist in maintaining the quarantine. They were arriving, Hezbon in the lead, at the nearest checkpoint to the main entrance of engineering. Without a word, or any visual cues, they immediately broke up into various tasks which included enhancing the existing defensive positions. They brought in heavy weapons, explosives, several turret mounts, and even a few fixed barricades. The Medjay seemed to have gone beyond the means necessary to maintain a quarantine and it appeared that they were staging for a front line assault instead. Maybe they were a little twitchy after their most recent mission.

Seba knew he didn't have long and that it was only a matter of time before the chaos nanites escaped. They were quicker and far superior to his own abilities, to prevent their departure. The only thing Seba could do was delay them, and hope someone on the other side of the main entrance was working on a plan to take them offline permanently. He didn't have the weapons necessary to fight them, nor did he have the luxury of being able to fully concentrate on the problem himself.

After the initial incident with the laser, the defensive personnel usually stationed in main engineering rushed into R&D to secure the area. Seba watched, from the main control console, as many of them were cut down by the rogue nanites. Seba tried hard to ignore the distractions in his peripheral vision. He needed to focus on stopping the nanites while he still had time. He rapidly accessed the basic security protocols via his H.U.D., on an encrypted channel, and sent out a burst transmission in order to not draw the attention of the nanites. The burst transmission included changes to the base code that mandated increased shielding around main engineering, as well as maximum encryption on any entrances both to and from engineering.

Observers who were just outside the quarantine observed the activation of the shield and knew it couldn't mean good news. The Medjay went about their tasks with increased sense of purpose while Hezbon made his call to the mountain's control center, correctly assuming that Kandake Nzinga would want this update. Meanwhile, even more explosions were heard from within, and they were growing with intensity.

As soon as Seba had encrypted his handiwork, he observed the shield manifest itself into existence and the indication lighting on every door in sight shift color. The colors shifted to indicate their status. Green meant full access, red meant restricted and the new color of black meant totally secure. The nanites could not escape. Then Seba physically disabled all access to the system by destroying the command console. Now the only way for the nanites to escape was to directly access his suit.

By this time the nanites had formed a loose silhouette which resembled the stature and size of Duro-Aina. It moved and walked just like she did and, currently, it was staring menacingly at the main entrance. It *knew* what Seba had done, or did it? Seba watched, as it repeatedly hit the door until it flew off its hinges. The door, six inches of solid steel, flew into the shield and then rebounded back into main engineering. The door flew through the air, right through the nanites and destroyed the rear wall of their lab. The nanites could simply make themselves less dense so that any object could pass right through. However, the solid wall could not and suffered considerable damage.

Upon seeing what they thought was Duro-Aina, the Medjay all reacted with weapon's fire. They fired in unison, heavy weapons and all, directly at the chaos nanites in the doorway. Every weapon, even the Shango heavy weapon system, was ineffective against the shield. It bounced back and impacted several security personnel who were stationed just outside main engineering. The nanites smiled a crooked smile and then turned directly to where the control console had been, in full recognition of what needed to be done.

However, the nanites didn't see Seba standing there when they turned to focus on the control console. He had quickly ducked down and hid himself, as small as he could, inside the nearest storage space he could find. As soon as he saw the nanites turning his way, Seba knew he had to hide both himself and his suit. Seba was now their only key to escape. When the nanites arrived at the main control console, they visually inspected it to gauge the extent of its damage. Then they went about the, relatively quick, process of rebuilding the console. Seba watched, from the safety of a crack in the door to his hiding place, as they restored the console using materials from nearby machinery. When the console had been restored, the first thing it did was enter a diagnostic routine. That meant a full system reboot and an automatic increase in security protocols. Seba was not surprised when the door to main engineering rebuilt itself out of fresh nanites.

The chaos nanites, however, were not so pleased with that result. Nor were they finished with their work as they attempted to override the security in the main console. Realizing that it was a futile effort, the nanites looked around for anyone in R&D that might still be alive. It didn't see Seba, but it did see the next best thing. The nanites grabbed the wounded engineer who had been assisting Seba during the initial scans. She was far from dead but gravely injured and unconscious. The nanites made the decision to repair her damaged body, then force her to rescind the security protocols.

When she was awake, Seba watched as her relief turned to surprise, then shock as she realized what the nanites had done. Then they grabbed her, aggressively, and forced her to the console. It pointed a very angry finger at the main entrance. Then it pointed to her, then it pointed to the main control console. When it was understood what the nanites wanted, they applied a small amount of electrical charge to their victim in order to make their point known.

The engineer turned around defiantly. She had no way of knowing how to bypass Seba and lift the lockdown. Even if she did she would never willingly betray the mountain in such a way. She stood strong in her comfort zone and refused to access the control console. The nanites charged up a large ball of potential electrical energy until it crackled and popped toward the engineer in a threatening manner. Still, the engineer did not move, and would have been the subject of a very devastating electrical burn had Seba not burst out of his hiding place.

Seba pointed his weapon directly at the chaos nanites. He knew any attack he could make would be ineffective but he still had to buy for time. For what, he wasn't sure yet. They still had no real plan but, maybe if they had Oya they'd have a chance. That was as good a plan as any. Seba decided to distract the nanites while he tried to restore the A.S.E.

"Get Oya back online," Seba whispered.

Then he took several shots at the chaos nanites, which had absolutely no effect. The nanites began to retaliate but hesitated. Seba saw the recognition play across the *face* of the nanites as they scanned him. Instead of attacking him, the nanites decided on a less lethal, yet quite debilitating attack. Seba was left unconscious and laying on the floor nearby the command console. The nanites then decided to go to the laser. After several moments of restoration, they had rebuilt the laser and even made it more efficient. One activation of the laser melted what remained of the door's frame with ease. A few dozen moments of directed energy forced the shield wall to attenuate, just enough, to allow the escape of the nanites.

Hezbon had seen enough. He opened a channel directly to the Kandake. "Status?" She asked.

"Breach, Kandake," Hezbon informed her. "Breach is imminent."

"Plan of attack?" The Kandake pressed.

Hezbon wasted no time giving his opinion on the matter. "Either we go in now or it comes out in the next several minutes. I'd prefer to catch it off guard, not the other way around."

"You have a go," Kandake Nzinga confirmed. "Primary directive is to pull Seba out of there. He has intel valuable to these nanites and how to fight them. You are also ordered to destroy these nanites by any reasonable means necessary. As always, secondary objectives include the rescue of all non-combatants or any injured security personnel. You have your orders Commander."

Kandake Nzinga switched off the comm in order to allow Hezbon to carry out her orders, and he did not delay. Now that the shield was weakened at a specific focal point, Hezbon directed all of the Medjay's firepower to that point. The attenuation in the shield wall began to grow and a sizable hole was now evident. That was their way in.

Hezbon turned to his Medjay and gave his final orders. "The Sovereign's brother is in there," He began, "We're going in there to pull him out. Along with any other survivors. Kill anything that doesn't speak Meroan. Finally, watch your fire. Remember, we don't know what we're walking into here. Visibility is going to be low and we've got a lot of friendlies in there."

The heavy weapon specialist wielding the Shango platform, directed it into the hole of the shield and directly at the doorway to main engineering. He fired one shot and a throw stone burst out of the weapon to lodge itself directly onto the shield's surface. A moment later, a synthetic bolt of lightning leapt from the Shango toward the shield. It was following the most direct path it could, in order to reconnect to the opposing charge contained in the throw stone. Due to the requirement of the throw stone, it was believed by many to be too short range of a weapon. However, a dissenting opinion was always offered by anyone who had been in close proximity to it as it fired. If, that is, they survived to tell the tale. The Shango weapon built up an electrical charge that was stored inside the weapon itself. The positive charges remain inside the weapon while the negative charges were contained within the throw stone. When the throw stone is fired at its target, the positively charged particles discharge from the Shango weapon in an attempt to rejoin with, and neutralize, their negative counterparts.

The result of firing a Shango weapon was a genuine, synthetic, hue-man made lightning bolt. The effect of which, formed a horizontal spiral of flames that traveled the length of the lightning bolt, igniting the air around it. The accompanying shockwave was strong enough to incapacitate any unarmored units lucky enough to avoid being ignited by the flames it produced. Synthetic lightning leapt out from the Shango and impacted the door, obliterating it. The handheld version of this weapon was usually enough to hit anything, of comparable size, once and destroy it. Yet when it hit the nanites, it failed to destroy them completely. A loud shriek could be heard emanating from the nanites upon impact, they contorted, stumbled backward and then dodged away from the entrance.

Both significant electrical and fire damage had been done to the door, entryway and interior of the receiving room. The H.U.D. on Hezbon's faceplate flickered with static as a result of the overwhelming charge that hung in the air. Hezbon signaled for the Shango to be warmed up again and every unarmored base defender ran for cover. They were fortunate that the weapons platform was only able to produce about a third of the destructive force of a real lightning bolt. And so the accompanying heat was reduced to about a third of what was to be expected from a real lightning bolt as well. The Shango only produced about six thousand degrees of heat while the real thing had temperatures upwards of about twenty thousand degrees Celsius.

When the weapon was ready again, the Medjay rushed the entrance without hesitation. But they did not find their enemy waiting inside. Instead, they found a level of destruction that they weren't expecting. The electrical damage had done the most harm to the rogue nanites. Even though they were shielded from electrical interference, the Shango was able to easily overcome those defenses. However, the nanites were completely protected from the heat and destructive power of the Shango, which washed over the entirety of the small entryway. The entire room, and adjoining observation lab, were destroyed. Of the researchers stationed here, there were only two survivors.

Hezbon pulled Seba from the rubble that had once been the storage space he'd used for cover. Though shaken and wearing badly damaged armor, he appeared to be okay. His assistant, however, was a little worse off. Having been closer to the door when the Shango was fired, she had taken a much more direct amount of damage than Seba had. One of the Medjay medics immediately moved to assess her condition. She was unresponsive, but alive, and her vitals were spiking. Hezbon glanced at the Medic just long enough to be sure that he was pulling her out.

Then Hezbon turned his attention back to Seba, helping him up to his feet by the arm. "Status?"

"It went that way," Seba managed to say, pointing toward the main control room.

"What is it?" Hezbon asked.

"Damaged nanites," Seba breathed, "Recovered from Sovereign Azubuike."

"Are there any other survivors?" Hezbon pressed Seba for one last question, the possibility of other survivors would both change the nature of his strategies and limit the amount of force he could bring to the engagement.

Seba began to shake off his disorientation, and had regained enough of his senses to see where the conversation was going. "You must not destroy it Commander. We must recover enough of these nanites to reconstitute Oya, or she will be lost to us forever."

"Well they don't pay us to do the easy jobs do they," Hezbon sighed, "Do you have the means to get them under control?"

"From here?" Seba asked incredulously, "Not even remotely. If you can get me to an intact console with command access, I may have a plan to disable them."

"The Main control room then?" Hezbon asked.

"That's the first place it went." Seba corrected. "I suspect it was trying to override the lockdown. We'll have to try the auxiliary control room. I can gain command access from there but, I warn you, the rogue nanites are probably thinking the same thing."

"And they have a head start," Hezbon agreed. "If they couldn't get through us then the next logical option would be to attempt to override the lockdown. They'll be free to go around us. We must pursue them."

"They must not be allowed to escape, their capture must become the highest priority." Seba sensed that he and Hezbon were now of the same mind.

Convinced of what his next course of action should be, Hezbon posted a squad at the entrance they had just secured. "Call for reinforcements, make sure they have another Shango weapons system. If anything other than us comes back this way, destroy it. Under no circumstances do you allow it to get by you."

Having given his final orders, Hezbon decided the time had come. The Medjay moved, as one unit, and advanced deeper into the engineering complex. What they found astonished them. There was no need for guess work. They were able to follow a clear path of destruction which clearly indicated which way their adversary had gone. Hezbon subtly looked to Seba for an assessment.

"I can't be sure," Seba admitted, "but it could be arcing residual kinetic energy due to battle damage and stress. Judging by the evident increase in damage, the farther we go in, I would say the nanites are becoming more and more unstable. Time is of the essence, Commander, and you must be sure to prevent their total destruction."

Hezbon understood his responsibility. Although these requirements were necessary, they were exposing his Medjay to increased risk. Yet Hezbon knew his duty. The Kandake had given him specific orders to subdue any threat and to rescue as many as he could. In order to rectify this with his own conscience, Hezbon put himself on point, exposing himself to the most risk. Further inward they pushed. As they went, they could see the dead and, eventually, hear the screams of the dying as they met their end somewhere in the distance. There was no mistaking that scream, the blood curdling sound of one who was about to transition against their will.

Hezbon accessed his active sonar suite and hoped the sound had been loud enough for detection. It was.

"Seba?" Hezbon called. "Distance – 80 meters. Direction – North by northwest?"

"Auxiliary control," Seba confirmed. "We must hurry."

With a clear indication of distance and direction, the Medjay increased their speed and wasted no further time to reach their target. Upon entering Aux control, they immediately identified the chaos nanites and their intentions. The nanites were in a quasi-solid configuration, hovering over the aux control console. They resembled a gas, even though the nanites themselves were solid matter, and they were in motion. They moved in a flowing manner, in and amongst themselves, in and out of the control console. The Medjay watched, for a few seconds, as the gaseous cloud of rogue nanites continued to swirl and rotate around itself. It was completely ignoring them. Then they saw it, no *him*, a technician assigned to the aux console was bent over the station in pain. It was evident to all what the aim of the rogue nanites were. They were trying to force the technician to override the lockdown, while simultaneously hacking into the system themselves.

The Medjay could actually see the rogue nanites interacting with the nanites which made up the suit protecting the technician. Whatever they were doing to him was causing the man a great amount of pain. Entire sections of his suit were degrading, and then attempting to repair itself, right before their very eyes.

As soon as the Medjay crossed the threshold separating themselves from the rogue nanites, the nanites leapt into action. The mass of nanites attempting to access the aux console burst into a frenzy of activity. The whole cloud increased their movement speed. Their increased speed generated an excess amount of heat, which caused the air around it to shimmer. Electric sparks began to generate within the cloud's mass. The nanites who had been tormenting the technician abandoned their task of torturing him into compliance, leaving the man to collapse in a heap. Instead, they dispersed and moved themselves among the several dead Meroans who had already been given their opportunity to comply. The assumption was that every one of the people tasked with maintaining this room had politely refused the chaos nanites, and paid for it with their lives.

When the nanites interacted with the deceased Meroans, the dead began to rise. Of course the nanites were not actually bringing the dead back to life, they were simply reanimating dead tissue as a distraction. The true goal, was to delay the Medjay while the core mass of nanites intensified their efforts to override the lockdown. That said, their dead allies began to wriggle and writhe as the nanites reintegrated themselves into what was left of their suits. Several dead Meroans awkwardly, and unsteadily rose to their feet. Then they began to move toward the Medjay.

Hezbon and his Medjay all took condition one stances. Their training kicked in immediately, as usual, on instinct. They shouldered their weapons, identified their targets, anticipated the recoil, leaned into it and prepared to fire. Yet, with fingers on their triggers, no one fired. Even as the new threat advanced toward them.

"Commander…?" One nervous Medjay asked the question no one else would, even though they were all thinking it. Even though he didn't finish his sentence aloud, all knew the question. All awaited the answer.

"Can they be saved, Seba…?" Commander Hezbon asked.

"I…." Seba hesitated. There was no way he could know. He would need a working research lab, Nosizwe and plenty of time under controlled conditions to answer that question. "I don't know."

"Fire!" Hezbon commanded.

Hezbon did not even wait to hear his order acknowledged. He understood the emotions of those under his command. Even though most believed the Medjay to be completely emotionless. So he fired first. He would bear the responsibility. He would shoulder the shame of opening fire on his own brothers and sisters. The order was his and so too would be the brunt of the repercussions. Hezbon cut down one of their fallen compatriots, which agitated the rest. The reanimated Meroans rushed the Medjay, which responded by opening fire en masse. However, they did not decide to fire in unison and without hesitation. This was evident by the fact that many of them did not open fire immediately.

Realizing that time would not allow for the completion of an override, the core group of chaos nanites changed tactics. They would make another attempt to force their way through the main entrance, collecting the bodies of Meroans as they went. The distinction of life was not a concept nanites could understand and they made no distinction between the dead and the living as they attempted to control the armor of the Medjay. Several soldiers fell, covered in chaos nanites. The stored kinetic energy from the failed override attempt was charging, aimed and about to be released in the direction of the Medjay.

"Move the Shango up!" Hezbon yelled.

"Commander!" Seba objected, in response.

"Fire!" Hezbon ordered, then he turned to Seba. "Make a decision."

The raw, unfiltered power of the Shango leapt forward once again. It impacted the mass of nanites dead center of target, however there was no explosion. The gaseous cloud of chaos nanites were swelling, expanding as a result of their impact with the synthetic lightning. Everyone looked to the Shango weapons system operator, who was frantically trying to shut the weapon down. Somehow, the chaos nanites were not only absorbing the kinetic energy, but they were also preventing the connection to that energy from being severed. Fortunately, they quickly reached the maximum capacity for which they could collectively store this energy. Discharges of energy, varying in size, were seen building up within the mass of nanites then arcing out in random directions.

The chaos nanites could not disengage from the Shango weapon either and recognized the danger posed by this prolonged exposure. Every reanimated Meroan shifted focus to the Shango operator.

"Cover fire!" The Chaos nanites had backed themselves into a corner and Hezbon was ready for it.

This time the Medjay did open fire in unison. The Shango heavy weapons system was a two man assignment. One would fire the big bulky weapon and the other would protect the exposed operator. He was usually equipped with a short range weapon with a fast rate of fire. Tinashe fulfilled his duty and rapidly fired at the nearest targets approaching his defenseless operator. He focused only on the nearest targets and allowed the rest of the Medjay to deal with the more distant ones. A forth dead Meroan approached Tinashe's position. He turned to fire on it but couldn't. His finger froze on the trigger as soon as he recognized his old training partner.

Tinashe and Masawi had entered training together. They were inseparable and were often seen competing in the simulators together. Yet, while Tinashe's strengths led to him being recruited into the Medjay, Malawi's strengths were more suited toward the sciences. They went their separate ways after the training had been completed, but made every attempt to keep in touch. Now Tinashe's old friend was advancing on his position, intent to take his life. No, not his life. His operator's life. Even as it pushed past him, it was no use. Tinashe could not shoot Malawi, not even to protect the mission. He wouldn't have to. Hezbon stepped in and dispatched Malawi for him. With one glance, Hezbon checked for the mental status of Tinashe. He was standing stiff, eyes hollow wide and breathing shallowly.

Seba realized his chance and ran for the aux console while everyone was distracted. He input the override procedure and initiated a diagnostic. Aside from the physical damage, none of the internal systems had been destroyed. His assumption was correct though, the chaos nanites had been trying to override the lockdown by any means they could. That wasn't all either, the techniques used were familiar to Seba, and they had the signature of Oya all over them. That information would surely be relevant later.

Right now, Seba only hoped there was enough time for him to do what needed to be done. Hezbon had been right. It was time to make a decision. Normal lighting in the room reestablished itself. Every piece of machinery activated at full capacity. Then the same events repeated themselves in the corridor just outside aux control. On and on this went until every room was too-brightly lit and all their machinery was operating over maximum rating specifications. At the same time the energy channeling from the chaos nanites got weaker. Seba was attempting to minimize an overload just long enough to access the base code of the nanites. The stakes were close, there was simply not enough time to accomplish both of those tasks. Then everything went bright.

No one knew what happened. Several moments later, everyone began stirring. Those who could got to their feet, and helped other Meroans suffering from various stages of injury. Seba and Hezbon attempted to restart a diagnostic on the aux console but there was no chance of that happening. The console would never power up again. The rogue nanites were still in their semi-gaseous state but they were frozen in place, drifting lifelessly above what remained of the console. The last thing Hezbon remembered was a loud hum that grew in intensity, just before Seba looked up to make eye contact with him. He had yelled one thing, EVAC. Even though Hezbon gave that order without hesitation, none made it out before the inevitable explosion leveled aux control.

Hezbon took the time to get an update from Seba, "What happened?"

I routed as much energy into the mountain's power grid as I could." Seba then gestured to the destruction all around them, "You know what happened to the rest. As for the rogue nanites, I believe I have been able to contain the bulk of them. Although it appears a small number of them have escaped."

Hezbon surveyed the immediate area, nothing unnatural was moving. Most of the Medjay were on their feet but the unit, as a whole, was no longer in fighting shape. This mission was over. Hezbon gave orders to pull out. The wounded that were not ambulatory were to be carried out, meaning portable stretchers had to be deployed. Fortunately, there were no casualties. Once everyone was organized Hezbon turned to supervise the final stage of their withdrawal, but Seba stopped him.

"We have to pull *all* of the wounded out," Seba reminded him.

"Do you have what you need to extract her?" Hezbon would only delay his wounded soldiers for a brief time. A team of engineers could always return for her, escorted by base security.

"Time. All I need is a few moments," Seba assured him. "My on-board engineering suite already possesses everything I need."

Hezbon turned to address his Medjay. His intention was to order them to evac without him. He, alone, would remain behind to assist Seba in completing the mission. However, the Medjay knew him all too well. The one nearest Hezbon spoke before Hezbon had the chance to "We're in no rush, Commander. The Medjay deploy and evac together. All of us."

The rest of the Medjay heard what was said and turned to face Hezbon as well. Another Medjay called out from farther back. Her voice just as determined as the first. "We all fought hard for this commander."

Hezbon gave a curt nod to the Medjay, acknowledging their decision to delay their own evac in order to see the mission through. Then he turned to Seba, "Let's do it."

Seba activated his H.U.D., accessed the engineering suite and initiated the process required to recover an A.S.E. from a failed system. Only an engineer had access to a built in engineering suite, so only an engineer could recover an A.S.E. whose containment system had suffered catastrophic damage. Tiny specs of blue light began to appear inside the gaseous cloud of nanites until there were too many to count. They flowed out of the cloud like wisps of air that joined into a current. It was all coming together to form one large ball of blue light at the end of that current. Once the mass hit a critical point, the light grew much brighter and took on the faint silhouette of, none other than, Oya. Many of the Medjay ended up polarizing their face plates in order to shield their eyes from the light. When there were no more tiny pieces of light to reconstitute Oya, what made up her entire essence drifted toward Seba and entered his suit through an auxiliary port.

It was done, she was safely inside Seba's suit, her new containment vessel. The harsh blue light that had previously covered every surface receded. Inside his H.U.D. the familiar feeling of sharing one's suit returned to Seba. Oya opened an encrypted comm channel between herself and Seba. The projected image flickered several times, before resolving itself into one of her choosing.

"Seba…." Oya spoke softly. "The debate, among Meroans, over sentience has raged longer than you have lived. Many life times, in fact. Regardless, thank you for saving my life."

Seba had no idea how to respond. He never once even considered that Oya might actually be alive. He made a mental note to find out more about the process which created her, when he had more time. Then, he searched for what he thought might be a proper response. Fortunately, Oya spared him the embarrassment of a further delayed response by adding Hezbon to the conversation and changing the subject.

"Is it done?" Hezbon asked. "Have we succeeded?"

"Yes, Commander," Oya confirmed. "After the events on Naijia I held little hope that we would meet on this plane again."

"I thought the same thing Oya," Hezbon admitted. "I'm glad to have been wrong. But Azubuike…."

"I already know," Oya interjected. "We'll need to get to the medical wing. I may be able to save them if we hurry."

There was nothing else to say, the Medjay pulled out and returned to engineering's main entrance. Oya, safely under the protection of Seba, radiated the cool sensation of safety and peace throughout his suit. When they got there, a medical team and base defenders helped transfer the wounded. Before anyone knew what was happening, a commotion between the Medjay and several base defenders could be heard escalating.

Tinashe grabbed one of the base defenders, thinking he had somehow seen Malawi. The base defender, more afraid than anything, pointed his weapon at the disturbed Medjay. Tinashe was vehemently apologizing for murdering him, then welcomed him back from the dead. In fact, even Tinashe realized his mistake. Everywhere he looked, he saw the faces of the four he had "killed." So he closed his eyes tight, yet their faces haunted his mind's eye just as easily as they had just a moment before. It took four other Medjay to disarm and restrain Tinashe. They held him down while the squad medic administered a mild sedative to calm his nerves.

"What the hell happened in there?!" The base defender could be heard demanding an answer through a shaky voice.

"The Duat could not contain the dead…," Hezbon began his answer in a tone that indicated that his comments weren't being directed at anyone in particular. "So they returned to life."

What did that even mean? Having decided the Medjay, and their Commander, had finally fought one over-the-top battle too many, he signaled for reinforcements. More base defenders arrived with their weapons drawn, to back up their own squad mate. Which only made the Medjay respond in kind, creating a standoff. The difference was, the Medjay operated on a hair trigger even under the best of circumstances. They were the most disciplined fighting force in Meroan society, but they were about to show these base defenders that they responded to threats against their own in only one way.

"Stand down…. NOW!" Everyone knew that voice. All immediately lowered their weapons and relaxed their posture. The Kandake usually never used a tone such as this one. She rarely ever had need of it. Yet the events at the first line of quarantine were spiraling out of control.

She closed the distance, moving at a glide's pace, and gracefully put herself between Hezbon and the base defenders. She spoke first to Hezbon, her statements did not leave room for feedback or input of any kind. "Disarm the Medjay immediately. Every member must report to the Medbay where they will be confined until they pass a full battery of psychological evaluation. You will go first, be on my encrypted channel for debriefing as soon as yours is completed."

"It will be done Kandake," Hezbon gave the royal salute and departed, without another word, to carry out her orders.

Then she turned to the base garrison, "The quarantine has ended. Clear every corridor between here and the Medbay. Seal the adjoining corridors until the Medjay have completed the transfer of all wounded. No one but the Medjay are to be in these walkways during this operation. I don't want them interacting with anyone. That includes any base defenders. There's no need to risk agitating elite soldiers who are clearly suffering from battle shock. Am I clear?"

"Understood, Kandake." All base defenders present answered in unison, then departed to carry out their task as well.

With that situation diffused, the Kandake could turn her attention to locating Seba and Hezbon to get some answers. Both of whom, were already standing there awaiting her attention.

"The Medjay look a little worse for wear, Commander." The concern for her most dependable unit was evident on her face.

"We'll pull through Kandake. The Medjay will be

back at fighting strength after a solid block of much needed R&R. And," Hezbon continued, "We have a gift for you."

"A gift from the Medjay?" Kandake Nzinga asked, a slight tone of surprise in her voice. "That alone should make it interesting. Were you both successful in your missions?" Kandake Nzinga asked.

"We were," Seba confirmed. "There is much to tell you," Seba nervously looked around at all the eyes that were on them, "but I believe you will appreciate discretion once you know the details."

Kandake Nzinga understood what Seba was implying. They needed to debrief in private. Kandake Nzinga paused in her steps to allow the Medjay to pass. They had refused to allow anyone near Tinashe, and were carrying him all the way to the Medbay themselves. Every one of them had blank, hollow stares that seemed to go on for miles. Even though they didn't seem to be focusing on anything, they were all locking their gazes straight ahead.

"Let's get to the Medbay, Kandake," Seba spoke the reminder in order to bring Kandake Nzinga's attention back to their debriefing. "I think there's someone there you'll want to meet."

Sabayt mDu Sfx

Nosizwe and her dedicated team of healers were still working toward restoring Azubuike. It had been several hours since the events in the hangar bay had taken place and they were still working tirelessly to restore him. Nosizwe had exhausted all known efforts to heal Azubuike's physical injuries and the Meroans were rewarded by her repeated attempts. Nosizwe was successful at treating Azubuike's wounds but, unfortunately, still could not wake him. So Azubuike spent the last few hours under her strict observation. Nosizwe quickly dismissed any suggestion that she rest or even leave the medical wing, so her staff erected a small bed for her to rest on just next to Sovereign Azubuike.

That is where Nosizwe's friends and family found her when they entered the Medbay. Kandake Nzinga, Councilor Melisizwe, Commander Hezbon, Seba and even Priestess Oluwaseun. They all observed her getting a much needed rest as soon as they entered the small room. Seba silently pointed out that her cup of tea, with lemon, was still warm and loosely held in her hand. Signaling that she had only, likely, recently dozed off. All was quiet, so Kandake Nzinga intended to keep it quiet. She decided to review Azubuike's medical findings with them on an encrypted channel, so as not to disturb Nosizwe. While she organized the comms set up and accessed Sovereign Azubuike's secure medical files, Seba took the opportunity to gently remove the cup of tea from Nosizwe's hand and place it atop the nearest food tray. None of the food looked like it had been touched and Seba made a note to come back to that later. He was concerned about what kind of effect this was all having on his sister.

Kandake Nzinga gave everyone in their encrypted chat access to Azubuike's medical files. Then she started skimming. She was specifically, interested in Nosizwe's findings and her medical opinions regarding Azubuike's treatment. Essentially, her progress had been stalled after she'd restored him physically. Although, without the source, the chaos energy was steadily abating. Every hour he was checked, the level of Isfet energy was deteriorating along with the intensity of the glow from his chest wound. She'd gotten word about Seba's warning just in time to prevent that disaster. Yet without nanites, there was little else she could do. So Nosizwe had prescribed time and observation as the next steps in his treatment plan. Kandake Nzinga pointed out the current circumstances, and relative good news.

"Look here," Councilor Melisizwe alerted the others to a specific section of the mind scan, sounding troubled, "This has been the case since he was brought here today. Two impressions on the mind scan results. One indicating coma like conditions, the other growing slowly stronger over time and showing a simple sleep pattern."

"We may have a solution for that." Seba chimed in. It was time to bring everyone up to speed on the plan that was forming. "Oya believes she can help."

"How would she do that?" Kandake Nzinga asked.

"I'm not entirely sure what the process involves," Seba admitted, "but she spoke of a digital representation of the fourth dimension."

"What did any of that mean?" Hezbon wasn't sure he heard a tangible solution in what Seba was saying. He never had any reason to doubt Seba, but this plan was sounding like one of his most extreme plans to date.

"I know what he meant...." Councilor Melisizwe began, "What you say is an insult to the NTRU. I want the son of my daughter back more than anyone, but only the ancestors have the power to request such a thing."

"They have already granted it." Priestess Oluwaseun understood that she was a new comer, and did not want to offend. She spoke in an even tone when she contradicted Councilor Melisizwe. "I have been given a sign on the battlefield. This is the right decision."

A shadow of doubt began to form on several faces. All except Hezbon, "I was there," He stated flatly. "Azubuike was dead. Whatever else happened is inconsequential to that fact. I can't explain how, but he was far into the transition when something, or someone, reversed that. Now we are faced with a crossroads. To trust this Priestess or not. Priestess Oluwaseun has my respect as a warrior and, for what it's worth, my full confidence."

Kandake Nzinga didn't need to hear anymore. She had only heard Hezbon make a statement like that one other time. So she knew the weight he placed on those words. "Then she has my full confidence as well."

"We are decided," Councilor Melisizwe added, to show his willingness to follow the lead of his peers.

Nosizwe noticed the gestures and mannerisms as she drifted close enough to consciousness and slowly opened her eyes. When she realized many of her extended family were in the room, clearly discussing Azubuike, she rose with a start. It was time to give her report. They needed to know about the mind scan results….

Nosizwe accepted her invite into the encrypted chat and uploaded Azubuike's medical file. A silhouette of her image joined with the several others who were already in the chat. She began to bring up the mind scan results when Kandake Nzinga gently interrupted her. "We know, Daughter. And we have a plan to revive them."

Everyone brought Nosizwe up to speed on the idea, over the next several minutes. When she had all the details they had, she couldn't help but feel less than convinced. "Are we going to go forward with this without even knowing what Oya plans to do? Is anyone going to give me any specifics or details to this part of the plan?"

This time it was Oya who contributed to the conversation. "Sovereign Roha is lost, and I have the means to find her."

"What do you need, Oya," Seba took the opportunity to change the direction of the conversation as soon as it presented itself.

"A new set of command armor," Oya began, "and several uninterrupted moments, if you can give them to me."

Oya's plan was a simple one. She had seen this condition one other time before, when Sovereign Roha had undergone her advanced command suit training. The instructors warned of the consequences of straying too far from the body when traveling. She suspected that this was the situation Sovereign Roha was in, forced upon her by Duro-Aina's attack. In one of the training demonstration's videos, one student had gone too far and his Ba could not find the way back to his body. Many instructors were involved in his rescue, it took several of them to search him out and return him home. While Oya did not have several instructors to assist her, she did have a unique connection to Sovereign Roha due to the process which created A.S.E. units.

Oya ran a quick diagnostic on all systems to be sure she was fit for such a rescue operation. She finished her task just as Seba finished coding the new nanites to Azubuike's physiology. Now they were ready. Well, almost ready.

"One last word of caution," Oya knew that she wouldn't be able to relay commands once she had entered the digital representation of the fourth dimension. "I will not be able to communicate with you for the duration of this operation but do not fear. No one wants my counter-part back more than I do. Nosizwe, you'll need to give them something for the pain. You will know when."

Then Oya was gone. Seba felt her presence withdraw, taking her radiant feeling of serenity with her, as she transferred herself into Azubuike's new command suit.

Tones from the medical equipment and comm silence were all they had to listen to, yet everyone dutifully waited without exiting the room. None wanted to have the unfortunate bad luck of being absent when Azubuike finally awoke. Minutes turned to hours as they waited.

To pass the time, Sovereign Azubuike's family and friends discussed the events that had taken place over the past few years. They focused on topics that held personal importance to both them and Azubuike. Each one told a personal story. Councilor Melisizwe, Azubuike's elder by blood, spoke of the time they spent subjected to interrogation at the hands of Lieutenant Wynch. Seba, Azubuike's brother by blood, spoke of the ill effects The Bennu Project had taken on Azubuike's state of mind. Everyone held a silent moment for Ime, who went missing during the operation that had completed The Bennu Project.

Kandake Nzinga retold the story of how she first met Azubuike, by having her personal guard shoot down Wynch's transport. Which was in high pursuit, intent on recapturing Azubuike. Hezbon observed the group, they were celebrating Azubuike's life by retelling stories of the times they'd suffered and escaped death together. When it became his turn, he couldn't help but participate. He and the Medjay were reformed out of the highest ranking soldiers training under General Themba. They presented themselves to Azubuike just after he was officially made Sovereign. The Medjay personally pledged themselves to the protection of the Sovereign, a vow that hadn't been made in several thousand years. Then they followed Sovereign Azubuike into some of the fiercest fighting taking place at Elmina base. For her part, Nosizwe spoke of her iconic marriage proposal that brought everyone together just prior to Azubuike's departure to assault Elmina base.

To everyone's surprise, the voice of Ayoka permeated the encrypted comm channel, "When Seba was gravely injured on our first mission outside of the mountain, our blood brother was willing to risk everything to save us."

"Ayoka…." A slight tone of impatience crept into Kandake Nzinga's voice. "How many times…."

Kandake Nzinga didn't even bother to finish her sentence. She would have to have another one of those "talks" with the Isoba commander. Detached and distant, Ayoka had trouble socializing with others. The nature of isolation often associated with Isoba missions already made most Isoba this way. In the absence of Oya, to keep them in check, the Isoba were taking a few too many liberties with their stealth abilities throughout the mountain. Nothing serious was happening, yet it did happen to provide a minor annoyance when an Isoba decided to randomly appear right in the middle of a conversation that most thought to be private.

"My apologies, Kandake Nzinga," Ayoka was genuinely sincere in her words, "I just wanted to quietly wait for him to come back."

Kandake Nzinga seemed to accept this violation of her own security status, making an exception for the fact that Ayoka, Seba, Melisizwe and Nosizwe could likely have another cause for grieving soon. This was not the time to stand on protocol.

"I have a story," Priestess Oluwaseun had yet to be heard. "While I did not know him personally, it doesn't take long to know the character of a man like Sovereign Azubuike. When all hope was lost, he personally threw himself into harm's way to save many Naijian lives. I would not be standing here, were it not for him."

The room burst into a chorus of organic laughter, which at first confused Oluwaseun. When she didn't understand the source of everyone's humor, Seba offered an explanation. "That would be the number one characteristic he displays. He leads from the front, inspiring all those behind. I can't tell you how many times he's done that, jumping into the unknown with no regard for himself, or how many times I've followed him in…."

"I see now," Oluwaseun understood the inside joke, "That would be exactly how he got these injuries."

Several warning claxons announced themselves, in the most startling way, in order to disturb the peace. One by one, each machine set to monitor Azubuike's condition began to alert the group that something was happening. A hissing sound could be heard as the automatic medical dispenser warmed up. It was about to administer some form of painkiller. In fact, many things were happening at once and Nosizwe rushed to determine the cause. First she checked the mind scan, which showed a flurry of activity from the more dominant mind observed. Pain levels were steadily rising, going off the charts, and approaching extremely unsafe levels. A collective gasp could be heard from all in attendance, as Azubuike could be seen visibly trembling.

This was the time Oya spoke of. Nosizwe knew that there could be no other moment for her to administer a pain killer. Based on, what she was certain to be, excruciating pain, she made the decision to provide Azubuike with the maximum dose allowable. It was either that, or induce a coma and she had no idea how that might affect whatever process Oya had initiated. Even so, if it had been a viable option, Oya would have mentioned it. It turned out to be academic anyway, after several tense moments. The pain levels began to dissipate and Azubuike could be seen physically relaxing.

Kandake Nzinga thought the silence should be broken with a small word of encouragement. Pain meant he was alive. In the moments of that pain, all of his body had tensed up and moved. That likely meant that he was not permanently paralyzed. But before she could articulate any of this, the attention of the entire room shifted to Azubuike. Not only was he making sounds, but he was also moving again. He was still laying completely down on his back but his arm was rising. This time he moved his hand toward his chest and placed it on the souvenir Duro-Aina had left him with. Then his eyes attempted to open, repeatedly blinked harshly at the bright light and then rose to the seated position to face everyone.

Everyone rushed toward Azubuike, but the image of Oya appeared, projected before him, to halt their advance. "Not all at once," She cautioned.

Realizing the necessity to refrain from overwhelming Azubuike, everyone attempted to contain their excitement. Nosizwe cautiously checked the mind scan again and feared what the results told her. How could he be awake? She had given him enough dosage to sedate a small capital ship. Still, she asked the question anyway, "Azubuike…. Are you alright?"

Priestess Oluwaseun did not need the answer said aloud. She'd felt the rise of feminine energy as Azubuike was waking up. She raised her right fist, placed it onto her heart and lowered her head to signal the royal salute. Hezbon, had felt this energy on the battlefield, during the time all had seen the silhouette of an ancient Meroan project itself from Azubuike to protect him from Duro-Aina. He quickly put two and two together and followed the example of the Priestess.

Azubuike immediately spoke, to answer Nosizwe's question. He spoke in one of the oldest, most rarely used dialects of ancient Mdu Ntr, which made him sound very formal and proper. "I am Roha Taharqa, Sovereign of M.A.R.S., and Commander of all Meroan forces."

Agallu, the A.S.E. tasked with the security and normal operation of the mountain, broadcast a system wide update to all Meroan forces who could receive the transmission. It simply read, "To all Meroan forces, receive and acknowledge recent updates to the chain of command.

Addendum to be added: Sovereign Roha, defender of the people."

Everyone in the room gave the royal salute upon hearing the declaration. Only Hezbon, who was already displaying the royal salute, went further. After holding the royal salute for several seconds, and to the surprise of Kandake Nzinga, Hezbon knelt to one knee and spoke the Medjay's pledge. "Once again and for all in attendance to bear witness," He began, "On behalf of the Medjay, I pledge our loyalty to your service. To your personal safety and to the fulfillment of your agendas. Whatever they may be, the Medjay will see them through and ensure your personal protection. The Medjay are yours to command, Sovereign Roha: Defender of the People."

Sabayt mDu Xmnu

Sovereign Roha had spoken enough with Azubuike, so that she was able to understand the new words and changes to the sacred language. She didn't need Oya to translate. What she needed was to get to the command center, but since her torso felt like it was on fire and she was having trouble focusing, she would certainly need Oya for that.

"Some disorientation is normal," Oya informed Sovereign Roha on an encrypted channel, "You've been through this before."

"Yes," Roha admitted, "I have. But not like this. An errant part of the process has caused extreme drowsiness and impedes my ability to focus beyond short periods of time."

"That would have been Azubuike's wife," Oya did not have to guess. She already knew who was responsible. "She administered nearly unsafe levels of sedative, for the pain, out of concern for Azubuike."

"I see," Roha searched the faces that she had seen through Azubuike's eyes until she found Nosizwe. "Oya, supplement the nanite's healing ability with my own DMT reserves. In time, both issues will abate normally."

"Of course, Sovereign." Oya had never been happier to comply with an order from Roha.

When Roha felt the cool sensation, indicative of the start of the enhanced healing process, she decided it was time to get herself off the table. She was unsteady at first, due to the sedative but also due to the fact that she'd never controlled Azubuike's body before. Oya was right on top of it and supplemented the bulk of her weight by using the suit itself to support her. This made standing upright much easier for Sovereign Roha to accomplish. Even so, her stature was still of power and grace. She was royalty, after all, and no amount of pain could alter her natural gait. She stood straighter, taller and noticeably more confident than Azubuike did.

The first words she directly spoke to anyone were directed at Hezbon. "Your words honor me," putting a hand on his shoulder, "But I have already *seen* your actions. Your undying loyalty to him and to the Medjay, at great personal expense. Please rise, distinguished Commander of the Medjay, and protect me as you have protected him."

Hezbon did rise, and when Sovereign Roha stepped back to allow the room, she nearly lost her balance. Hezbon was forced to grab her shoulder to provide some stability. Roha, normally determined to carry her own weight, allowed herself to make this exception. She kept her hand on his shoulder for the duration, for the balance. Standing erect for too long began to take its toll on her chest injuries, so she slightly hunched over and kept her right hand gently placed there to ease the pain back.

Then, she turned to Nosizwe, "Thank you for the care you have provided. We would not be standing here were it not due, in part, to your efforts."

"I always want what's best for Azubuike," Nosizwe was not afraid to make her motivations known to all. "It is my honor to serve you."

Roha wanted to reassure everyone in the room once more before she departed, "I know how much all of you mean to Azubuike and I will respect his wishes in all cases." Everyone seemed to visibly relax the worry lines on their strained faces upon hearing this. So she continued, "For now, I must get to the command center."

"Please allow us to arrange transport, Sovereign Roha," Kandake Nzinga stood on ceremony and used the very dialect Roha was using. "You are far too injured and must await assistance."

Sovereign Roha almost chuckled to herself. If she'd had a ship for every time she'd been told that, the war would have ended with a different outcome. "Thank you

Kandake Nzinga, but I have never been one to wait, too long, for any reason."

Sovereign Roha exited the Medbay with the assistance of Hezbon and made her way to the command center. As they walked, the discomfort became a little more evident.

"Sovereign Roha...," Nosizwe began.

"Again, young Nosizwe," Roha interrupted her, "My time here is limited. I intend to take every step myself, and enjoy every physical sensation, no matter how painful."

Nosizwe seemed to accept this and continued to walk alongside Roha, just in case.

"Well, nearly every physical sensation," Oya joked with Roha on a private channel, in order to broach an uncomfortable subject.

"Of course not *every* physical sensation," Roha agreed, "This is Azubuike's body, not mine, and that must be respected. Do you have any suggestions?"

"Nanites have already been tasked with waste management," Oya informed Roha, "It is the very same process we use on long missions. You'll never notice a thing and Azubuike's privacy will not be violated. However, you're on your own if you were to, say, lose one of his limbs.... You'll have to explain any new physical injuries or scarring to him yourself."

"We all have our prices to pay, don't we…?" Roha spoke almost absent mindedly, consumed with thoughts of how much Azubuike had already sacrificed. She had realized long ago that the two of them were not, at all, entirely dissimilar.

Roha decided to continue this line of thought, which led to a verbal reassurance to Nosizwe, "All is not lost, young Azubuike is with his ancestors."

Everyone was visibly relieved at Sovereign Roha's reassurance, yet Nosizwe asked the question everyone else wanted to. "Do you know when he will return to us?"

Roha thought about the best, honest answer to give them. She didn't want to give them false hope, but neither did she want to leave them demoralized; with nothing to fight for. So she gave them the truth without any extra information which might lead up to follow up questions. "That is between young Azubuike and his ancestors. They have already approved, but he must make the final decision."

When they approached the command center's main entrance, Roha reduced the full protection of her nanites. She had only enhanced its protection because Azubuike was something of a rock star and their slow progression never would have made it to the command center once word got out that he was "back." In addition to that, clearing the corridors would have drawn too much attention, and nobody was ready to attempt the fantastical explanation for why Roha was returned.

When she entered the Command center, a rush of euphoria instantly overcame Roha. She had given her final evacuation orders from this room and then disappeared. That stage of her journey, concluded. She went right to her command chair and took up her station. Sovereign Roha sat in that chair like it belonged to her, because it did. She'd had the original swapped out with the command chair from the Aha Mena, once it was clear that ship would never fly again. At least not without a major refit operation and a complete overhaul. Still, she liked to think of it as a long term goal.

Roha raised a hand and, to the surprise of everyone stationed in the command center, a separate console rose from the floor to supplement the existing command console. "Authorization RT02062848603078937." In response to her words, the console projected a small blue light that scanned Roha's biometric readings and confirmed her identity.

"Sovereign Roha, Defender of the people. Full

access granted." The mechanical voice of the mountain's A.S.E. unit could be heard projecting itself throughout the command center, "Command access level: Double Restricted, applies to most of these files. None of the personnel in this room, aside from yourself, are cleared to view the information contained within. Please consult the council, or the latest publication on Meroan law, regarding security access."

"Override," Roha was not surprised in the slightest. After all, she was personally responsible for the robust security measures.

"As you command, Sovereign Roha," Agallu took little time in delaying Roha any further than was necessary. "What is your query?"

"Stellar map," Roha spoke, "display all active facilities."

A map of the local star systems popped into existence as the lights in the command center slowly dimmed. Several stars had icons next to them, with details of the accompanying installations or Meroan worlds in those systems. Any star with a Meroan presence was given a purple hue to indicate its geopolitical allegiances. Of course this was a snap shot of the situation as it was when Roha had last used the station to initiate the lock down and it was far out of date. "Display all installations classified: Double Restricted. Break radio silence procedures, ping all active installations for updated status reports."

The holographic display, previously full of motion, was now frozen as Agallu updated it with the new information. Whereas it previously contained stars that projected solar flares and comets or asteroids in motion, nothing moved and the soft light from each star had dimmed. Then each light brightened again and the motion returned. The update was complete and Roha did not like what she saw. The entire government and culture had collapsed some time ago. Many of the installations were offline and not responding.

"Where am I, Oya," Roha paused to correct herself.

"As I said," Oya reminded her, "Some disorientation is normal."

"*When* am I," Roha finished. The slight frustration becoming evident.

"You are currently on KSH, Great Year 155.4262994," Oya thought it would aid Roha if she were to hear a specific answer. "KSH is currently in the fourth precession of its equinoxes."

Sovereign Roha considered this for a moment. That would mean five precessions had passed since she gave the order to evacuate this room, and the mountain. No one thought or expected this much time would have come to pass. The Bennu Project did not have this amount of extended time as a consideration when they designed it. It was no wonder there were a few glitches. And now to see the full extent of the devastation done to her beloved Meroan Republic, it was almost too much to bear. The good news was that at least a few top secret installations were still operational. She only needed one…. Roha took manual command of the map and focused on one region of space in particular. It had a new icon on it, a gold star. This was to indicate that an installation, previously undisclosed, was in the system. She enlarged, and then scrolled through the data for all to see. This particular installation was active, reporting operational status and displaying all of its parameters in the green. It was as good a choice as any.

Sovereign Roha only needed to check one thing, "Inventory."

The data screen everyone had just looked at updated to include a new tab. When Roha switched to this tab it displayed a list of ships, their tonnage, approximate speeds, crew compliments and armament. There were several ships in various stages of repair or construction.

"Forgive me Sovereign, but are we looking at a list

of functioning ships?" Sea asked. "In real time?"

"This is one of our minor, automated refit and repair installations," Roha explained. "At least that's what it appears to be on the official record. The reason it is on this highly classified list is because it also doubles as an experimental ship building facility. We test several types of weapons and ship building techniques here. I chose this one due to both its isolated and automated nature. If we're ever going to push back your Ezalin, or establish regional control for yourselves, you're going to need these ships.

"Now," Sovereign Roha specifically addressed Hezbon, "How are you going to get me there?"

Sabayt mDu Psd

Of all the crazy ideas Seba had come up with, this one may have been the one to finally, completely catch Hezbon off guard. It was a great idea and had completely impressed Hezbon. The only thing that bothered him was that the Medjay would miss the bulk of the planetary engagement. Councilor Melisizwe had argued against the Medjay's involvement, citing battle stress. Nosizwe agreed with him and, no matter how much he didn't want to, so did Hezbon. The plan involved several phases that all depended on each other if they were to achieve overall success.

First, Oya would use unmanned Impundulu drones, named Ushabti, to mask their approach to the Ezalin blockade that appeared in Agallu's scans of Naijia. They had a few thousand of these drones, under Oya's personal command, floating harmlessly toward the Ezalin blockade. They knew the general deployment strategy used and where their target was located, based off scans from a recently reactivated micro satellite in orbit over Naijia. Seba had chosen to "borrow" some of the drones stored on the Aha Mena, Sovereign Roha's ancient flag ship, because a similar strategy had worked during the battle for Elmina base.

He had also chosen their target, based on the limited intelligence they had on Ezalin ships. Fortunately, the mission requirements weren't very high. They needed a disposable ship. One that was large enough to carry their entire raiding party, enough to crew several Meroan ships. However, the ship also had to be strong enough to survive their initial attack and, if all went according to plan, it would have to survive Ezalin retaliation as well. Yes, they were going to steal a ship. Seba had suggested one of the medium sized support vessels that hung near the outer edge of the blockade.

The plan was simple, the drones would act as disposable cover for two flights of Keftiu drop ships. Two flights, two missions. The first flight, held nothing but Meroan soldiers and supplies meant to reinforce Kandake Anima. The medical supplies and reinforcement were much needed by her overwhelmed Egbas soldiers. The other flight, under the command of Sovereign Roha, were on a separate mission to commandeer an Ezalin ship and use it to get to their destination.

The two flights and their escorts floated toward the blockade using natural inertia, so as not to alert the enemy sensors. When the time was right, they would all spring into action. Oya spent the duration of the flight checking and updating the data. There were many moving parts to this mission and she wanted to be sure that everyone had their best chance for survival. She also found a few moments to infiltrate the Ezalin secure network. It was laughably easy. There were so many vulnerabilities to exploit that she didn't know which to choose from. Ultimately, she decided to use them all. Oya began by triggering the self-destruct mechanisms on several ships throughout the Ezalin fleet, which forced them to spread apart. Then she wreaked havoc on their defense network. She activated fire suppression systems, pinged false positives on their active scans in order to create ghost ships for them to chase, and she was even able to send the bulk of them into an emergency diagnostic. That meant dozens of ships were floating lifelessly while their main engines cycled toward full restart. Their main computers were also going to have to cycle through a full restart.

When they were close enough, Oya made her declaration. "Phase one complete. The bulk of them are blind and defenseless. The time is now, sovereign."

Sovereign Roha looked to Hezbon, who signaled that he was ready. The pair of them looked back to Oya, to confirm their ready status. On Oya's command, all Ushabti fighters burst forward into a full burn. The two flights of

Keftius went into a max burn as well, in an attempt to keep up with the fighter drones. Oya did not hold any back, she knew the numbers were good and there would be plenty of time to take up defensive positions once the Keftiu flights were in range. She wanted all operable Ezalin ships to focus on her attack and she would only get one opening salvo. She intended to use maximum force in her initial attack.

The first of the drones reached their targets unchallenged. Four ships, in a tight cluster, had not been able to return fire, flee or even deploy their own fighters. They were completely defenseless. Sovereign Roha and Commander Hezbon watched as their view port grew closer and closer to the hull of one of these ships in particular. The drones were ignoring it but the other three ships were being devastated. Fighter drones swarmed in and around their formation, destroying their turrets, targeting their engines and generally disabling critical ship components when they found them. Hezbon could now see details on the ship as they grew closer. It had suffered minimal damage, compared to the other three, and some text painted on the side that he could not recognize. Just underneath that, were several bay doors, obviously meant for embarking or disembarking the ship. When the doors

suddenly slid apart, Hezbon's suspicions were confirmed.
They were approaching the ship's main hangar deck.

Several of the fighters took their chance to escape
the ship that had trapped them. When they cleared the
hangar bay doors, they immediately made a bee line for the
Keftiu drop ships. Only they never got close enough to do
any real damage. Oya re-tasked the Ushabti fighter drones
to defensive positions. Sovereign Roha could see the
expressions on the faces of Ezalin pilots as the drones
closed in on them and destroyed them. There were only
three hundred meters to close the distance between them
and their landing zone inside the ship which, combined
with the Ezalin fighter attack, meant that it was time for
Oya to switch to phase three.

The fighter drones split into two groups and took up
defensive positions around both Keftiu flights. The first
group escorted the ground troops and supplies toward their
destination, counting on the fact that the Ezalin commander
would have far more important concerns to worry about.
They were right, most of the ground contingent made it
down with minimal casualties. Do in no small part to the
fact that the bulk of the fleet was occupied. The fighters
that did manage to harass these drop ships were quickly
dealt with. Even more so, their direct attacks on the

dropships were intercepted by fighter drones who intentionally flew into missiles meant to down Keftius.

"You're making this too easy for us, Oya," Hezbon made the small talk in order to pass the time, "I was expecting a real fight here."

"You may still get it, Commander," Oya was disgusted at the ease with which she'd infiltrated the Ezalin defensive network. "These attacks are rudimentary, pathetic. But there is no reason to believe they will not recover from them in due time. We'll need to be gone by then."

When the ground assault force reached the orbital insertion point, Oya alerted Sovereign Roha and she sent the final transmission to all Meroan forces on the local net, "The people of Naijia have allied with M.A.R.S., now their fight is my fight. Our fight. They could have chosen differently, yet they fight on our behalf. Now we will fight on their behalf. Go forward, secure and reinforce all defensive positions. Protect Kandake Anima until our return. Honor to our ancestors."

Oya broadcast the inevitable reply across the local net as well. "They died in our name," could be heard echoing from the comm as thousands of soldiers gave the response. Then they could be heard no more.

Electromagnetic interference from Naijia's natural atmospheric shield blocked all transmissions. Once they entered the upper atmosphere, they were on their own. All had been briefed on this part of the plan and completely expected to lose communications at this stage of the plan. The invasion force would have to get to ground the best way they could, and join the fighting until Sovereign Roha could bring relief.

Hezbon watched as the last of the Keftiu drop ships disappeared into the Naijian atmosphere, with the escort fighter drones returning to join the attack on their new capital ship. It wasn't theirs yet, Hezbon still had a job to do. Hezbon momentarily thought about the invasion force. There wasn't a single Medjay going to ground, along with that mission. Councilor Melisizwe, along with Kandake Nzinga, had argued against their involvement in that part of the mission. Citing, "battle stress and fatigue." Although Hezbon politely reminded them that the Medjay were under the purview of the Sovereign, Roha had ultimately agreed with them. It was all academic anyway, Sovereign Roha had a different mission for Hezbon's team. Which included getting her to the ship yards. She was sure the Medjay would be in fighting form after the extended trip their mission would take them on. After they were safely away from the Ezalin, the Medjay would be on mandatory down time for the duration.

The members of the ground invasion force were not the only ones Hezbon thought about either. Priestess Oluwaseun was less than enthusiastic about remaining in the mountain while others fought for her home world. In the end, she agreed to help councilor Melisizwe establish a temple within the mountain. The Temple of Hru, remade in the image of the original, would train inductees in the ways of Kemetic spirituality, Kemetic science. When completed, and training underway, it was hoped that the first wave of recruits would grow into a fighting force that could challenge Duro-Aina. The Priestess had reluctantly agreed that her time would be best spent establishing this new temple. After all, how could she refuse a direct request from Sovereign Roha?

"It's our turn," Oya spoke directly to Roha and Hezbon to alert them that their boarding action was imminent.

"Right," Hezbon acknowledged their new status and turned to address the rest of the Medjay. "As of two minutes ago, ground force invasion teams penetrated the atmosphere of Naijia and are expected to make land fall within the next twenty. As of that moment, we're on the clock. The importance of our mission cannot be overstated. Any delay, or setback, will certainly contribute to the lives of our brothers and sisters on the ground being lost. Naijians, Kushites…? Irrelevant. Individual planets no longer matter. As members of M.A.R.S. that makes us all Meroans!"

Oya began the landing sequence and tasked several of the Keftiu pilots to launch a volley into the hangar bay. Nothing serious, in fact, Shango weapons had been withheld from this attack. She wanted to clear the area and keep any defender's heads down, not destroy the ship.

As the view into the hangar bay rotated behind him, Oya dropped the bay doors so all could disembark.

They were seconds away from insertion. The black expanse of space and the distant stars that had been visible, were now visibly obstructed by the hull of their target ship. Hezbon knew it was go time, so he concluded his statements by giving a specific overview of their goals. "Forward, Medjay! Force them back, eliminate all hostiles, and secure our ship! For Naijia, for KSH, for M.A.R.S.!"

Several drop ships waited for the initial volley to subside. When it had, their pilots briefly hesitated to ensure that there were none left to return fire. Two to three seconds of observation showed no movement, aside from the wounded who were about to make their transition. Then the incursion began. The Medjay were in the hangar bay in under a minute, as they disembarked their Keftius in waves. Hezbon had brought the entire contingent of Medjay on this mission and none had previously seen such a high number deployed on one engagement. They secured the hangar bay, along with all obvious exits, both quickly and efficiently.

The Medjay immediately went about the business of setting up a triage station inside the newly seized hangar bay, along with a temporary command center. Pre assigned fire teams did not wait for further orders. Time was of the essence and the Medjay were expected to be mindful of their speed. The faster they secured the ship, the less time the defenders would have to sabotage or scuttle it. Three fire teams of ten Medjay moved out in different directions. One, which included Seba, moved aft toward main engineering, while the other two moved toward the bridge and toward the enemy Medical department.

When engaged in any boarding action, it was of vital importance to secure the bridge and to secure engineering. This was why Seba's inclusion in that fire team was such a high priority. Hezbon was well aware that most ships could still be controlled from main engineering, but he was also aware that any defenders would attempt to slow his progress by destroying their own ship. At least they would attempt to do so, once it was decided that their battle to repel boarders could not be won. As for the medical wing, any good ship captain would have a contingency plan for last hold outs to rally in their Medbay. It had stockpiles of medical supplies, food and a nearby weapons locker. It was of great importance to the Medjay to secure the enemy Medbay or else they could wind up facing a prolonged battle for complete control of the ship.

Immediately upon entering the hangar bay, Hezbon personally transferred Oya to the nearest console that would give her access to the ship's defensive grid. In fact, Oya quickly had command access to the entire network. Now that she had direct access to their target's main computer, this ship practically belonged to her. She immediately locked the Ezalin bridge crew out of everything, including the self-destruct sequence they were in the middle of initiating. For all intents and purposes, Oya had just made herself captain of their new ship. Which she learned was referred to as "Old Ironsides," meant to be a tribute to one of their most revered, ancient war ships.

Whatever they called it no longer mattered, they had failed to properly defend "Old Ironsides" and now they were losing complete control of the ship. The entire crew was now fighting to escape or scuttle it. As a counter measure to sabotage, Oya then moved on to seal all passages on the ship. Aside from those needed by the Medjay. That meant the Ezalin defenders were restricted to whatever rooms and passageways they were in when Oya infiltrated their network. They would remain trapped there for the duration of the mission. Oya saw absolutely no reason to risk any Meroan lives to eliminate them, when they could remain safely isolated in storage lockers or berthing areas.

Oya took a moment to survey her new prize, before she gave the information to Sovereign Roha, and she was not impressed. By all indications, Old Ironsides was a primitive ship. Slow, bulky and relatively weak by Meroan standards. It actually relied on ancient missile technology as its primary weapons system. Oya hoped she wouldn't have to fight anything that could pose an actual threat while the Meroans were crewing Old Ironsides. Luckily for them, Old Ironsides happened to be considered the pinnacle of Ezalin technology and that wasn't saying much.

Sovereign Roha walked the corridors, confident in Hezbon's ability to keep her safe. She was surrounded by Medjay and protected at all times, while they escorted her to the bridge. Thanks to Oya's intervention, they met with little resistance while they were en route. The few defenders they did see were quickly dispatched. Hezbon lacked both the time and the desire to take any prisoners, so he didn't. The route to the bridge was lightly defended by those few who were unfortunate enough to be there when Oya had initiated the lockdown. They, in their desperation, hid behind hastily erected barricades. The Medjay had little trouble destroying their cover, which consisted of desks and filing cabinets.

When they arrived at the bridge, they quickly dispatched the guards posted there. They were out in the open and trapped on the outside of the bridge's main blast doors. Hezbon inspected the door, it was far too thick to use explosives on. Any explosion large enough to damage the door would also do significant damage to the surrounding bulkheads. Which would almost certainly compromise the hull's integrity. Hezbon wouldn't risk unnecessarily damaging the Sovereign's new ship. There had to be another way in. "Can you get us through?"

Oya displayed a three dimensional representation for all to see, in response to Hezbon's question. She highlighted the door they stood in front of and an error message displayed in the Ezalin native tongue. Then it translated to Mdu NTR, to inform the Meroans that the motor which drove the door had been physically disabled. Another, smaller, route highlighted itself with an entry point just to the rear of where they were standing. It appeared to be a service hatch that would allow access to the bridge for maintenance purposes. Although convenient, this meant they would have to double back to the next junction and leave the main blast door lightly defended.

"We *have* another option." Oya delighted in the fact that she could detect what most others couldn't. She had been aware of their extra member ever since they left the hangar bay.

"Looks like the path forward is clear, brother." No one was surprised when Ayoka dematerialized directly in front of the hatch. She was much further down the passageway and broadcasting to Hezbon on an encrypted channel. "I will secure the bridge."

Without waiting for a reply, Ayoka slid into the service hatchway. She was small and slender enough to fit into this hatchway, where no Medjay could, and maneuver through it. She consulted Oya's map and made her way to the bridge in a matter of moments. She only used seconds to survey the bridge from the safety of the service hatchway. From several feet backward, she listened to the Ezalin discuss their defensive situation. They were in a

panic, bridge officers were being reminded of their duty
and a few infantry guards had made it inside the bridge
before the lock down. One of them had been posted to
guard the service hatch while the other three were in
defensive positions closer toward the main blast door.

Ayoka waited for the guard closest to her to yawn
and stretch one more time, then she was out of the service
hatchway. She had discarded her sniper rifle just inside the
hatchway for safe keeping and, instead, opted to use a
simple blade. The guard never had a chance. All he saw
was a blur exit the service hatchway with amazing speed.
As quietly as she could manage, Ayoka made the service
hatchway's grate into a weapon, jamming the edge of it
into the man's wind pipe. Now that he would do her the
courtesy of passing on quietly, Ayoka gently put him on the
deck of the ship as he gasped for air. Then she made short
work of him, quietly, using her blade.

The semi-transparent image that was Ayoka peered
over the nearest console to get a better look at the
defenders. They were on the other side of the bridge, all
facing the opposite direction. They were evenly spaced out
and using bridge consoles for cover. Ayoka wasted no time
formulating her plan. She pulled out a stun grenade and
threw it at the furthest two. When it exploded, so too did

she burst into a flurry of movement. She was on the one
remaining guard before he could properly train his weapon
on her. He was forced to take wide shots, none of which
were remotely close to hitting their target. She, on the other
hand, silent and efficient, was far more accurate. Ayoka did
not restrain herself when she confronted the bridge guards.
Speed was her ally and she intended to make the most of it.

Slashing as she went, an invisible blur moved to all
three guards before both disarming and dispatching them.
Then it was time to deal with the bridge crew. They were
not in combat gear and only lightly armed with small
caliber weapons. They had nothing large enough to
seriously threaten Ayoka. As deadly as she was, she knew
she could not eliminate the bridge officers. Hezbon would
certainly want to interrogate some of them. So Ayoka opted
for non-lethal injuries. She moved in and among them,
relieving them of their weapons and even breaking an arm
or two. Of the seven bridge officers, only one of them was
barely on his feet and Ayoka didn't know which of them
would turn out to be the ship's captain.

Oya provided Ayoka with a new icon on her H.U.D.
to indicate her next objective. When she focused on it, her
H.U.D. zoomed in to show her a manual release that had
been pulled to disable the door. Ayoka moved to the target

and put all her weight behind pulling the underused lever, which settled with a solid mechanical click when she finished. Everyone on the other side of the door rushed in as soon as the main blast door opened. They spread out, secured the bridge and established a guard for the prisoners.

Hezbon took one look at the bridge, surveying what had been done. "Nice work," he admitted.

"As always," Ayoka attempted an awkward smile, before departing the bridge.

Oya broke the awkward silence with a general announcement, "Sovereign Roha, the bridge is under your command. What are your orders?"

"Have our people secured Engineering?" Roha asked.

"Seba's team is reporting success," Oya reported, "The ship is yours."

"Give me a map of Naijian space," Roha, requested. "Tactical overlay."

Roha viewed the current tactical situation outside their new ship. Several ships in the Ezalin blockade were active and moving in her direction. However, the bulk of their blockade still lay lifeless. She briefly considered whether she could get away with it…. Roha discarded the map and took up the command chair. Her decision was made, "Bring me to within radio range of all Meroan forces on Naijia. Deploy all drones to preassigned attack runs. Choose your targets."

"Uh Sovereign Roha," Hezbon interrupted Roha privately, on an encrypted channel. So as not to question her in front of everyone else. "This isn't part of our plan."

Sovereign Roha smiled to herself before responding to Hezbon, "I'm aware, young Hezbon. I do that occasionally."

Oya joined the conversation in an attempt to make light of the fact that Roha was long used to hearing her subordinates remind her that she wasn't operating according to plan, "Just go with it Hezbon. It's part of what makes her so effective."

"None can question that," Hezbon admitted, "I am ready to follow Sovereign Roha into any situation she may get us into."

Sovereign Roha silently acknowledged Hezbon's undying commitment. Azubuike was definitely going to need that if the ancestors were right. She thought about what Wsir had told her in the house before Azubuike arrived. "He will be the one to rally our descendants, to defeat the Ezalin and rebuild M.A.R.S.

"How much longer do I have, Oya?" Roha hoped

she could accomplish as much as she could for Azubuike. The more she accomplished now, the easier it would be on him later.

"The very same medical indicators that signaled your return are beginning to manifest themselves again," Oya explained. "You have a couple of days, a week at most."

"Disappointing," Sovereign Roha took a deep breath to help accept the situation. "Then we will have to settle for delivering his new fleet. There are some thoughts I would also like to leave for him."

"I understand." Oya kept it simple. She knew her human counterpart was preparing her goodbyes and she also knew that Roha was never any good at it. "I'll arrange it."

Old Ironsides, under the command of Sovereign Roha, made a low pass over Naijia. As it did, Oya made several near instant decisions. First, she updated Hezbon on the tactical situation by sharing the data she was retrieving from their microsatellites. As well as the data from their ground forces. Then she used that data to assign bombing runs to the drones. All high value targets. All while initiating the low pass, Oya gave the floor to Sovereign Roha.

"This is Sovereign Roha," Roha kept it brief, she knew there were only minutes before the more distant Ezalin ships would arrive to overtake her. They would only have time for one bombing run and a few words of encouragement. "To all Meroan forces, we will return for you. On my life I swear it. *I* will return for you."

As she spoke, thousands of drones entered low orbit and broke into squadrons. Thanks to the undetectable microsatellites, there were no line of sight restrictions. Ushabti drones were able to hit targets all over the planet. They destroyed refueling stations, fuel depots, power generation facilities, enemy base camps, anti-air installations, forward operating bases and even convoys. Oya wished she could hit more targets aimed at disrupting their supply lines, however some of the drones assigned to attack their supply depots had to be reassigned to active high priority scenarios.

She needed to use those drones to support friendly troops who were on the losing side of some pretty desperate looking battles. Oya knew they would be happy for the reprieve the drones were providing. In fact, as Old Ironsides began to pull away from their optimal angle for extra-orbital observation, Oya was able to see the tide of many battles turn in their favor.

"We're out of time Sovereign," Oya informed Roha. Expecting a rebuttal, Oya continued. "The nearest ships will be within weapons range within three hundred seconds. And I'm out of soft targets. Any further bombing runs will be ineffective and only serve to put us at increased risk."

"Very well," Roha ceded the point," Get us back on track."

Old Ironsides pulled away from Naijian orbit completely. Outbound on an unknown destination to all who weren't onboard. All Ushabti drones that weren't destroyed were seen breaking low orbit to rejoin their base ship. Only to be redeployed to deal with the pursuing Ezalin ships. Old Ironsides was last seen, at extreme range, easily outpacing its pursuers, who were engulfed in fighter drones/bombers.

Sabayt Mdty

Azubuike was back in the farmhouse, situated at the base of a rolling hill, somewhere in the Field of Reeds. During his time there, he had learned much about Meroan society, Kemetic Science and even himself. "We are our ancestors," took on an entirely new meaning for him. Where it once had stood as a spoken testament to honor his ancestors, he now realized that, via genetic memory, he actually was an ancestor. The closest approximation to understanding this concept was explained to him by Wsir. In it, Wsir explained that Meroans routinely transgress the ancestral plane and the hueman plane. In most cases, during repeated hueman experiences, Meroans lose all memory of their previous experiences on the hueman plane. The hueman mind lacks the capacity to retain all of that information, however, genetic memory will retain some of those experiences directly in the DNA structure of the body. Hence the phrase, "Genetic Memory."

Time was irrelevant, yet his Hue-man existence wouldn't let him completely let go of the concept. He didn't know how long he'd been there, but Azubuike spent the bulk of his time both speaking to and learning from the others who were present. One of his most frequent visitors was none other than Siphiwo, who came to Azubuike often. Siphiwo had taken an interest in teaching Azubuike about himself and about their heritage. Azubuike had long suspected that Siphiwo was trying to prepare him for something and, judging by the unusually large number of people in the farm house clearing, today may be the day to find out what. In fact, everyone was watching Azubuike as he tried to avoid drawing any more attention to himself than usual.

So Azubuike decided to go out into the clearing and redirect the attention into something helpful. Closing the door behind him, he approached a new face in the clearing, intent on introducing himself. He thought he might learn the state of the situation on Naijia if he asked someone who had just arrived. It was a good idea, that is, until Siphiwo appeared and cautioned him against it.

"I wouldn't recommend that," Siphiwo warned. When Azubuike appeared to be confused, Siphiwo offered an explanation, "The Field of Reeds is a transient space unlike any other. His arrival is from a point in space time that occurred after yours. His people won't remember any specifics about your battle on Naijia. To ask him any questions about his time or to give him the wrong knowledge from your time will put both of you at undue risk. Not to mention the intentions of the NTRU."

"How exactly do I discover the intentions of the NTRU," Azubuike asked in earnest.

"Come, young Azubuike." Siphiwo gestured toward the farmhouse door, "They're about to tell you."

There was no mistaking Wsir. Aside from the green skin, which he was most known for, his white Atef crown was one of a kind. Wsir stood just inside the farm house door, which was now slightly ajar, patiently waiting while inspecting his Crook and Flail. He took his seat when both Siphiwo and Azubuike entered the farmhouse to join him.

"Welcome, honored ones." Wsir was as pleasant as ever. "The time has come."

Siphiwo and Azubuike took up their seats. Azubuike felt a little uneasy so he looked to Siphiwo, in an effort to gauge his demeanor. Siphiwo didn't look like he had any more information than Azubuike did. Yet he was calm and collected. Azubuike was amazed at the type of Meroan Siphiwo was. The man was celebrated as a HRU everywhere he went. Yet, he avoided the praise and preferred to live a humble existence. Although, at the current time, Siphiwo was far more concerned about what they were going to do next. Azubuike decided that he should be as well.

Wsir continued speaking when his guests had settled into their seats, "It is the will of NTR that both of you be returned to the Hueman existence. Each with separate missions, yet neither can succeed without the other. Wsir looked into the eyes of Siphiwo as he spoke, "One will return Ma'at to a state of cosmic balance." Then he shifted his gaze, so he could look into the eyes of Azubuike, "The other will find and protect him, until such time as he is ready."

"M Hsst Ntr, In reverence of Nature," Siphiwo understood his mission. He rose from his seat, prepared to depart, but hesitated when Azubuike did not move.

Siphiwo began to speak, in an effort to answer Azubuike's unvoiced questions. Yet it was Wsir, himself, who addressed Azubuike, "You have questions young Azubuike."

Azubuike struggled with how to even ask the first question, "How could I protect the Hru of Installation Sisu…. He is far more powerful than I am."

Wsir handled the question with ease, as he had been expecting it for some time, "He will not be the Hru of Installation Sisu when you find him. The process for his return is quite different from yours. You will return to your body, Ba will return to the vessel you left behind. However,

Siphiwo must be reborn into a new vessel. While you may, or may not, retain most of these memories, Siphiwo will most likely *not* remember them. Therefore, when you meet again, he will most likely have no knowledge of you, me or his past life. He will be defenseless and he will be your responsibility.

"But first," Wsir held up a hand and displayed a visual of current events occurring in Azubuike's point of reference in space-time. Azubuike could see an Ezalin ship, crewed by Meroans, conducting bombing run operations on the surface of Naijia. "Your friends and family need your help."

That was all he needed to see. He was ready to go back and continue the fight, on behalf of his people. Azubuike had learned to trust in the ancestors. However unrelated these events seemed to be, somehow, the NTRU always had a plan. Still, there was one thing Azubuike had to know. "Will I ever see you again?"

Wsir serenely answered the question he had answered for countless generations. "For you, the next time we meet will signal the end of *this part* of your Hue-man experience."

Azubuike had no problem accepting this answer. These things were uncertain and, at the same time, they weren't. All things were as the NTRU intended them to be. Ma'at would shift back toward balance as the cosmic pendulum swung back toward a neutral position. The trio went out into the clearing, just as Sovereign Roha had before. This time, everyone in the clearing approached both Siphiwo and Azubuike. They wore the same solemn faces as they had when Roha departed the safety and serenity of this place. They spoke similar words of encouragement and unfamiliar phrases in ritual tones. Azubuike could feel his ethereal body deteriorating. Replaced by his own ethereal energy, black in color, because a physical body would no longer be necessary.

As everything began to blur and swirl out of existence, his surroundings also began to disappear. First, the farmhouse. Then the field itself. Then the people started to disappear. The last of which, Wsir, remained in the transient space to see them off. Azubuike could see that Siphiwo had transitioned back into the bright gold energy that far outshined his own. It also outshined anyone else's for that matter. At least anyone that Azubuike had ever known. However, Azubuike was at peace in the knowledge that his own energy shined as brightly as it could. That he had a mission to complete, which could result in his inner light shining even brighter. Azubuike was at peace until he had a troubling thought, that is.

Azubuike collected his thoughts and directed them at Siphiwo's energy which, by this time, was charged full of activity. "How will I find you? How will I know who you are?"

The golden energy, sparkling and crackling with electrical charges, sent its own thoughts back. "The NTRU will guide us to each other's paths. Trust in them, and when they deliver me, you will know who I am. Search for this light. No matter how dim it may be, you will know it is I! Siphiwo, The Hru of Installation Sisu!"

Sabayt Mdty Wa

Commander Themba had the unfortunate luck of having been deployed when Sovereign Azubuike returned from his mission. He was out on a training mission, evaluating potential recruits for the Medjay regiment when he got the news. By the time he got back, he returned to tales of Sovereign Roha and malfunctioning nanites. Everything he'd heard was incredible. Aside from the parts about Azubuike throwing himself into harm's way. That part was believable. He'd been doing it ever since before Themba met him.

Now they were off, or so the Kandake had told him, to an ancient Meroan installation to recover an advantage to use against the Ezalin. As a result of this, he was charged with the defense of Naijia until such time as their return. Themba had no idea how long they could hold out without Medjay and air support. The way things were going thus far, he didn't know how much higher the casualties were going to be either. Still, he had traveled to Naijia to do his duty. As commanded, by the Queen Mother.

Under his command, several divisions were deployed to Naijia in advance of his arrival. He slipped on-planet through the blockade established by the Ezalin, by using dead spots in their orbital patrol routes. Judging by the condition of their fleet, Sovereign Azubuike had left them without enough ships to maintain proper patrol routes. Once landed, he quickly observed the desperation of the situation. The Ezalin blockade and orbital bombardment were both devastating. Hunger and even starvation were widespread among the civilian populations. The "monster" everyone spoke of was a wild card, attacking in random locations at will. Her forces, the Biafar traitors, were only halted by the same orbital bombardments that were affecting Kandake Anima's Egba soldiers.

It was a good idea he'd had extra flights of Keftiu drop ships fitted with nothing but weapons and supplies, to be sent alongside the ground side force toward Naijia. Now all they had to do was hold. After Kandake Anima's forces secured the Temple Authority's guards, the city was put on lock down. All Egbas and reserve soldiers were called to service in this city and every other city under Kandake Anima's control. The national security status was raised to its maximum level and all citizens were alerted. Under this elevated defensive posture, all citizens would have enough time to get within the walls of any Naijian city to seek shelter. After such time as the doors to each city are ordered shut, they will remain sealed until after the duration of the emergency.

While the temple authority traitors were easy enough to subdue, Kandake Anima's loyal forces were still having trouble dealing with the Biafar traitors. Especially now that they seemed to be working with the one called Duro-Aina. Whatever else she really was, she was efficient and effective. Seemingly unstoppable and attacking at will, her advances were only slowed by the Ezalin bombardment aimed at both sides. While she seemed unstoppable, the Biafar traitors were not and she had to accommodate their need to survive an orbital bombardment.

For their part, the Ezalin seemed to have made a permanent enemy out of Duro-Aina. Commander Themba had assumed that they could be working together in some way, but reports were coming in that indicated otherwise. Eye witness accounts report that an invisible monster was making sport out of eliminating Ezalin scouts. Then making brutal examples out of them. Especially if they were broadcasting their war propaganda.

In order to further demoralize the hungry Egbas soldiers, the Ezalin were broadcasting one of their favorite propagandists. Under the advice of Lieutenant Wynch, they allowed one of their most accomplished Ascari propagandists, LuhBee, to take to the airwaves of the battlefields. LuhBee was incredibly affective at demoralizing her own people. Born with black skin but raised to behave as an Ezalin pet, LuhBee led a very privileged life. She, among the Ezalin, uniquely knew how to identify Naijian insecurities. She knew the traditions, behaviors, customs and lifestyles, and she knew how to exploit them.

She took personal pleasure in this. Undermining the freedom of her own people and aiding the enemies of her ancestors. On and on she went, repeating the rhetoric promoted by the former oppressors. She would brag about how her family sold other Meroans into slavery. How they personally chained and delivered other Huemans to the Ezalin. Her family even encouraged young girls to undergo the highly controversial skin whitening process, which had a high rate of failure resulting in cancerous tumors.

One of LuhBee's personal favorites, was to mock the descendants of the enslaved. The very people, whose ancestors her great grandparents threw away. "Akata," she declared them. A word based on the terrible concept of being compared to a wild and senseless beast. Indeed, she had little self-respect and even less dignity. In fact, about the only thing she had very much of was self-hatred. She was filled with it, to the point of overflow, and she radiated that self-hatred out in all directions. LuhBee despised anyone or anything to do with being pro black or even freedom from Ezalin cultural influence. To be honest, LuhBee had no interest in being free of the former oppressor and wanted nothing more than to serve her masters. So she did so at their whim. LuhBee was willing to say and do anything to support the Ezalin war effort. She knew full well that she was a pariah and her family would not be able to depend on the continued protection of the Ezalin, if Naijia was free.

Unfortunately for the Ezalin, Duro-Aina did not take to LuhBee's rhetoric too well. She made her displeasure for LuhBee's antics known by attacking the broadcast stations and destroying them. Out of habit, Duro-Aina never took prisoners and when it came to these radio operators, they were no exception. She often left their mangled bodies on full display on top of their destroyed radio equipment.

Commander Themba thought about all this as he pondered the odds while considering that they may be able to temporarily convince Duro-Aina to agree to a truce. Just long enough for both of them to attack the Ezalin. The Biafar traitors loved the Ezalin but Duro-Aina obviously did not. If they were lucky, the truce could last long enough for Sovereign Azubuike to return with help. In any case, he would have time to think about all that later. The all too familiar warning siren screamed to life in order to alert him. The Biafar traitors were approaching the outer wall again. Commander Themba looked up from an old tactical map laid out across the war table. He walked over to the window and spied a glimpse to where he knew Kandake Anima's position was. He could see smoke rising in the distance and could hear gunfire erupting at the same location. He hoped her plan would work. Either way, he grabbed his weapon and headed for the outer perimeter wall. He wasn't going to find out by sitting in the war room.

Sabayt Mdty Snu

Kandake Anima waited patiently, thought about all the preparations she'd made, and hoped her plan would succeed. She had recalled all military forces and non-combatants into the cities, via planetary distress signal. Each city had its own defense plan, provisions, bunkers and a city-wide reserve commander who would oversee the defense. She was grateful for the last minute arrivals, the forces sent by her counterpart, Kandake Nzinga. They brought additional food and weapons, which were essential. Especially now that the Ezalin were using a blockade to try to starve her cities into submission.

They came from the sky, accompanied by a deafening sound, which signaled large scale ship combat in high orbit. They had chosen an insertion point which would allow them to spread out all over the continent. Mainline Meroan soldiers joined the battles of any nearby cities. They all had orders to integrate themselves into the defensive plans of whichever city they landed closest to. Their commander came much later, and established his command and control center in an empty office within the palace. An older, far more reserved military veteran, Kandake Anima wasn't sure if they were going to be able to successfully work together. Whereas Hezbon would have embraced her plan, this new Commander, Themba, was a lot more cautious. Still, she had convinced the new commander to support her with his troops and now everything was set. The Biafar traitors were coming back, everything was in place and there was no turning back now.

Kandake Anima knew she couldn't hold the walls. Especially not if Duro-Aina showed up. Fortunately for Kandake Anima, the "monster" hadn't yet made an appearance in the area. Her plan was simple, bait the Biafar traitors in the exact same manner that they had trapped her before. They were charging the wall en mass, intent to overrun the outer perimeter wall with sheer force of numbers. However, eight foot deep trenches were dug outside the perimeter wall and covered with simple boards. Unbeknownst to the enemy, a large number of Egbas soldiers were hiding in these trenches as their enemies ran overhead. Each foot step pounded down on the boards and released a bit of dust overhead but everyone remained absolutely still.

Kandake Anima's trench was the closest to the wall, where the bulk of the confusion would occur. She waited, listening for the sound of battle to indicate when she should spring her trap. After the surprise bombing run had disoriented her enemies, they thought twice about attacking the cities. Yet, eventually they came. Anima knew they would and she used the time to upgrade her defensive capabilities. After the air drops from the Meroans, more turrets were installed and the food rationing program was adjusted accordingly. Then she waited for the inevitable charge and, when it came, they were ready. While their enemies ran overhead, the Egbas soldiers calmly waited for one thing.

As soon as she heard the exchange of gunfire, including the distinctive sound of Meroan weapons, Kandake Anima knew it was go time. She started a low, repetitive hum sound that would help deal with the adrenaline spike. She increased the tone and intensity of her repetitive hum until all had joined her. The sound of gunfire and nearby explosions masked their war cries. When Kandake Anima was certain that all had control of their fight or flight mechanism, she looked the nearest soldier right in the eye for assurance. When it was returned, she burst out of the trench into a chaotic environment.

Smoke and dust had reduced the visibility down to nothing. The Egbas soldiers were right on the heels of their Kandake but no one could see anything. The prepositioned explosives had decimated the forward line of the Biafar traitors. They were in complete disarray and nearly blinded by the debris. Kandake Anima and her Egbas soldiers exploded outward in all directions. They pursued the traitors up and down either side of the wall, indiscriminately engaging both active and support elements of their army. Anima's plan had worked perfectly. Their front line had pushed into the city and taken up positions in the first few streets, leaving Anima to spring her trap on the support units. Officers, supply crates and transport vehicles made up her targets.

The Biafar front line consisted mainly of scouts and light infantry, who could not disengage from their battle in the streets with the Meroans. By the time they realized it, their entire flank had been exposed. The Egbas soldiers stole the vehicles they could, planted explosives on the ones they couldn't, and fired at the vehicles that were attempting to make an escape. All Biafar scouts and infantry were either killed or captured, but none escaped Anima's plan.

Commander Themba supervised the surrender of the Biafar traitors his men were still capturing. He could see the Egbas soldiers reentering the city gate and, when the smoke cleared a little more, he could also see Kandake Anima with them. Commander Themba approached, in order to deliver a word of congratulations, "I have to admit, Kandake Anima, an excellent strategy."

"An effective strategy," Anima corrected, "Our casualties were still higher than I'd hoped. Still, we got the job done. They won't try that again for a while."

"But they will try it again," Commander Themba considered the options, "*If* we wait for them in here."

"You're right," Anima agreed, "You've got something don't you?"

"An idea," Commander Themba admitted, "Next time we push them back we need to hit them hard. The Sovereign will be back, it'd be nice if we could take out some of those Anti-Air turrets they've been building recently."

"The scouts have been giving increased reports of new surface to air missile battery construction," Kandake Anima held up a map with rough estimates of AA emplacements drawn on it.

Commander Themba studied the map. Since the Sovereign's bombing run, enemy missile emplacements had been going up all over the place. They were certainly, trying to prevent another surprise attack of that kind. Even though Themba knew their enemy's inventory included nothing that could threaten a capital ship in orbit, the emplacement of the missile batteries were a major threat to drop ships. Something would have to be done if he expected reinforcements. Furthermore, doing nothing would only empower the Biafar traitors to repeatedly attack them and wear down their defenses. "Do you plan to use the trenches again? That could be the perfect mask for a surprise counter attack."

Kandake Anima thought about it. She never did the same thing twice and preferred to remain unpredictable. It was part of what made her so effective, when dealing with her enemies. "No, that won't work again. However, I think there may yet be a way to reuse the trenches to our advantage. We'll pack them with explosives this time...."

Commander Themba immediately recognized her intention, "....and when they inspect the trenches on their next push, they'll get more than they expected. Kandake Anima, I like the way you think."

Kandake Anima and Commander Themba both departed in order to finalize the details of their plan together. The preparations for their counter attack took several hours to prepare. Explosives had to be set and primed, soldiers needed to rest and rearm, and the most practical targets had to be identified. When they were ready, everyone took up positions on the wall. Day turned to evening and, as Anima expected, their enemy had planned another attack to coincide with nightfall. This worked perfectly with Kandake Anima's plan to deceive the enemy, so she ordered all wall lights to be disabled, further adding to her deception.

All was quiet on the wall when the first Biafar scouts became visible. They bounded from cover to cover, in an attempt to conceal their movements. When they were convinced that there was an acceptable level of risk, they began to hastily inspect the trenches for hidden troops. They were not looking for, and missed, the small sets of explosives hidden inside. The scouts signaled for their forward line to move up, and into Kandake Anima's second trap.

As the Biafar scouts confidently moved forward, one lone Egbas soldier quietly activated his radio and transmitted from his observation post on the wall, "They're in the kill zone."

Kandake Anima stood next to Commander Themba, in an O.P. (Observation Post) farther down the wall. She could barely make out the distinctions of patterns moving to and from cover just outside the perimeter wall but, still, she could see them. Her reply was curt, and unsympathetic, "Now."

Multiple large explosions tore through the night, shattering the façade of serenity. Lulled into a false sense of safety, provided by the lack of sound and obvious movement on the part of the Egbas Soldiers, the Biafar traitors were caught off-guard. They were completely unaware of the danger until the first of the explosions went off. Precision shooters popped up from defensive positions all along the wall and started targeting the confused Biafar traitors.

However, Kandake Anima's plan still was not complete. As those closest to the wall turned to flee, more explosions, in the more distant trenches, began to go off. Triggered by remote detonator, the Egbas soldiers were free to set off the explosions when they would be most effective. The wall defenders made short work of the new wave of attack, but that was where this plan went even further than the previous one. Kandake Anima, alongside a well-armed battalion of elite soldiers, was staged to go on an excursion outside the wall. Her target, several surface to air installations that would prevent future reinforcements or resupply.

Kandake Anima knew that if she was going to get off-world assistance, she had to create an opportunity for it. Commander Themba had been right when he suggested the counter attack. The orbital bombardments had temporarily halted when Sovereign Azubuike was in orbit and Ezalin air superiority hadn't yet completely recovered. Now was their chance to conduct surface operations without fear of orbital bombardment. Even more so, Kandake Anima knew that no friendly drop ships were getting in or out of her airspace unless she took down part of the anti-air grid. She had no idea how they planned to get past the Ezalin blockade a second time, though. That part, she would leave up to Sovereign Azubuike.

In the meantime, she weighed her options. Regardless of all other considerations, her only option forward was clear. Disrupt, distract and disorganize the two opposing factions who were currently fighting on her world. Until such time as reinforcement could arrive, to help her drive them all from Naijia for good. To do this, she would have to fight several guerilla style battles. The types of battles her family had great experience fighting in. However, they were also battles, of which, Commander Themba had limited experience. When he'd suggested this counter attack, Kandake Anima decided it was time to make the best uses of each other's strengths.

Commander Themba was an excellent garrison commander. So it was decided, and he agreed, to command the defense of the city while Kandake Anima took her best soldiers behind enemy lines. And behind enemy lines they went. All soldiers burst out of the main city gate and rushed right at the disoriented Biafar traitors. Their enemies never stood a chance. Most of them surrendering without even putting up a fight. When everyone got to a reasonably safe distance, the Egbas soldiers under Kandake Anima's command continued forward. While the soldiers under Commander Themba's command stopped. Naijian and Meroan alike, the soldiers under Commander Themba's authority handed over extra ammunition and field rations to those who intended to go forward. Kandake Anima departed the city in a light wheeled troop transport vehicle. Several, of which, had just arrived to transport her soldiers to their next battle.

Sabayt Mdty Xmt

Several days had passed onboard the stolen Ezalin ship, Old Ironsides, and Oya lamented her displeasure to Sovereign Roha. She knew it was slow, by comparison, but wasn't prepared for the emptiness that would coincide with such a long journey on such a primitive ship. There were no holo-simulators for training purposes. There were no extensive historical references, painted on elaborate designs, built right into the bulkheads. There weren't even any complex computer systems onboard for her to run diagnostic evaluations. Anything to pass the time.

The Huemans had found ways to entertain themselves, though. Seba isolated himself, along with Ayoka, and spent the bulk of the down time studying Meroan capital ship designs. Using information provided by Oya, Seba distracted himself from the anticipation of seeing actual ships made of Meroan construction. Meanwhile, the Medjay were given full medical reviews during the down time, and that was when they weren't reviewing basic training techniques in the hangar bay. They played games, told war stories and competed against each other in marksmanship exercises. Oya had been watching their progress for troublesome medical indicators ever since that unfortunate Tinashe incident and she found none.

For her part, she had quickly grown tired of scouring the Ezalin database on Old Ironsides. She had a complete record of the ship's log, to include everything from previous deployment action to current action. Old Ironsides had been redeployed to Naijia from another world even further from the interior. It seemed that the Ezalin were having trouble maintaining direct control over all worlds under their sphere of influence. The world in question, Isandlwana, was another world embroiled in civil war. As per usual, there were those who did the work of the Ezalin and there were those whose interests were in freeing the people from foreign rulers.

The rebel faction, known for their iconic red war paint, had grown tired of being treated as second class citizens on their own world. So they revolted against the foreign invaders, and anyone who supported them, in an attempt to rid themselves of the Ezalin once and for all. Oya found video and audio files detailing the most recent incidents. In the classified reports, Oya learned about some of the more violent acts of aggression committed by the Ezalin on this distant world. They had created a system, in which they would live as kings while the Huemans would live as slaves. The original people of the world were stripped of all rights and any claim to equal treatment. That is, until a large enough segment of them had had enough.

In honor of their ancestors, they painted their faces, along with their helmets, in bright red war paint and adopted an aggressive posture. However, they did not resort to sabotage or other underhanded techniques. They openly attacked hardened military targets through sheer force of numbers. They were over eighty percent of the population on their world and had no need of secrecy or half measures, so they indulged neither. The previous captain of the Old Ironsides had issued a kill order on the rebel leader. Mamale, the strongest among them, was seen as their highest priority threat. The secret files on Mamale included up to date photos, in which Oya saw a man with conviction and nothing else to lose.

Oya played the video associated with the photos of the man called Mamale. In it, she could see the same man delivering a powerful speech to his followers. Oya did not recognize the language but the Ezalin had already gone through the trouble of translating it for her. "Only death will stop us." Oya intended to make sure to send a delegation to this world. She was certain they would be much needed allies in the war against the Ezalin.

Oya also had access to Old Ironsides' entire

maintenance logs. Blueprints, structural diagrams, loadouts, inventories, crew compliment, and complete maintenance records were all available to her. Oya spent a considerable amount of time implementing ways to make improvements to her ship while simultaneously developing ways to undermine Ezalin technology. Ezalin technology was highly susceptible to electrically charged attack and digital exploits. So Oya focused on streamlining her hacking attempts against their networks. She found as many weaknesses in Ezalin ship design as possible and then formulated the most efficient ways to exploit them.

Oya was running another power efficiency simulation when the navigational computer's proximity alarm sounded, to break the monotony. Oya checked their location to be sure that they were still approaching the outer beacon for their hidden refit station. The time for preparation and planning had finally come to an end. Oya already knew they were close and had alerted Sovereign Roha nearly six hundred seconds prior. She and Roha had been reminiscing about the height of their culture and how it could be rebuilt. They speculated on how future generations might repeat the mistakes of the past, or how they might avoid the same pitfalls. They even collected some of Roha's personal thoughts on current events and saved them as a text file. Roha planned to come back to these files and update them as a personal journal.

However, the time for dwelling on the past had come to an end. Hezbon joined the pair on the bridge, in response to the proximity alarm. He looked out the main viewport and saw- nothing. Save for the empty expanse of space, dotted by the occasional star. There were no other celestial bodies nearby, aside from one orange gas giant. Hezbon knew the gas giant couldn't be their destination. Gas giants are nothing more than dense collections of gasses that have no tangible surface. Hezbon looked again, still not seeing anything jump out at him, and considered checking another view port.

"The gas giant is the distraction," Oya offered an explanation. She'd often forgotten that some information that she took for granted still needed to be explained to her Huemans. A few short years ago, they were still technologically regressed and had much more to learn. "That gas cloud, comprised of cosmic dust and gas, is our true destination."

Hezbon looked at the cloud. It was large, as far as he could see, and they were heading right for it. He didn't understand how they could navigate inside the cloud, since he was unable to see inside the cloud at all. His first instinct was to clarify what he'd heard, "How will we navigate if we're blind?"

"By auto beacon," Oya replied, "Those clouds are fairly extensive. The first explorers were lost in clouds like this one for years before we developed the auto beacon system. Beacons have been pre-placed, like ancient buoys, to transmit the appropriate course. All done on encrypted Meroan channels. Even better, the beacon system will only activate when in close proximity to M.A.R.S. ships. This is a deterrence to pirates, who will never even hear the signal without a standard, military grade M.A.R.S. receiver."

"Ezalin ships don't have M.A.R.S. receivers," Hezbon pointed out, "How will we overcome this small set back?"

"I double as a receiver," Oya joked, "I have the means to access any Meroan system, and bypass them if necessary."

"These security measures, Sovereign Roha chimed in, "Were put in place to prevent anyone from stumbling upon any hidden Meroan installations, unless they already knew of their existence."

"Very effective, indeed," Hezbon had to admit it. Sometimes he often wondered just how his ancestors were undone, when they possessed such a high level of technology.

Old Ironsides was about to breach the threshold of the gas cloud and Sovereign Roha wanted her final assurances, "Can we make it Oya?"

"While this ship is damaged and lightly armored," Oya began, "I believe it will hold up long enough to reach our destination."

"And if it doesn't?" Sovereign Roha asked, "Do you have a plan to prep another ship for our use, in case of emergency?"

"I won't be able to initiate remote contact until we're clear of the clouds interference," Oya explained, "Which is why I recommended all hands board their assigned Keftiu drop ships."

Sovereign Roha looked to Hezbon for confirmation. "All deployments are complete," Hezbon confirmed. "By your authority, Sovereign."

"And the stowaways?" Oya was inquiring about the Ezalin holdouts who were still isolated in various parts of the ship.

"Leave the stubborn to go down with their ship," Sovereign Roha was clear in her response. I have other priorities."

"Handshake established," Oya confirmed, "Taking

us in.

The next stage of their journey took several hours to complete. This particular cloud had a maze large enough to require over fifty evenly spaced beacons. Any one of which could direct them toward a fake course if Oya did not respond to the individual challenges correctly. What's worse, Old Ironsides was literally falling apart. The highly corrosive effects of the gasses held in the cloud began taking their toll on the old ship, almost immediately.

Entire sections of Old Ironsides' battle plating were slowly dissolving and deteriorating. Leaving the hull of the ship exposed and compromised in many locations. It was, in fact, a great suggestion on Oya's part, to have all Meroan personnel already onboard their Keftius. They would get as far as possible in Old Ironsides and, if necessary, abandon ship when it became a floating derelict. Oya had no personal attachment to what she had been referring to as her, "Ezalin life boat." There was nothing especially important about the ship and it had served her purpose. She only hoped it would serve her purposes long enough to get her Huemans close enough to the station. Since she wasn't exactly sure how long a Keftiu could last under such hostile environmental conditions.

Fortunately for Oya, she didn't have to worry about

it. The beacon they were approaching notified Oya, after successfully passing its challenge, that it was the final marker. It gave her the final approach vector for the station and, fifteen minutes later, they were free of the cloud. However, Old Ironsides did not share their fate. Mere moments before they exited the cloud, Old Ironsides began to shake and vibrate dramatically. Loud mechanical groans could be heard throughout the ships as it slowly tore itself apart. Its main supports, too weak to keep the ship together, were snapping and warping in on themselves. Sections of the ship were breaking free of its core frame, of which, the smaller sections were immediately dissolved and absorbed into the gas cloud.

It was time to abandon the primitive ship, and travel the final distance via Keftiu. Sovereign Roha wasn't too disappointed. She was of the logic that no foreign ships should ever disgrace their legacy, by appearing in such close proximity to their classified installations. Even if she, herself, had commandeered said ship, and personally flown it there. Besides, as far as Roha was concerned, she was about to depart the hidden installation in far better technology than she had arrived in.

Dozens of Keftiu drop ships departed both the primary and secondary hangar bays located on Old

Ironsides. From a great distance, their departure resembled that of fireflies buzzing around a bon fire. When in reality, nearly a hundred Keftiu drop ships were fleeing a doomed capital ship as it imploded on itself. Secondary explosions forced the ship to rock back and forth until, finally, its main reactor had suffered enough abuse. Long after all drop ships were clear of the blast radius, Old Ironsides accelerated at an unnatural speed. Likely the sign of a runaway power plant, the ship's surface also began to glow bright orange. All Keftiu view ports auto dimmed, in order to protect the eyes of their occupants. No one was ever encouraged to look directly at a nuclear reactor as it went critical. Even had it not been the only local light source, bright lights of such luminosity, against the dark expanse of space, would almost certainly cause permanent blindness.

All Keftius were accounted for and, as a result of Oya's remote commands, fell in line behind the command shuttle occupied by Roha, Seba and Hezbon. Automated defenses tracked their flight of Keftius but did not engage them. Once the danger of extreme luminosity had passed, Oya had the view ports readjusted and stood by for their reactions. Everyone was amazed. The first, and most obvious, thing to notice was the neat rows of ships that were in the ship yards just outside the station. Every one of them was dark and inactive but they were massive in size. They also looked like nothing any modern Meroan had ever seen in person.

The silence was deafening as everyone took in the view provided by the station. Everyone except Oya, who started providing helpful information in order to break the silence. "Inventory lists forty one ships, but we only have enough crew for about twelve of them. Those would be skeleton crews, barely enough to operate in a prolonged engagement."

Sovereign Roha recognized the station design and, while she hadn't personally visited this particular station, she knew the landing bays did not have enough room for all the Keftius they brought. "Keep all Keftius in a holding pattern until we board the station," Sovereign Roha ordered, "We'll initiate the cold start procedure afterward, and they can board their ships directly."

"What are the odds that we may run into anyone out here?" Hezbon was really asking if there were any other surviving Meroans who could have used this station as a refuge.

"Unlikely," Oya answered, "The station was largely automated to begin with. It had a few high level researchers who would have deactivated all processes and left the station abandoned. If, that is, they followed the established protocols."

"Repositioning Keftius to their ship deployments," Oya confirmed. She then displayed a list of available ships, and their capabilities, for Sovereign Roha. "Which ships would you like to requisition, Sovereign?"

Roha scanned the list and considered her options. Every ship she saw would easily have an advantage over Old Ironsides. The problem was, they were at a top secret Research and Development installation. That meant most of these ships were prototypes. She wouldn't recognize them and that meant they would be completely alien to her new crew, who'd only ever prepped for starship duty in Mount Roha's simulators.

"Nothing fancy," Sovereign Roha decided, "Only choose ships I'm familiar with or, in the very least, are not radically different from what the crew will be familiar with via their simulations."

One lone Keftiu, gold in color and adorned with royal emblems, began a final approach vector for the main landing bay. Commander Hezbon and Seba were accustomed to traveling in the Sovereigns personal Keftiu. Ever since Azubuike had "re"-discovered it in the Aha Mena, the three of them had been using his personal Keftiu on all of their off world missions. This was no different and, as they approached, the hangar bay doors slid open without any hesitation.

"The Sovereign's personal Keftiu is equipped with a challenge package," Oya offered, "The station's automated countermeasures are expecting us."

The station itself took on the typical characteristics of Meroan engineering. Sleek surfaces, seamless entry points, primarily automated, grand in scale and highly advanced. Predominantly painted in red, black, green and purple colors, no one could mistake this structure for anything other than of ancient Meroan design. They always built big, as evident by the various spires that rose up above the rest of the structure. There were four main sections to the actual ship yards, which were constructed on each adjacent wall of the central command center. Therefore, each individual shipyard was commonly referred to as its degree number (a designated angle respective to the command center). For example 90, 180, 270 and 0.

In each shipyard, the ships were kept in neat rows of bays that were evenly spaced from their neighbors, with enough room to conduct complete overhaul operations. The trio, and their escort, were standing in the primary hangar bay. Not far from the command center, the crew would only need to travel a short distance to reach their destination. The receiving bay, or main hangar bay, was large in size and largely empty. Aside from the overabundance of maintenance gear, and seating options, there wasn't much to look at. The receiving bay was primarily designed to serve one purpose, to temporarily hold large numbers of transient passengers as they moved to and from their assigned ships.

For the convenience of senior level personnel and VIP's, the Command Center for the station was not located too far away from the receiving bay. In fact, the entrance to the restricted area could be seen on the far side of the receiving bay. It was eerily quiet as they crossed the distance. Normally, someone of Roha's stature would have been formally greeted, with full honors, by the station commander and his staff. However, at least it wasn't eerily dark at the same time. The automatic lighting system activated whenever it detected their movements. Still, nothing moved anywhere in the receiving bay aside from the three of them. Before long, Roha, Seba and Hezbon stood in front of the main control console and prepared to activate it. Roha would need to give Oya direct access to the console, which she did by using a small auxiliary port just to the side of it.

Once she had access to the system, Oya pulled up various schematics, diagrams and ship summaries to display. One such diagram showed the power distribution system for the station and the adjacent ship yards. Every ship had been completely powered down and inactive for centuries. They required a cold start procedure which could be most easily initiated with the assistance of the station. The station, itself, had several powerful main reactors which could jump start ships. The station's main power grid would be required to initiate any docking and undocking procedures as well, so Oya initiated the startup procedure for the stations main power systems.

It would take from several hours to a full day for the station to achieve a full power status. However, with one reactor online they could provide power to initiate the cold start procedure on a few of the ships in a single ship yard. The only thing to do was make the decision on which shipyard. Oya thought the shipyards at ninety degrees would meet the requirements set by Sovereign Roha. Based on that previous assumption, Oya used the first fully powered reactor to bring that shipyard to life. Docking clamps, lighting and various machinery powered on and resumed their natural states.

"The station has begun the cold start procedure on

eight ships. We're going to be running skeleton crews as it is, but eight was as many as I felt comfortable with." Oya was already concerned with how well the crew would react to real world fleet action. She didn't want to overwhelm them as well. "Given the uncertainty of the crew's abilities."

"Agreed," Roha did not hesitate to ally her opinion with Oya's. "Have you assigned my temporary flag ship?"

"Temporary?" Seba and Hezbon both asked in unison.

"Absolutely temporary," Sovereign Roha confirmed. "The Aha Mena will always carry my flag. No matter its condition. There is no ship that can even remotely compare…."

"I still agree with you Sovereign," Oya politely cut in, "However, there's been some *recent* improvements to the frame and design of the ship. Please come with me, Sovereign. I have a surprise for you."

Oya projected herself, in full size, in front of the Huemans under her care. The four of them walked to shielded glass and observed the ship she indicated. "Designated, the Memnon. This ship is the only known prototype of its kind to exist. It was solely designed to replace the Aha Mena as the current pinnacle of Meroan technology. A prototype, it is only about three quarters of the full size of what the final design would be. Still making it one of the largest ships in your new fleet. However, it lacks the size and armament of the original Aha Mena. Damage output and shield ratings will all be lower than what you're used to. The main selling point of this platform is its dual cores. While the over drive still exists, you should have much less *need* of it now. Due to the fact that there are now two fully independent cold fusion cores on board. That means the hard light shields and main engineering are each powered by their own reactors."

"Wait a minute," Roha interjected, "Are you telling me someone designed a new ship for me and gave me **two** engineering departments?"

Sovereign Roha thought about all the battles she'd ever been in, about what she could have achieved if she'd been at the helm of an Aha Mena that had two hearts in it. Her moment of serenity was cut short by Oya's minor correction, "Not two engineering departments, Sovereign, but a new type of cold fusion process which entails components of the antimatter research that I am not privy to. The result, of which, allows two slightly weaker "twin cores" to operate within the same containment vessel. They can even be operated in tandem to create a barely controlled state of overload, which should result in even higher levels of energy production. Even more impressive is this, the the slightly weaker cores are justified by the fact that each one is powering a primary system individually. Meaning they should be much more effective at those tasks than when a single, more powerful reactor, was providing the power source to them simultaneously."

Oya finished her point with a bit of humor, since her three charges were clearly convinced of the superiority of this ship, "All things considered, it is still not the Aha Mena but it is a close second and, in my opinion, is a remotely close comparison."

"I have to admit it, Oya, I'm impressed." Roha smiled at the prospect of taking such a ship into battle. If only the Aha Mena had these upgrades during the final stand at KMT. The battle could have turned out so differently."

"Just wait until you see the stories they've told about you throughout these corridors," Oya joked, knowing full well that Roha detested the spot light that came with being featured on one of these corridor's walls. All Meroan warships had murals on the bulkheads, which told of their greatest triumphs. Usually, the stories were involved, in some way, with the figure the ship was named for.

However, Roha was a little curious as to how the scribes tied her failures and accomplishments to the mythical stories of Memnon of Troy.

"You know me so well," Roha replied, with genuine interest. "When will we be ready to board? Can we go over now?"

Oya had already prepped the docking procedure for the Memnon, "Come Sovereign, your chariot awaits."

The flight over to their new ship wasn't a particularly long one. During which, they could see the Memnon enter its pre-ignition phase. Indicated by the soft glow of main engineering's main coils, which were intensifying as they warmed up. The cold start procedure used a series of A.P.U. (Auxiliary Power Unit) generators, located throughout the ship, to power the main engines. Once powered themselves, the A.P.U.s would require a minimum of ninety minutes to provide enough power to attempt ignition. During which time, the Meroans used the delay to transport and situate each crew.

Seba, Hezbon and Sovereign Roha were on the bridge of the Memnon having a discussion about their troop placements when the duration of that ninety minutes finally elapsed. Oya interrupted their conversation with an update, "All ships have completed their pre-ignition procedures and all diagnostic reports indicate we're in the green. We're ready for ignition."

"Give me the other ship captains," Roha wanted to address them personally.

When they appeared in her H.U.D. Roha spoke one last word of confidence. "I've reviewed all of your training simulation's statistics. You are the right men and womb-men for the job. Are there any concerns? Now is the time to voice them."

Sovereign Roha waited for anyone to speak up. When no one did, she continued, "Then you are cleared for ignition. Engage in undocking procedures in sequential order from my flag. After we've cleared the shipyards Oya will provide your course."

Sovereign Roha cut off the connection between her and her ship captains. Then, turned her attention to Hezbon. "We don't know what we'll be walking into once we get there. I want the simulators running nonstop until we get there. Make sure the priority goes to those who need it most."

"It will be done, sovereign." Hezbon gave the royal salute and left the bridge to get the Medjay into a training cycle.

Now, it was Seba's turn. "Young one…. running

my engineering department can be a bit, *demanding*. Do you think you're prepared for this task?"

"I do, Sovereign," Seba replied, confidently. "My record speaks for itself."

"Indeed, it does," Roha agreed out loud. "And it should. This is one of the children?"

Roha directed her question to Oya and waited for the reply. "Yes, Seba is one of the children directly impacted by The Bennu Project."

Seba heard it for himself and, yet, he wasn't so sure, "But I don't have any memories."

It was Roha who offered the explanation. "We only possessed the capacity to send one mind, but there was plenty of room for necessary skills. We've long known how to program experience into the minds of the young."

Roha could see the doubt leave Seba's face as he considered this. So she continued, "We chose from the greatest minds. Generations of specialists contributed their thoughts to this database. Yes, young Seba. You too, are touched by The Bennu Project."

Seba had reached another conclusion and wanted his assumption confirmed. "Does this mean that we're all touched by it?"

"It does," Oya replied. "Consider what sending a

mind forward would mean if there were no support. What sort of help would a Sovereign need for the project to have a favorable outcome? Based on these assumptions I chose a Satiu Archer, an Engineer, and a Medical specialist but there are many patterns stored here."

Seba was stunned. He never once considered that he was part of the honor directly associated with The Bennu Project. After a long pause of thinking it over, he realized the Sovereign was waiting for him to speak. "My apologies Sovereign Roha but, yes, I think I can handle this."

"I've heard many engineers say that before," Roha joked. "Just keep your calm and do your best to keep up with me. And don't take anything personal, young Seba."

Roha directed her next comments toward Oya, "You will be responsible for relaying my commands to the bridge crew. They are to treat this as a live fire exercise and follow all of my commands immediately. If there is any delay then you are to initiate the command. Work with young Seba for the duration of our trip back. He is to know everything he can about these twin coils and the anti-matter elements inside of them."

"He will be ready, Sovereign," Oya agreed.

"Thank you, for this honor, Sovereign Roha." Seba gave the royal salute, before exiting the bridge.

As her subordinates went about their tasks, Sovereign Roha consulted her medical data. The readings were increasingly moving toward worrisome results. Indicating that her remaining time was draining faster than she'd anticipated. She hoped she could get back to that planet to keep her promise this time.

Sabayt Mdty Fdu

Several days of both intensive training and study passed onboard the Memnon as they made their way back to Naijian space. All ships were still operating well into the green and their projected time to arrive inside Naijian space was under forty minutes. Long range scans were beginning to pick up contacts at extreme range but it would be another few minutes before the Memnon's Heru turrets would be in range.

"Oya, choose and prioritize Heru turrets to high value targets as soon as we're in range," Sovereign Roha ordered.

"If I may," Oya objected, "With your permission, this may be the time to display that surprise I mentioned."

When Roha didn't object, Oya ordered an oddly shaped ship to increase its speed so that it pulled out in front of the formation. All other ships stopped short of it when it took up a firing position. Oya made sure there was plenty of space around the ship so that there would be no collateral damage. Then she opened a comm link to the captain. "Fire the weapon," she ordered.

The shield on the oddly shaped ship dropped, leaving the ship unprotected. A moment later the hull of the long, skinny ship began to hum with a bright blue tint. The humming grew in frequency along with the intensity of the blue tint until the tint became hot white. A bubble of distorted space time began to form around the ship, collapsing the gravity well around it. It was fortunate that Oya had taken the precaution, any ship in the vicinity of the prototype weapon would have been damaged. Wisps of energy, origin unknown, were appearing within the bubble and then rushing to be collected by the ships hull. This went on for several seconds until the energy around the prototype ship attenuated and leapt out toward its target.

A familiar energy began to spark and crackle along the entire length of the ship. This new weapon was a Shango weapon, someone had taken the Shango heavy weapon and made it into an entire ship. The occupants of the ship could feel the static electricity building up around them as a result of the weapon's charge. Those on the ships nearest to the experimental weapon saw their screens and H.U.D.s flicker with distortions. That bright, white-hot light operated as a throw stone for the charge of electricity that was building within the ship.

Sovereign Roha rose from her chair and moved directly toward the end of her raised platform. Like many of the bridge crew, she wanted to see this weapon fire with her own eyes. When it finally did, the resulting amount of energy that was released was absolutely terrifying. Roha wasn't surprised. Any weapon that drew its energy from an unknown power source in subspace was going to be impressive. However, the ship had some limitations. The ship had to be isolated in combat due to the high chance of collateral damage. It had no other long or medium range weapons. Because of this, and the fact that it would be immediately designated as a high value target, the designers had stacked as many defensive options onto the platform as they could. The ship was more than capable of defending itself from any medium sized ship of comparable armor and it had enough anti fighter turrets to deter several flights of fighters. The problem, and main liability, was in the delay of time it took to re-activate the shield after the weapon fired. Not to mention the slow recharge time. It really only left one tactical option for the ship. Allow it to fire the first few salvos and then use it as bait when the enemy closed the distance. If they didn't, they were fish in a barrel.

A giant bolt of bright hot energy leapt out of the ship, arcing and twisting as it went. It followed the general direction of the line of travel set by the white-hot light and impacted the Ezalin ship it encountered there. The shields briefly attenuated before they popped like a fragile bubble in the breeze. The armor that wasn't destroyed on impact was boiled away as the remaining energy discharged from the ship. The duration of the weapon's firing sequence was fifteen seconds. During that time, the initial target ship served as a conduit and doomed the ship nearest to it. The powerful energy arced away from the original ship to include the next target into its stream. Now both ships were being hit by the energy. Sovereign Roha was impressed by the fact that the weapon's energy could leap targets in the middle of its firing sequence. A third ship was even impacted, but not destroyed even though it suffered moderate damage.

The Ezalin fleet reacted exactly like she thought they would. By predictably charging a superior weapon in an attempt to cut off its greatest ally, distance. "Charge the weapon again," Roha commanded. "Form a firing line on either side of the Shango ship, be sure to leave enough room. Oya, you have the Heru turrets. Prep all fighters but, do not launch!"

The fleet moved into position, creating a firing line with the Shango ship at its center. Three ships were on either side of it, with the Memnon slightly above and further back. The Ezalin fleet had called in support and increased the size of their fleet. That didn't bother Roha in the slightest, she wanted a larger fleet so she could send a larger message. The entire blockade on the near side of the planet reacted to the firing of her terrible weapon by moving into attack formation and closing the distance. Oya issued firing orders to all ships in the fleet. They were to use their Heru turrets to pick off any ships on the wings who strayed too far from the center of their formation. She wanted them as close to their core as they could be.

Twelve minutes later the incredible energy from the Shango ship fired again. Hitting another seven ships in the center of their formation, distributing the energy evenly among them. When the bulk of those affected ships imploded, the enemy fleet commander must have figured out the strategy. All of their ships were ordered to loosen their attack formation and enforce an evenly spaced distance from each other. Yet all of them were still on a collision course with the Shango ship. Judging by their attack speed, Oya estimated that she would have one more cycle of the full firing sequence. Before they would be too close.

The weapon charged again, but this time the Ezalin were inside firing range and loosed their entire initial salvo at the Shango ship. To their own disappointment, all of their missile and projectile weapons fell short of impacting with their target. Instead, they were warped and destroyed by the distortion in time space created by the Shango ship's firing sequence. Along with the first two waves of fighters and bombers, none of these weapons were able to penetrate the sub space bubble. The weapon fired again, this time finding an isolated battleship. One of the largest capital ship designs in the Ezalin fleet. It was the highest priority target, a suspected command and control ship, since the enemy was no longer grouping together.

As suspected, the Shango ship was momentarily defenseless and the enemy was far too near for Sovereign Roha's comfort. "Deploy all fighters," She ordered. Hueman fighters form a screen around the Shango ship until it is capable of rejoining the fight. Impundulu fighters are with me."

"And where are we going Sovereign?" Oya asked.

Sovereign Roha retook her seat on the raised platform and opened a channel to her ship captains, "All ahead at full power. Follow my lead."

Sovereign Roha closed the channel to her captains and opened another on the frequency designated for emergencies. "To all Meroan forces this is Sovereign Roha. Anyone on the ground please respond."

There was no response. At the same time, there wasn't any static either. Oya ran a diagnostic on the communications equipment. When it had completed, she reported the situation, "I've resent the signal across all known Meroan frequencies. We're transmitting just fine and they're receiving you as well. We're getting incomplete return packages, increased signal degradation. They're likely being jammed at the source."

"So they can hear me," Roha thought to herself, "To all Meroan forces, signal yourselves if you are in immediate need of reinforcement. We have returned to aid you, but you must aid us by clearing landing zones and crippling their anti-air capabilities."

Sovereign Roha briefly consulted her H.U.D. to retrieve the map Hezbon had made based on his time spent reviewing the micro satellite's most recent images. "Consult the attached and stand ready. More to follow in six hours, mark."

Sovereign Roha consulted the micro satellite for any indication that her message was received. Hundreds of purple flares could be seen from orbit shooting into the sky. They were quickly followed by a flurry of activity. Both attacks and counter attacks were launched by all sides participating in the ground conflict. She had made it, her promise fulfilled and personal guilt assuaged. Roha took a moment to enjoy the feeling of relief but was interrupted by a dizzy spell, one she quickly tried to hide from everyone else. One she never could hide from Oya, either.

"Another D.M.T. suppressant," Sovereign Roha said, flatly. She was in no mood to have this conversation with Oya, who'd been monitoring her vitals.

"You can't prevent this," Oya said, in response, as she administered the medication. "The maximum safe dosage in such a short time is two uses, and you're on three."

"I just need a little longer," Roha forced her words through gritted teeth.

The Ezalin capital ships were close enough to move alongside Roha's own ships. There was even one on a direct course for the Memnon, a collision course. Roha waited until the Memnon was much closer to the enemy ship, to be sure he wouldn't alter course, "Z-35, now!"

The Memnon "descended" in space to a point where it was directly beneath the enemy ship. "Fire all starboard batteries! Quarter rotation to port. Give me a revolution matching its speed, around the target."

Roha was looking for the "seam" on every ship. The location where the turret's defensive fire coverage was at its weakest. The result of her commands, was the Memnon revolving around its target as it repeatedly gave broadside barrages to it. Everything on the ship unexpectedly listed. Objects, and even people, were sliding toward the bulkheads.

Down in engineering, Oya appeared to an increasingly nervous looking Seba, "This is just the beginning." She spoke to him as she administered a mild sedative. Then she lowered his suit temperature by four degrees Celsius. "You're going to have to relax a little more before the end of this."

Back on the bridge Oya reappeared to Roha in a slightly humorous manner, "It's their first time, Sovereign. Maybe not so fast."

"I wasn't expecting it to be so quick," Roha admitted. "It doesn't have the weight."

Sovereign Roha continued her revolution until she found the seam. Then halted her ship's movements until they matched that of her target. The ship began to break apart while Roha collapsed to the floor. Oya appeared just over her as she spoke her final commands, "Help him, Oya. He will need you to teach him how to command the Aha Mena."

"Good bye, old friend," Oya knew this day would

eventually come, yet she never considered what she would actually say when it did.

"Would they tear me from this life, even though my task is incomplete?" Sovereign Roha forced the words until they came out, until everyone on the bridge had heard them.

"It is not your task to complete," came the lone reply from some place just off the bridge of the Memnon.

Three lights, two extremely bright, were on the bridge of the Memnon. Unseen by anyone else as the lights existed somewhere between the current plane and that of Sovereign Roha's mind. The bright light of Siphiwo was accompanied by that of Azubuike and Roha. Roha, now free of her Hueman constraints, took on a slightly less urgent tone in her words, "I have done all I can, the rest is in your hands."

Azubuike had considered a life without Roha many times. Never, once, did he ever consider that he would actually have to face the day when it would happen. "I don't think I can do all this without your help, at least not on my own."

Roha moved closer to Azubuike and concentrated on directing her thoughts to him, along with a soothing urge to reassure him, "You will not be alone. Oya has patterns of my memories, for your use. The experiences we've given to your friends should begin to manifest themselves even more effectively."

Sovereign Roha directed her next thoughts to Siphiwo, "Always in passing."

"Agreed," Siphiwo's words were saturated with regret, "But at least this will be the last transition for you."

"For a while, at least," Roha agreed.

Siphiwo collected himself and directed his thoughts in a more hopeful tone, "Our time to depart has arrived, and may the fortune of the ancestors guide our choices and the rest of our Hueman experiences."

Azubuike couldn't figure out why, but he had to ask a question that had been nagging him ever since he'd first made a transition to meet with his ancestors. "Roha, Why are our colors different? What do they mean?"

Roha thought about it and opted to go with the most direct answer she could give, "Each color is different because it reflects the different motivations of each Meroan at our core. The most common of which are Red for the blood of our people, Gold for the Kemetic Sciences, Black for the Meroan Republic and Green for life. The brighter your light shines, the more in touch you have become with the Ntru."

Siphiwo offered one last word of advice before the three departed to their own paths, "When you find me, young Azubuike, I will be with one whose light shines green."

The three lights moved away from each other, simultaneously, and then disappeared.

Sabayt Mdty Diu

Azubuike awoke several hours later, in his private quarters, alone in his thoughts. The moment he did, Oya joined him without delay. As if she'd been waiting for him to rejoin the Hueman experience. Azubuike was grateful for her company, any company really, because he had questions that needed answers. The only thing he knew was that he was in excruciating pain and that some events in his memory weren't quite adding up. He felt disoriented and confused, yet reassured by the fact that Oya was there waiting for him. The first thing she did was assess his vitals and administer a mild pain reliever.

"What happened?" Azubuike spoke, as the medicine did its work to take the edge off.

"That, is a very vague question sovereign Azubuike," Oya began. She decided to give Azubuike the relevant data without sugar coating anything for him, "After your defeat in the battle against Duro-Aina, Roha was empowered temporarily. She took up the fight and, she too, was defeated. Under her guidance we traveled to a hidden installation to procure the ships that make up your new fleet. Sovereign Roha made her final transition during the initial battle to break the Ezalin blockade. That battle

concluded in an Ezalin retreat to the other side of Naijia.
Our position is in high orbit above the main city, where
we're currently supporting a number of campaigns-"

Azubuike shot straight up, the painful look on his
face was unmistakable, "We're involved in active
campaigns on the ground at this very moment??"

Azubuike did not wait for a response from Oya.
Instead, he keyed his wrist device and generated a three
dimensional holographic representation of their fleet. The
fleet's position, relative to Naijia, the Ezalin fleet and the
surrounding space were displayed. He then zoomed in on
the planet and adjusted the display filters to show only
active combat scenarios. There were hundreds of them, in
various locations all over the planet. It seemed as if the
entire planet was in conflict. Azubuike was watching, in
real time, the state of their counter invasion involving
Naijia. Some of the hotspots displayed were of low priority
because they were isolated incidents indicative of scouts or
recon activity. However, other hotspots were of significant
intensity. Usually located near cities or military
installations, these hotspots were of the highest priority.

Azubuike had seen enough, "Where are my
commanders?"

Oya keyed Azubuike's H.U.D. then tagged the

locations of Hezbon and Themba. She also included the locations of Seba and Ayoka, so that he could see all four of them on his holographic map. Seba was in engineering and Hezbon was on his way, along with the medic usually posted to the bridge. Commander Themba was in the main city below and Ayoka was unable to pinpoint, as per usual.

Hezbon entered Azubuike's private quarters and ordered the medic to assist him in transporting the Sovereign to the bridge.

"I'll be walking under my own power," Azubuike politely refused any assistive devices. The nanites were doing enough to help him stand upright as it was. Besides, the pain was already subsiding and his thoughts were becoming clearer. "I could use a shoulder to lean on, though."

Hezbon positioned himself to the left of Azubuike so that he could put a hand on Hezbon's shoulder. Once Azubuike could rest the bulk of his weight on Hezbon's shoulder, he was able to walk without much more assistance.

"Oya," Azubuike turned his attention back toward his A.S.E., "How did you-"

"Your adrenaline was spiking," Oya interrupted him, "Your vitals were also increasingly sporadic. I knew that you would want to deploy and there was little chance of changing your mind. So I arranged transportation for you as soon as you realized we were running active operations."

That was enough to satisfy Azubuike's curiosity. Apparently, Oya was beginning to know him just as well as she had known Roha. He wondered, to himself, where and when Roha currently was. Then he reminded himself, almost in a humorous tone, that time was relative. So he resigned to simply say a prayer to his ancestors on behalf of Roha, hoping that she was okay. They arrived to the bridge before a bewildered bridge crew, and they needed some sort of explanation. Azubuike could see his subordinates, and the confusion set on their faces, all the way from the raised platform.

"In the interest of time," Azubuike spoke as loud as he was able, "I'll have to keep this brief. I know that many of you are confused by recent events that have taken place onboard this ship. I don't have an easy explanation for you. All I can tell you is that Sovereign Roha has gone to her well-deserved, time honored rest. She is walking amongst the Ntru and will not return to us. Our ancestors have done all they intend to do, at this point, and the rest is up to us. I'll need all of you working at your best, in order to help me honor them by succeeding here."

The bridge crew seemed to accept this explanation and moved with a sense of urgency. Everyone went about their tasks with renewed vigor, at the thought of Azubuike's return. The fact that he sounded confident, and had a plan, served to energize those under his command. Azubuike and Hezbon took up their places around the bridge's holographic map. While they waited, Seba joined them on the bridge and immediately moved toward the raised platform. He had to stop himself from embracing his brother, once he saw the apprehension in his body language.

"I've been there," Seba said, "It will pass in time."

Seba and Azubuike both shared a meaningful look, regarding the time Seba fell victim to an artillery blast, as Ayoka materialized on her side of the holographic map. No one even flinched at her appearance, they were all too used to her entrances by now.

Ayoka wasted no time opening an encrypted channel to Azubuike and her other brother. "Don't ever do that again, brother."

"I saw what you did for me sister," Azubuike's response was genuine and grateful. "Your aim and calm demeanor saved my life. Both, of which, I will need once more. Will you join me again?"

"Of course, brother," Ayoka did not hesitate. "Where you go, I go. On one condition," Ayoka joked, "Call your wife first."

The three siblings had a laugh before they cut the private channel. Azubuike, making a mental note to actually call Nosizwe before they were groundside. He didn't know when he would have the chance to speak to her again. He knew she had to be worried. It was explained that she'd seen, and cared for, him during his journey to the Field of Reeds but he had not personally seen her since he left Mount Roha.

Now that they were all in attendance, it was time for Azubuike to make his intentions clear. "Hezbon, what is our strategic outlook for this invasion? Where is the highest priority?"

Hezbon reached for the map and zoomed in on the capital city beneath them. Afterward, he moved the map just to the outside of the city to show a fresh attack taking place. Commander Themba and his defenders were keeping the Biafar traitors at bay, but an entirely separate army was approaching from the opposite direction. Made up of Ezalin soldiers, Azubuike knew they had to act fast or else Commander Themba would have to fight two armies instead of one. A prolonged siege, with two armies fighting each other over the city, would not go well for Commander Themba and his soldiers.

"You intend to reinforce the city?" Azubuike asked.

"Actually, no, Sovereign." Hezbon moved the map slightly outside the city so that a new installation appeared. Just behind the approaching Ezalin, Azubuike could see their forward base of operations.

Azubuike was beginning to realize Hezbon's plan, "A bold move. How are we going to get there? Those anti-air gun emplacements are pretty well constructed."

"We'll come down in four waves," Hezbon moved the map so that everyone could see the great forest which ranged from the city's outskirts all the way to the Ezalin forward base. "Using the tree tops to mask our approach, I am reasonably sure that we can get as close as twenty kilometers before we're detected. Each wave will have a different objective but all of us will rendezvous at these coordinates."

Hezbon moved the map one final time. It displayed a clearing large enough to double as a foothold for a forward operating base of their own, if they could get to it.

Azubuike had seen enough. He now understood the entirety of the plan and the only thing left to do was for him to order the mission. So he did, "Let's go, I want to have

Commander Themba reinforced before the end of today's cycle."

"Sovereign Azubuike…," Oya attempted to caution Azubuike about his medical condition but never got that far.

"If we lose this city we lose everything," Azubuike made his declaration as plain as he could make it. "This is our only major foothold on this world and only our direct intervention can salvage this situation. As I have said, I'm ready to depart."

Azubuike surveyed each one of them as he decided how he wanted to deploy them. He knew he was injured, so he planned to keep Hezbon close by. At least until he was in full fighting shape, himself. "Hezbon, you're with me. We're riding the first wave in."

Azubuike also knew he would need Ayoka in the field. Her ability to wreak havoc behind enemy lines was incredibly useful. "Ayoka, you're in the second wave. Get to ground, and hit that enemy column hard. But only hit them once. After you've halted their advance, make your way to the rally point."

"I understand," Ayoka agreed. "We'll slow them down."

"Good," Azubuike confirmed. "After you've gotten

your platoon on track to the rendezvous, try to hit some of those fixed gun emplacements along the way."

"Seba," Azubuike usually kept his little brother in the back, away from the bulk of any direct conflict. "This time will be different. I'll need you on the ground in the vanguard. Bring up the rear, deliver our heavy vehicles to the field and construct any hasty defenses you can. We'll need a fall back point and you're it."

"You can count on me to be there, brother." Seba was more than confident in his words. Which was a good sign, Azubuike was sure he would come to depend on Seba's abilities once they were in the thick of the battle.

When there were no more tactical questions, everyone departed for the hangar bay to board their assigned Keftiu drop ships. Hezbon's wave would go first, clearing the way for Sovereign Azubuike to come in just behind. The third wave consisted of Ayoka and her troops, while Seba brought up the rear. Azubuike made a small detour to the bridge's armory in order to upgrade the nanites that comprised his protective armor. While Oya was taking care of that, she also took the time to administer a slightly stronger pain reliever. She did not want Azubuike's senses to be dull, so she only used a low grade medication meant to block the pain receptors. He would still feel his injuries but they would be dull and much less intense.

Azubuike boarded his Keftiu, saw the familiar faces of his closest guards and immediately hailed Hezbon. When Hezbon's image appeared in his H.U.D., Azubuike brought up the Medjay's newest member. "What has happened to Tinashe? That look in his eyes...."

Hezbon gave Azubuike a brief summary of what had occurred in the mountain, regarding the chaos nanites. To his surprise, Azubuike didn't seem that shocked by the story. "You're not surprised by this new threat, Sovereign?"

Azubuike thought about everything he'd been through recently, "The things I've seen Commander.... Speaking of which, I know what you did for me back on Naijia. You have my deepest gratitude."

"And you have my deepest apologies," Hezbon immediately added, thinking about the way they had been so ineffective against Duro-Aina. "The Medjay will not fail you like that again."

"I'm glad you feel that way Commander," Azubuike smiled, "Because we're about to test that vow very soon."

Azubuike spent the duration of the trip easing into his new set of armor. Breaking in new nanite suits was always a hassle because the new nanites tend to give wearers an "itchy" sensation, while they adjusted themselves to the skin of the new wearer. On the bright side of things, the pain in his body had nearly subsided completely. He caught himself thinking a thought to Roha before he realized she was no longer there to answer him.

"Is she gone for you too?" Azubuike said aloud.

"Indeed, she is," Oya responded. "I do not mourn her, though. Roha deserved to transition, and this should be viewed as a joyous accomplishment for her. She earned her right to walk among her ancestors many times over."

Azubuike did not find the comfort he was looking for, in Oya's words. Azubuike felt an incredible emptiness without Roha's guidance and he was having some difficulty dealing with it. Giving up on finding a solution to that problem, he decided to call Nosizwe on an encrypted channel and attempt to get a message to her. They spoke of nothing of consequence. Nosizwe could tell that Azubuike wasn't quite himself and she'd seen the backdrop of his Keftiu enough to know when he was going on a mission. She decided to keep the conversation on lighter topics, so they spoke of other things. She brought up their childhood, Azubuike's grandfather, Councilor Melisizwe, and the day Nosizwe had proposed the joining of their families. They were in the middle of discussing Nosizwe's intention to have Azubuike take a much needed rest, when the collision alarm sounded.

"My attention is needed," Azubuike let out a sigh as he prepared to say goodbye to Nosizwe. "Mr.i Tu Hmt.i"

"Be safe, my love," Nosizwe replied. "Aha Tu."

Azubuike shut off the encrypted channel and mentally prepared himself for combat. "Status, Oya."

Oya appeared with a map ready for Azubuike's view. "Hezbon has come under intense anti-air fire. Newly constructed and very efficient. His flight path is compromised, we have to deviate."

"We're going in right behind Hezbon," Azubuike was firm yet calm in his decision. "If we deviate now we'll be scattered to the wind."

Oya reassessed the gun emplacements and found that she agreed with Azubuike after all. The enemy gun emplacements were deployed in such a way that they created a kill zone of anti-air fire. They were in it now and Azubuike had the right idea: stay calm and fly through. Any deviation now would increase their risk of being shot down. "I absolutely love when you speak to her before missions, she does wonders for your vitals." Oya added.

Hezbon was in one of the lead Keftius at the front

of the first wave. Much farther ahead than Azubuike, which meant he was getting the brunt of the anti-air fire. He keyed a warning back to Azubuike, yelling over the numerous alarms and explosions attempting to drown him out.

"Sovereign!" Hezbon's words were cutting out, due to the distortion caused by nearby explosions, "We're under heavy fire! We're not going to make the insertion point without additional air cover."

Oya checked the troop deployment schedule and re-checked the holographic map, even though she already knew they didn't have any assets near enough to make the difference. She showed Azubuike the bad news in his H.U.D.

"That's a negative on the air support, Commander," Azubuike informed Hezbon. "We'll have to move the L.Z. up."

The Keftiu next to Hezbon was shredded in a hail of anti-air shrapnel while he consulted the back-up L.Z.s on his holographic map. Hezbon quickly shut it down and chose the best one he'd seen thus far. One of the closer ones. Hezbon tagged his current location as a possible search and rescue site. Then he tagged Azubuike to alert him to the hastily chosen landing zone. Finally, Hezbon opened a comm channel to the pilot of his dropship, "Get us down now!"

Hezbon's drop ship never made it to the landing zone. They were shot down on approach, six kilometers short of their destination. Azubuike passed the word about the change in plans to both Seba and Ayoka. Both, of whom, were now also under heavy fire on approach. Ayoka, was diverted further into the tree line. Her mission did not need to put her at undue risk. With her reasonably safe, Azubuike tagged the S.A.R. coordinates for her. Her new orders were to swing by there, and check for survivors, on her way to the new rally point. After she'd harried the enemy's rear guard.

Seba, on the other hand, had all the heavy weapons and vehicles in his flight of Keftiu drop ships. Azubuike was entering the kill zone of anti-air fire and could feel the increase of explosions all around him. He called Seba immediately, "Turn back, L.Z. is hot! Do not land!"

"Where else are we supposed to go?" Seba, incredulous, looked at the holographic map of his tactical situation. There was no turning back. His drop ships were too slow, with the added weight, to try to make it back through the way they came. His best chance to make it out of this was to punch right through, and try to make it as close to Hezbon's position as he could. Survivors would need a nearby fall back point and Seba had to get deployed fast if he was going to help them.

Ayoka came down in the trees after fast roping out of her drop ship. She wasted no time getting her platoon of soldiers oriented to their target, before they set off on their mission. Thanks to the thick canopy, her soldiers were masked from enemy air patrols as they moved slowly and carefully thought the forest. She hoped Hezbon and her brothers were okay. She'd heard Azubuike's attempts to redirect the others as well as Hezbon's distress signal. However, she was much too far away to do anything about either of those situations. The only thing she could do now was trust in her brother's plan and carry out her part of it. Ayoka paused and halted her platoon. On her signal, they all hugged the nearest trees and became as still as they could be. An Ezalin drop ship was making a slow, low pass just over their position. Its spot light was made useless, by the thick branches on the tallest trees. As soon as it gave up and moved on, Ayoka moved her platoon back on track. Determined now, more than ever, to catch up to the rear guard of the army currently marching towards Commander Themba.

Azubuike tracked Hezbon's last known location and had his pilot aim for those coordinates. It would be a fool's decision to fly directly onto the same path that got the Commander shot down. However, Azubuike would follow it long enough to get an idea of where the missing drop ship was. The crew needed to be located and, if possible, rescued. Azubuike's drop ship was heavily damaged and it was decided that they would abandon it and carry out the rest of their mission on foot. After departing, the Keftiu pilot flew in the direction that would take him around the far side of the great forest and away from the bulk of the main fighting.

"Status on the other three waves, Oya," Azubuike asked.

Oya took a moment to check the status of all other Keftiu drop ships that took part in their mission. ."Ayoka has gone to ground and is on mission. Seba has gone to ground far to the rear of our position. He's deployed Wepwawet troop transports and is attempting to construct a fallback position."

"What about the first wave," Azubuike pressed.

"Most of them survived the impact," Oya assured him. "Commander Hezbon signaled distress himself. Which way are we going? To the fall back point or to Hezbon's downed Keftiu?"

"You have to ask?" Azubuike joked.

"I like to be thorough," Oya chided.

"Direction?" He asked.

"North by northwest," Oya double checked to be sure. "Two point eight kilometers. Rough terrain."

Azubuike and his survivors knew they only had a certain amount of time to clear the area, before more Ezalin forces moved in to search for them. They'd be looking for survivors just like he was. Azubuike knew he just had to get to them first. As opposed to the greenery that Ayoka was graced with, Azubuike and his platoon were traveling across rocky, mountainous terrain that provided little cover and even less to look at. The only reasonable cover to expect were the large boulders and the occasional crevice on the hillsides. They made their way, in a staggered formation, across the largely open terrain. Just like they had the very first time Azubuike approached Mount Roha.

Hezbon had a lot of injured soldiers to evac after they were shot down short of their target destination. He hoped that his warning got through to the others and they had time to adjust their plan of attack. With no clear communication with the others, Hezbon prepared to get as far away from the crashed Keftiu as he could. In as little amount of time as was Huemanly possible. Unfortunately, the nature of many of the injuries and the condition of the unsalvageable Keftiu made a quick evac nearly impossible. The occupants were caught in the middle of trying to pull the worst cases from the wreckage, when the Ezalin attacked. One of the medics survived the crash and began pulling other survivors back into the wreckage, so he could care for them while being reasonably safe. Hezbon rallied those who could still fight and they created a perimeter around the downed ship. The berms created by the crash made the best firing positions. They were no longer mobile, so Hezbon hoped that someone had heard his distress call.

Seba came down well behind the crash site of Hezbon amid, reasonably, light anti-aircraft fire. He hadn't made it to the worst of it and, by comparison, got off a little light. Seba was the fallback position and wasted no time prepping the immediate area for his defense. First, he deployed his Wepwawet tanks into a large circle so that everything inside would be reasonably safe from attack. The tanks would draw enemy fire and return fire at any targets who were considered a threat. Then, he had his medics establish a triage area right in the center of all the tanks. They established hasty defenses out of portable shield wall barricades that they brought with them. They even had portable turrets to deploy in-between every vehicle. The infantry soldiers in Seba's small army took up defensive positions around, and even on top of the tanks. In order to use them as cover. They carried sniper rifles, Shango heavy weapons systems, portable anti-aircraft weapons and even heavy lasers. Seba was constructing a heavily fortified defensive position. All he had to do was wait for his allies to show up, or his enemies. Either way, Seba was ready.

Epilogue

Duro-Aina had been absent from the bulk of the recent fighting, as her interests lay elsewhere. With the help of Ausar, she was able to locate the planetary stronghold that held her prey. An Ezalin officer could have been anywhere on the planet, it was fortunate that he happened to be so near the capital city. She watched and waited for her target to appear, or for some reasonable assurance that he was in the vicinity. This would be the fourth Ezalin stronghold she'd infiltrated without finding what she was looking for.

"Is that him?" Duro-Aina asked Ausar her question as she gestured to another Ezalin officer who was entering the complex.

Ausar used his facial recognition technology to match the facial features, body language and gait to a reasonable certainty, "It's him."

Duro-Aina abandoned her position on the small cliff face to approach the main entry gate. She no longer needed a good vantage point for her observations. What she needed now was to keep up with her target before he disappeared inside the larger base. Using her stealth technology, she was able to walk right through the gate, unchallenged.

Fortunately for her, the Ezalin at this base were a bit preoccupied with repelling a three pronged attack from the Medjay.

The fighting was intense and there were heavy casualties on both sides of the conflict for the city itself. Duro-Aina also briefly observed one of the drop ships come down in a fiery crash. From a distance, it looked like the gun emplacements were using wide-arcing sweeping motions to keep the survivors pinned down. They were also providing Duro-Aina with the perfect distraction, which would allow her to infiltrate their most robust defenses.

Once inside, she followed the young officer at a safe distance, being sure to keep enough space between herself and anyone else. Into one of the secure buildings they went, down into the holding area where there were many prisoners being held. The young officer, Wynch, was about to do a prisoner transfer. His authority, and intention, clearly evident by the document he brought with him and the reaction the other soldiers gave to his presence.

Duro-Aina was careful to survey the route on their way in. With most of the base on alert, deployed or engaged with the Meroan attack, the brig was only lightly defended. Now was as good a time as any. She calmly walked down the isolated tunnel that made up this wing of the brig, then closed the distance between herself and Wynch. There were two other guards who were permanently stationed in the brig and they were only lightly armed. If she could find a way to kill them quietly, she may be able to escape, undetected, with her prize. Her opportunity presented itself when one of the guards escorted Wynch to a particular cell, while the other guard remained behind to man the main security station.

Duro-Aina killed that guard as soon as the other's backs were turned. There was no audible sound as she used her double edged blade to quietly eliminate him. From behind she attacked, covering his mouth and suppressing his attempts to struggle. When he stopped struggling, she lowered his limp torso to the desk, careful not to make any noise. Then she turned her attention to the remaining two Ezalin. Unaware of the imminent danger, they proceeded to continue the prisoner transfer process. Wynch was granted entry into the cell while the guard waited just outside, hand on his weapon.

Duro-Aina approached that cell and grabbed the man's arm so he could not reach for his weapon, pulling it free of the socket. Before he could scream in pain, a purple mace crashed down to meet with his skull. Wynch, just inside the cell, did not reach for his weapon. Instead, he reached for a small device. One of Meroan construction which was in his possession ever since he'd realized the truth about Meroan technology. It had worked before on Azubuike and he was hoping, betting his life, that it would work again now. He pressed the button and the worst thing happened: nothing.

Duro-Aina almost chuckled to herself. She dematerialized the mace and rapidly closed the distance. Then grabbed Wynch by the neck, pushing him up against the wall. With her free hand, she took the small, severely outdated armor inhibitor from his hand. She held it up and inspected it, mocking Wynch. Ausar synthesized her voice so he could translate her words, "You savages have no understanding of our technology. Was this supposed to stop me? This was an obsolete model thousands of years ago."

Wynch was many things but a coward was not one of them, "It was only a matter of time before you finally caught me." He struggled to force his words through a constricted airway. "Had to try something."

Duro-Aina opened an encrypted channel to Ausar, "How could he have known we were tracking him?"

"He can't tell you if you kill him," Ausar's point was a fair one.

Duro-Aina relieved her grip around Wynch's throat

just slightly enough to allow his bright red face to relax.
Ausar translated her question and Wynch gave his reply, "I
moved him around intentionally, to draw out any would be
rescuers. We were previously at all four locations you
destroyed."

Wynch quickly realized his attacker wanted
something more than his death. If that wasn't the case, he'd
be dead already. Wynch had to make this interaction last
long enough for the shift change to occur, which was only a
matter of minutes. "I can't stop you from taking him, but
you won't get far. He doesn't possess your impressive
stealth technology."

"I came here for you," Duro-Aina corrected her new
prisoner. "He is not my concern."

Ausar was well aware of the shift change and
alerted Duro-Aina to the danger. Realizing that time was
running out, Duro-Aina made herself clear, "Time is not
my ally, your reinforcement will be here soon. You have
some leverage on Sovereign Azubuike. Surrender that
information now and I will kill you quickly. Delay, and I
may consider keeping you alive as a pet."

"I won't tell you anything useful." Wynch was as
defiant as ever. He only needed to buy a little more time.

"Oh yes, you will," Duro-Aina tightened her grip

around Wynch's wind pipe, once again. At the same time, she generated her ethereal mace, held it high and moved to crush Wynch in one blow.

Wynch's hands went up, in submission, immediately, "Wait, wait WAIT! As I was saying, you may want to meet this man after all."

Duro-Aina slightly eased her aggressive stance and looked over at the Meroan who was sitting in chains. He'd seen better days and, by the condition of his injuries, some very recent interrogations. Yet, through all of that, she saw a tall and strong man who was the subject of brutal tortures designed to break the unbreakable.

"Why is this man relevant," Duro-Aina demanded.

"He," Wynch was losing consciousness again but managed to breathe out his last reply, "Ime, is the leverage you seek."

Duro-Aina needed to make her choice and fast. Ultimately, she decided she would take them both. She put the mace away and, without releasing her grip on Wynch, used her free hand to tear the chains off Ime's chair. She hefted him over her shoulder and marched toward the exit. Meanwhile, she dragged Wynch, by the neck in an awkward position. His back was toward the ground and the heels of his feet dragged along the surface as they moved.

Duro-Aina waited for an opportunity and prepared to exit the brig as soon as it was safe to do so. "I think I will keep you as a pet," Duro-Aina decided. She gestured toward the rocky and bland terrain that was strikingly similar to the Ezalin home world, "Look ice man, this is your true inheritance and I will send you back to the caves you came from."

Thank you for joining me on a journey through this story. I hope you have enjoyed the narrative I've created here.

Ankh Uda Snb

Printed in Great Britain
by Amazon

64585542R00236